Smitten Kitten

PRIDE · LUST · ENVY · GREED · WRATH · GLUTTONY · SLOTH

Chris Renee | Johnna B | Shadress Denise

Thanks for the support Sis!
Love you ALWAYS!!
C. Renee

Smitten Kitten

To Heather, always supporting with love, Shadress Denise

CHRIS RENEE | JOHNNA B | SHADRESS DENISE

Thank you Heather, Love always, Johnna

© 2016 Chris Renee
© 2016 Shadress Denise
© 2016 Johnna B

ISBN-13: 978-0-9981484-2-7
ISBN-10: 0-9981484-2-3

Editor | Progressive Learning Solutions, LLC
Book Cover Designer | Koraz Norman
Interior Design | LaQueisha Malone www.LaQueishaMalone.com

All rights reserved. This book contains material protected under International and Federal Copyright Laws and Treaties. Any unauthorized reprint or use of this material is prohibited. No part of this book may be reproduced or transmitted in any form or by any means, electronic or mechanical, including photocopying, recording or by any information storage and retrieval system without express writer permission from the author/publisher.

This is a work of fiction. Any references or similarities to actual events, real people, living or dead, or to the real locals are intended to give the novel a sense of reality. Any similarity in other names, characters, places, and incidents are entirely coincidental.

Table of Contents

Prologue — 1

Chapter 1 | *Welcome to the Smitten Kitten* — 9

Chapter 2 | *Love & War* — 20

Chapter 3 | *Nova Pussy Trapping* — 28

Chapter 4 | *Heart Strings* — 34

Chapter 5 | *Unapologetically Finished* — 48

Chapter 6 | *Red Moon* — 57

Chapter 7 | *Seduction* — 68

Chapter 8 | *Propositions* — 75

Chapter 9 | *Temptations* — 81

Chapter 10 | *Ultimatums* — 87

Chapter 11 | *Nova's Betrayal* — 96

Chapter 12 | *The Vow* — 102

Chapter 13 | *Next Lifetime* — 112

Chapter 14 | *Obsession* — 122

Chapter 15 | *Atonement* — 128

Chapter 16 | *Revelations* — 133

Chapter 17 | *Sloth* — 146

Chapter 18 | *Envy* — 153

Table of Contents

Chapter 19 | *Lust*	163
Chapter 20 | *Greed*	169
Chapter 21 | *Gluttony*	176
Chapter 22 | *Pride*	182
Chapter 23 | *Redemption*	195
Chapter 24 | *Wrath*	202
Epilogue	208

Sneak Peeks

Who Do You Love Now | *Shadress Denise*	215
The Devil's Pie | *Chris Renee*	219
P.O.V. | *Johnna B*	223

he loved sex and everything about it, even to the point it became his downfall……

Prologue
Azora Monroe | 17th Century

"Azora!"

"Yes, my queen," Azora answered meekly as she came running around the corner.

Scared, she bowed into a kneeling position. She hated when the queen yelled her name loudly, knowing she was never that far away. Azora felt she only did it to exert her power over her.

"Stand up! Where were you?"

The queen looked Azora up and down, envious of her rare beauty. When she first laid eyes upon the girl she knew she would do anything to have Azora grow up in her kingdom under her care. This included having Azora's native village wiped off the face of the map by unleashing a deadly virus that eventually killed everyone. Just before Azora met the same fate, the queen's men swooped in and snatched her from the arms of her dying mother. To prevent her from succumbing to the curse an antidote was given to Azora to save her life. The queen made herself sound like the hero in the story when she told it to hold leverage over the young and impressionable, Azora. She had no idea that the queen was the villain who went to great lengths to enslave Azora. She had plans for the girl that would eventually lead to her being one of the most powerful rulers of several lands.

"As you wish, my queen. I was just getting your bath ready," Azora replied, still looking down at the floor.

"Look at me," the queen demanded.

She licked her lips in a lusting manner. The queen was a beautiful lady who kings from near and far tried their best to sway her to marry them. Holding tight to her reins, she wouldn't budge. It was her greatest secret that she only had eyes for women. After searching for quite some time she realized she was unable to find someone she could love forever, until she laid eyes on Azora.

Azora was only thirteen years old when she came to be the queen's servant and a few moons pass seventeen when the queen decided she couldn't wait any longer.

Azora was left in a state of disbelief. She'd never imagined herself with a woman and most definitely not one like the queen. She was mean and spiteful even on a good day. It was no mystery to Azora why the queen was alone.

"I said look at me! You know what happens when I have to tell you the same thing twice!" the queen yelled louder than the first time.

Shaken by the threat, Azora nervously looked up at her. She tried to hide it, but nothing could stop the cringe that shook her body when she noticed the look of lust in the queen's eyes. She lay naked with the covers pulled up partially and a small, almost tarnished crown adorned her head. The thing always looked so ridiculous and Azora almost laughed out loud at the site, but she knew that would only cause her to receive harsh lashings.

The queen hated to be talked about or ridiculed but she heard the petty gossip quite often. People assumed that her reign was nearing its end. She would never admit it but, she had that nagging feeling that they were correct. No matter what, she still proudly wore her crown in case someone forgot what she was capable of. Lately, it seemed numerous people were trying her, at least that's what the paranoia in her mind told her.

For years, she heard the whispers and the rumors about her sexuality, especially when she was young and looked to please everyone in her kingdom. To keep them from talking she coerced, more like forced, a man passing through kingdoms to lay with her to procreate. She knew from the very moment it happened that they conceived a boy. She married the lonely drifter and kept him around for a few years before she killed him. Unfortunately, her

Smitten Kitten

son's spirit was of a gypsy. He ran away from her several times before finally leaving for good.

It had been years since the ten-year-old boy decided that he was a man and he wanted to take care of himself. They were never able to build a bond because the queen ruled him with the same tyrant, iron fist she was grooming him for. At his last departure, the queen did not put up a fight because in all honesty, motherhood was not something that she was cut out for. Besides, she now had a new plan for dominance. She was going to use her most precious possession, Azora.

"Just how in the hell are you preparing my bath and you are standing here looking stupid," the queen barked.

"I umm, you called me and I umm," Azora stammered through her words.

She too was almost naked but it wasn't by choice. The queen picked out her attire every morning. Azora noticed that the skirts had gotten shorter and the shirts tighter, if there was a shirt at all. Even though she was uncomfortable working in them, she dared not utter a word. Currently she wore a short silk wrap around her waist and a gold necklace that hung down to middle of her stomach. The strangest part of her daily attire was a red stripe that was hand painted every morning by the queen's main assistant. The red stripe went around her forehead, signaling she was off limits to everyone and that she belonged to the queen.

"No need for the bath. Just let the guards know that we will be leaving for Benin right away. We will return in four days' time."

"Yes, my queen," Azora said as she prepared to leave the room.

She was glad the queen had pushed her desires aside. Nothing repulsed her more than having to be the queen's pleasure toy. She rather she'd died in the village with the rest of her family. She was always so uncertain about why the Gods decided this fate for her. She thought dying would have been better than suffocating just a little every sun up and moon rise.

She was almost out of the room when that dreaded voice yelled out to her again.

"Azora, wait!"

Azora turned on her heels to find the queen with the covers now tossed to the side. She lay open and exposing her not so youthful body. Yes, she was beautiful in the face but her body told her real age. Although her stomach was flat as a board, you could see deep scratches, burns, and bruises that violently hugged the skin all over body. Her breasts were small but flat due to the milk that she produced while pregnant with her son.

Azora took a deep breath, and then answered, "Yes, my queen."

Azora forced the words out of her mouth as if they were filled with bile. She wasn't sure how much more of this she could take. She wanted a way out and would jump at whatever opportunity presented itself first.

"Come lay with me before we start our journey."

"Yes, my queen."

An hour later Azora and the queen, followed by a few of her guards, were on their way to Benin. Azora watched as the dirt roads and homeless peasants moved past her at a slow pace. She once lived in a place like that. She felt conflicted because there were times she was thankful the queen found her and saved her from dying like her parents but she was tired of being her lover and personal servant. On any given day, she would be ridiculed or humiliated for nothing at all. There were moments when the queen treated her well, kept her fed, and made sure no one did anything bad to her, well no one other than herself. Still, that never stopped Azora from dreaming of a life where she didn't have any worries or problems. As she continued to look out the window, she silently said a prayer for salvation.

The journey was long and uneventful and finally after several hours their carriage pulled up to the most beautiful palace Azora had ever laid eyes on. It was three times the size of the one she lived in. It looked as if the palace was made of gold and fully bloomed rose bushes covered almost every square inch of the long passage way leading to the door. Even though the scene was indeed breathtaking, she wondered what kind of horror stories would the walls tell. If this palace was anything like where she stayed, she could only imagine what frightening stories they held.

"Azora!"

"Oh, yes my queen."

She looked up to see the queen waiting impatiently for her to get out of the carriage. Azora made haste to climb out of the carriage, but she purposely walked a few paces behind the queen, taking in the beautiful embellishments of the inside of the palace. The walls inside were made of gold just like on the outside. The white floors were so clean that Azora could see an image of herself. There were several girls, young and old, who loitered along the hallways. They looked as if they didn't possess a care in the world and Azora envied that. She imagined herself living in such a space. She wanted to ask the queen who they were visiting, but she dared not to speak out of turn.

"Wait here," the queen commanded of Azora and her two guards once they reached a room in the back of the palace.

Glad to get a moment of peace without the queen breathing down her neck, Azora continued to let her eyes explore. She wished the guards weren't there so that she could walk around, but she knew they would tell on her if she did decide to venture out. The queen's guards were more loyal to her than Job to God. No matter what she did to them, they still sung her highest praise. The restless nature of Azora caused her to go to the wall just to examine it. The fact that it was made in gold really tripped her out. She had never seen gold up close and in person before.

"Beautiful, isn't it?"

Azora turned towards the voice and was startled by the short, small chocolate beauty that stood before her. They looked to be the same age but there was a certain grace that the stranger held that Azora didn't have. Azora wasn't sure what it was but she wanted some of whatever made the stranger feel like that.

"Yes, it is. Is this really gold?" Azora asked.

"Well, what else would it be, silly? My king is the richest man in the land. He has nothing but the best and soon it will be mine as well," the stranger said with a huge smile on her face.

"You are set to marry him?"

"Of course, I am the most beautiful woman he's ever seen. I was created especially for him. How could he not marry me? There's no one who even compares."

Azora found her comments to be arrogant and before she could give a response, the queen stormed out of the room angry. She tried not to show it as she walked with her head high and her shoulders back but Azora always knew when she was upset. It was the time when the queen treated her the worse. She started to fret, thinking over what she could do to make things right but her young mind froze in place when the door opened and out came the most handsome man Azora had ever laid eyes on.

He looked young, way too young to be king, but he carried the air of a man with a great force of power. It screamed, I am all man. His chest was exposed and glistened under the sunlight. His hair was long and locked to the back like thick black ropes. He put her in mind of the great warrior, Samson. Azora felt her mouthwatering but that did not compare to the wetness that secreted between her legs. She stood mesmerized by his beauty as she tried to move in order to follow her queen but her legs wouldn't cooperate with her mental demands.

He too seemed stunned by what stood in front him. His dark brown eyes bore holes into her soul. She wanted to reach out and touch him to make sure he was real. His dashiki rested on his body like a second skin and the sparkle from his crown gave his brown eyes a kaleidoscope effect. It was as if time stood still as they stared at each other. The attraction must have been felt by all who witnessed the two because the stranger cleared her throat in an unpleasant way before talking to the king.

"My love, is there anything you desire?" she asked.

Azora made herself busy with gathering her things but she also had one ear on the situation before her.

"Not now, Nova. Go and wait in the grotto until I fetch you," he ordered.

His word was definitely law as Nova didn't even give a second look back as she all but ran out the room and down the hall. The king then turned his attention back to his guests.

"Queen Anna Nzinga!"

"Yes, Oyo," Queen Nzinga said as she turned to him.

She was trying to figure out why his voice held so much urgency. She followed his eyes and saw that they were fixated on Azora.

"On second thought, I think we can come to terms if you are willing to make a trade."

"A trade? I'm not sure I understand," the queen replied.

"My eyes have finally rested upon the face of the prophecy," King Oyo muttered to himself but was heard by all.

Queen Nzinga and the guards turned to Azora. They saw nothing but a peasant and a sex slave. Azora's fire red locks of curls were pinned up into a bun, showing off her high cheekbones and naturally arched eyebrows that sat atop her midnight black, almond shaped eyes. With her skin matching the shade of her eyes and both resembling the feathers of the phoenix, this effect gave her a majestic look to the king.

"What would your trade be, Oyo?" the queen questioned uncertainly.

In his chambers, he'd refused her pleas for help and said she had nothing else of value to offer him. She was now curious as to what could have piqued his interest since she left him standing there with a pissing match against himself. She was not new to this chauvinistic world that questioned her ability simply because she was a woman. To the queen he was nothing more than an egotistical, little snot nosed brat who only got the country and the land because his parents were killed in an ambush by foreigners.

"I will give you my political sway in Yoruba and my army at your full disposal for her."

The king never took his eyes off of Azora. King Oyo knew he could've gotten Azora for less, but he needed her and Queen Anna Nzinga to know how bad he wanted Azora.

"Oyo, she's just a peasant. I can offer you so much more than her. I'm sure you aren't short on jilts," Queen Nzinga said, referring to his harem of women he had frolicking around the palace.

"Nonsense! None of them compare. Certainly, I would get rid of them all if I had her."

"She's not worthy all this," the queen said in a panic.

She didn't want to give up her precious Azora. She really was so much more than a peasant. She constantly reminded Azora to keep her in her place. She knew one day Azora's curious mind would want to venture out. They'd been together for years and didn't want to part with her.

"I told you my terms and I'm quite sure you see I am being relatively generous with my offer, queen."

"Yes, you are but why so much for a mere peasant?" Queen Nzinga looked over to Azora as if she could sway his intentions.

Azora beamed on the inside at the thought of being purchased by the beautiful king. Life couldn't be that much worse than with the queen she figured. *Why would he go through so much trouble to mistreat her?*

"I've never explained myself to a woman. Queen or not and I will not start today. Either you want my help or you do not."

The queen weighed her options. Did her sexual desires trump the needs of her kingdom? She hated losing, especially to a man. She would bend for now, but there would be some consequences that would be befitting for the king. Queen Nzinga swallowed her pride for a later date, and then reluctantly agreed.

"As you wish, King Oyo."

Chapter 1
Welcome to the Smitten Kitten

"Azora, your guests are set to arrive in a little under thirty minutes are you ready?" Azora's personal assistant Tina asked.

She looked at Azora with strong adoration. Everything about her was magnificent to Tina. She had never known a woman like her before.

"Yes, love. I'll bring the lotus in a few minutes," Azora replied absently.

As she finished picking the herbs she would need for the night's events, she looked up and caught Tina still standing there staring at her. She knew Tina was smitten with her but she'd left that lifestyle in her past life for the most part. When she told Tina that years ago, she seemed to take it well and she never tried again. Lately Tina wouldn't say anything but she would stare, like now. Azora felt a wave of annoyance wash over her.

"Is everything else in place, Tina?"

"Oh, umm, yes ma'am. I almost forgot. We're missing your secret ingredient."

"I'm gathering all I need right now. Has Nova arrived?"

Tina couldn't hide the immediate frown that covered not only her face but also her soul. She hated Nova more than any other person she could think of. To her it seemed as if something wasn't right with Nova. She couldn't really put her finger on it, but she could tell a dirty whore from anywhere. Hell, she used to be one herself. That was how she found herself indebted to Azora and the *Smitten Kitten*. Tina had done her husband dirty. She slept with any other man, including his family and friends, but him. The night they came to the Smitten Kitten had changed everything in her life. She would forever be grateful to Azora for saving her. She vowed to always protect her the same way that Azora had done her. So, if she had to keep a watchful eye on the manipulative and morally corrupt, Nova, she would.

"Yes, she is here. I saw her somewhere wandering around Lust and Envy, her two favorite spots," Tina forced the words from her mouth, but muttered the last part about Nova to herself.

The last time she mentioned anything about Nova to Azora, she almost lost her life. Azora didn't take kindly to anyone trying to tell her what to do nor how to feel. When it came to the relationship between the two women, Tina learned to just shut up.

"Good, then we are ready to begin."

"I'm sure everyone will be most appreciative of your presence."

"Well, I wouldn't dream of denying anyone of my radiance. I'll be right up."

The Smitten Kitten was launching a new tonic, and Azora couldn't wait to see what majestic adventures it would bring about in the house. She'd been working on it for a really long time and before she used it for its real intention, she wanted to try it out first to make sure it would be most resourceful.

Slowly, she rose from her knees with a basket filled to its brim with her special Lotus flower. She was expecting a house full, but tonight the focus would be on one special couple. Everyone in attendance was there for their own reasons, but Azora always picked out the one couple that needed extra attention. They needed her own special little guidance. She had a special knack for fixing troublesome relationships, one way or the other.

It had taken her almost six months to get her guest list to where she needed it to be. Nova wasted no time in gathering the necessary information. She was the best of the best when it came to what she does. She could effortlessly weed through all the lies and get to the root of the problem in people. Sure, there were sinful desires in everyone, but Azora needed the desperation and yearning to be breathtakingly desperate, and Nova had assured her that everyone was there.

"Aahhhhh yes, nothing like the feeling of fresh souls to play games with me," Azora thought to herself.

She could sense that her guest had started to arrive. The worry and anguish about what would happen during their visit tickled her spirit. All lost souls, heavily filled with lust and sorrow and that brought a heat to her body that made her smile.

"All praises to Hecate. I pray that you are satisfied with my selection for tonight, my lord."

Azora bowed as she tilted her head for her short prayer. Tonight's sacrifice was meant to please the God in hopes that he would eventually remove the dreaded curse that was bestowed upon her.

"Let the games begin," Azora said as she walked towards the door.

She looked herself over in the mirror. Her fire red hair was pulled tightly in her signature bun. The shimmering, golden, silk gown she wore clung to her curves to perfection. To top off her attire for the night, she wore a pair of black and gold Giuseppe Zanotti come hither and fuck me pumps.

"Not bad for an old gal, if I might say so myself."

She took one more look, winked at herself, and ran her hands down the front of her dress. She was now ready to go greet her guests of honor. She briskly walked towards the stairs, looking down at her guests. A moving darkness, peaking in the shadows to her right caught her eye. Without clear verification, she still knew it was Nova and this excited Azora.

"Welcome, to The Smitten Kitten. I hope tonight all of your desires are met," she seductively spoke while descending the stairs.

Azora took in her guests that were dressed to the nines for the gala. In total, there were three couples. Three men and two women who were single and all seeking different awakenings for the night. Yes, tonight would be perfect. Azora fought hard to conceal the excitement that pumped in her blood.

"For those of you that haven't had the pleasure of knowing me, I am Azora Monroe, your host for tonight's festivities."

"How could we ever forget you?" one of the male guest spoke out loud.

Most of the others joined in with laughter, all exchanging knowing looks of the powers that Azora held to captivate someone.

"Well, it's been awhile since I've seen a few of you. William is it?" Azora asked the man who spoke to her.

She could feel the lust oozing from his pores as he stood next to his wife, but practically eye fucking her. Yes, she had something special planned for him for the night. He had no clue that he was the one that she would give extra attention to. William had been a very bad husband to his wife. Years of lying, cheating, and empty promises is what unwillingly made him cross paths with Nova. He thought it was nothing but luck that he would bump into such a beautiful and seductive woman, but that would all depends on one's definition of good and bad luck. If Nova had you in her eyesight, your goose was as good as cooked.

Looking at him closely, Azora could see how he was such a womanizer. He was very easy on the eyes with a solid body and a handsome boyish face, plus she could see his manhood jumping in his slacks. From the looks of things, he planned to have a lot of fun at the party.

"Yes ma'am," he answered bashfully.

Now that the spotlight was shone on him, he was intimidated by Azora's attention. Most loud and boisterous men were really nothing more than wet pussy when a woman who isn't afraid of the dick is standing in their face.

"Yes, I remember you and your beautiful wife, Beverly, very well. Welcome," Azora extended well wishes to Beverly with a warm smile.

Azora's heart went out to Beverly because she understood the devastation of being promised everything by a man only for him to lie to her. William's own insecurities had forced Beverly to surrender and agree to have one night with him and his mistress, Raven as William knew her but Azora and everyone else called her, Nova.

"Tonight, I will do something different. There will be no tour of the palace. Your mind's internal compass will lead you to your proper places. This is where we will part ways. However, we will meet again later tonight. Oh, and be sure to take a treat from the bowl at the bar. They will help heighten your experience for the night, but please only take one. Believe me, I will know if you decide to be naughty and over indulge."

She shook her finger in a fake scold. Laughter filled the room again as the guests all walked through the golden doors into what they assumed could only be described as a sexual paradise. Unbeknownst to most, this would be a night that would forever change their lives.

Hmmm so many to choose from dear which one should we pick? Azora heard one wife ask her husband.

They were an odd couple that were completely opposite in looks. He was tall, midnight black with broad shoulders, a solid back, and a square jawline that made Azora want to sit on his face. The wife was a short, ball of thin pale skin. She had no ass and no tits, but she had beautiful ice blue eyes. She was also a whore and the reason they were chosen for tonight. Nova didn't find much interest in the husband because he was weak and broke, the two things she despised the most. She only recommended them to Azora because she felt sorry for him. Azora hadn't allowed a woman target to enter since the night she acquired Tina, but she felt a need to amend that due to the severity of how trifling the woman was.

I think I'm going to try this cigar first. I wonder what this does? I hope one of these hoes are down to give me some fire head,

One of the single men thought to himself. He was a young executive who never had time for anything but work. Most of the time, his sexual desires were satisfied by his hand as it forced his semen to spew into washcloths in his bathroom. When Nova walked into his office and presented herself as Lola his sexual needs were met, providing he purchased large amounts of ridiculous things for her. His obsession with her was just as strong as an addict's to any hardcore drug.

I wonder if Miss Azora likes women? Oh I love gummy bears. I wonder how her skin tastes?

The two single women spoke in silence to each other. They were living their lives in a sworn secrecy of lesbianism. Afraid to come out to the public, they found solace in each other, mentally and sexually. Nova's good girl alter ego, Cleo, had joined the church choir and was not surprised when she saw the two of them using their mouths for something more than singing. She could pick up on their uncertainty about their sexuality as soon as she walked in the church doors. They were unable to relax and live in the moment for fear of going to hell. Watching them go wild tonight would be a refreshing treat for Azora.

Oh, I haven't had a joint since high school. I'm going to enjoy this night I wish that pretty black bitch was participating tonight. I would wrap my hands around that red hair and fuck the life out of her.

Azora smiled to herself as she heard William's secret thoughts. Reading minds had been a little trick that she picked up along the way. She ducked off into her small prayer room, and kneeled in respect until the spirits she'd provided started to take effect.

"Hecate, please guide my actions tonight to mirror and please you. I pray I am doing everything in your image."

Once Azora felt rejuvenated from her prayers, she went to join in the escapades. She could feel that her guests began venturing out and she relished in the release of their uninhibited sexuality. The tingle in her spine sent electrical shocks to every nerve ending in her body as each second passed and her guests went further into the abyss of sinful desires.

"Tina, bring me my chalice and then you can retire to your quarters for the night," Azora said into the intercom.

She never let Tina stay and watch the activities. She knew this infuriated Tina, especially whenever Nova would join them but she still never let up. Tina had used herself enough as a slave to lust.

"Yes, Azora," Tina answered.

A few minutes later Tina walked in and placed a gold chalice filled with Azora's own personal cup of hell-broth. Behind her stood Nova in the doorway. She was looking beautiful as usual except she didn't have any clothes on. Her breasts were firm and her small nipples pointed north. The *V* between her thighs was shaved bald and glistened from a mixture of oil and glitter. Her smell was intoxicating, and Azora felt a yearning in the pit of her stomach.

"Thank you and good night, Tina. You did good getting everything together for me today."

"Thank you," Tina blushed. "Anything for you. Anything at all."

Azora didn't need to read between the lines because she could feel the lustful heat radiating from Tina's body. Tina had yet to turn around and saw Nova standing there.

"I'm sure," Azora smirked. "Get you some rest, Tina."

"Yeah get you some rest, Tina. We have things to do," Nova called out.

Tina spun around and glared at Nova. The energy in the room almost shifted into disaster, but Azora would not let the two of them and their pettiness fuck up her evening.

"Tina, get out! Nova, go back to Lust. I can feel you're needed in there."

Azora quickly dismissed them, and then took a sip from her chalice. She left the room and let the hot liquid flow through her body as she roamed the halls. Once she arrived outside of the room that she was certain most of the guest were itching to get into, she stood in front of the glass wall and watched as sex filled the air.

She opened the door and as she suspected, this was where the party had begun. She walked up and sat on the bed next to William and Nova who were fucking. William was hollering loudly as Nova was wearing his ass out. Nova looked at Azora and winked. William was completely oblivious that she joined them. Nova was the only one who could see her.

"She isn't your wife, William," Azora whispered in his ear.

He looked up at the sound of the voice but to his eyes no one was there. He continued his hard pumping into Nova who was throwing her ass back at him with no mercy.

"Fuck her harder, William. She's not yelling. William, give it all to her."

William looked up again, and still there was no one there. He figured it was the potent drugs he'd taken. Azora told him to take only one of them, but he was a greedy man and always wanted more than what was allowed. For that he would pay dearly.

"Shame on you, William. I told you to take only one and you had to have more didn't you? Do you know which deadly sin you are guilty of?"

Azora could feel his heart rate speeding up. The fire in the pit of his stomach made her own pussy ache. He was nearing an orgasm.

"Where is your wife, William? Look over to your left."

William looked over and saw his wife in bed with another man. His strokes slowed greatly. He couldn't believe what he was seeing.

"Is that what you want, William? Do you want to watch your wife to suck another man's dick? Look at how she swallows him whole like a pro."

The sight was hard to watch but hearing the whispers were downright maddening. William's hard dick turned flaccid instantly. He tried to get up from the bed but Nova tightened her pussy muscles around him, holding him in a firm grip.

"Oh, William, that's not how this goes. Keep fucking her."

"I can't," he whimpered.

"Why yes you can, daddy. You've fucked me plenty of nights when you thought she was at home waiting. This is what she was really doing," Nova said to him.

She started gyrating her hips, leaving him no control but to fuck her even though his eyes stayed on his wife. She had never sucked or fucked him like that before. He was shocked by the size of the man's dick and the easy way his wife took him all.

Azora could feel his heart breaking into pieces. His ego was shrinking as he got a glimpse of how his wife felt about his infidelity.

"Your wife once told you that greed would be your downfall, but you wouldn't listen to her. You had to have more. You had to have more money, more women, more cars, more, more, more. Greed will always be a man's downfall," Azora whispered more to herself than to William.

"Shut the fuck up!" he screamed.

"Now keep fucking her like you fucked all those other women even after your wife asked you not to cheat anymore, William!"

"Stop saying my name! Why do you keep saying my name?" he yelled.

Every time she said his name, it felt like nails going down a chalkboard. The screeching sound was driving him insane.

"Fuck her, William!"

His anger only fueled Azora's desire to destroy him even more.

"I can't dammit! I'm trying to get to my wife," he yelled.

The fact that Nova was throwing her pussy on him so tough had rendered him powerless. He didn't want to fuck. He just wanted to grab his wife and get the fuck out of there.

"Oh, but you have no choice, William," Azora chuckled.

"Please make it stop. Beverly stop!" he screamed.

His pain was radiating throughout Azora's body and she relished in the feeling. The sounds of his wife moaning while she sucked on another man's dick had driven William way past his breaking point.

"This is what you wanted, right? Look at her, William. Does she moan like that with you?" Azora taunted him as she watched the tears flow from his eyes.

His pain was bringing her such an amazing feeling throughout her body.

"Wow, did you see her swallow that whole thing. It's a such a big thing too, William. There is no coming back after that. How could you cheat on somebody that can do with her mouth? I'll never understand you men."

"Please make it stop. I'm sorry," he begged.

"I don't think so, Mr. William. It's not going to be that easy. Why would I stop her fun? She looks like she's loving every second of that big fella over there."

"Beverly, baby, I'm sorry."

He watched in horror as his wife looked like she couldn't get enough of the man that was shoving his manhood down her throat.

"Did I tell you to stop fucking her, William? Keep stroking. Don't give up on her now."

Azora place a hand on his shoulder and William felt his hips start to move again. He could hear soft moans that sounded like singing coming from Nova's mouth. It infuriated him and caused a massive rage to wash over him.

"You dirty whore!" William roared as the anger from watching his wife settled in the bottom of his stomach.

"You goddamn whore! How could you do this to us?" he questioned in a low tone, feeling defeated.

William had no clue that his wife could not hear him. No one could hear him. He was standing in his own twisted reality where he could see and hear only himself. Nova had finally released him, but he was still unable to move.

"Now, William, which would you rather be in this situation, the pot or the kettle?" Azora asked sarcastically.

"Please, I don't want to do this anymore," he said as his voice trembled with pain.

"You don't get a choice anymore, William. It seems Beverly was tired of your trifling ass and took that choice from you. Look at her, she's in heaven right now. I don't think she's gonna come back to you after this."

"What do you mean?"

"Oh, our dear Beverly made a deal with the devil. It was your life for her happiness. She just wants to be happy. You've been hindering her happiness for far too long, William."

"She wants me dead?"

"Gone, dead, in hell it's all the same thing. Really doesn't matter what angle you look at it from."

At the moment, he was wishing for his own death as well. Knowing the love of his life wanted him dead was too much. Sure he'd cheated on her for years, but he'd never stopped loving her and he'd never gave another woman his heart because it would always belong to his wife. It felt like the saliva in his mouth had evaporated and the air in his lungs ceased to exist. He couldn't seem to catch his breath.

"Are you sure that's what you want, William?"

William never said he wished for death out loud so he wasn't sure how Azora knew but he was glad that she put it out there.

"Oh, fuck me harder, daddy!" William heard his wife squeal.

"Yes, I can't take it anymore. I'm sorry, Beverly," he cried.

"As you wish."

In an instant the whole scene changed and William was in the dark room alone.

"For your sins, you've been sentenced to lifetime in hell."

William made no sound. He had already given up. Azora put her mouth up to his and began to suck the very essence of his being into her body. She watched as his soul was vacuumed out of his and stared into his lifeless body as she held him up by his face. Once she was sure she'd gotten all of his soul, she dropped him to floor and left him there. She felt temporarily satisfied.

"Tina!" Azora yelled into the intercom once she reached her praying quarters again.

"Yes, Azora," Tina answered immediately as if she'd been anticipating a command from her master all night.

"Let Diablo and Lucifer go play in the greed room. I'm done for the night," she said, referring to two oversized black panthers.

"What do you want me to do about the other guests?"

"They are free to do whatever. Nova will take care of them. Just make sure they are out of here before I'm awake and clean up the mess."

"As you wish, Azora."

Chapter 2
Love & War

Miranda had awakened another morning to see Israel hadn't come home. It was 9 a.m. and by the looks of his side of the bed, he hadn't even been home. Normally, if he came home late his clothes would be thrown across the chaise and he'd sleep in the guest room. To him, it was his way of being able to lie about the time he came home. Miranda knew better since most nights he would be walking in about an hour after she had gone to sleep. At the time, she would be up until three or four in the morning waiting for him to walk in. Gone were the days where she would wake up in the middle of the night to see if he had come home.

They had been married fifteen years, and she was finding it harder to stay each day. They had been to a professional therapist, their pastor, and even a few marriage retreats. No matter what she tried, it seemed her husband always found his way back to his whorish ways. She wished she had the nerve to step out on him just one time. She wanted to know what it felt like to feel sexy and wanted by another man. For once, she wanted a man to treat her like a savage and ravish the inside of her body like no man could. Regardless of who or what she fantasized about, she didn't believe in adultery or divorce.

Lately, Israel had been telling her that he was working on a big project and that's what was keeping him in the city and away from home some nights. If she was the woman she was ten years ago, she would've been in the city verifying that story. Now, she was more mature and much more tired. She had no more energy to drag him or his side pieces out of any more hotel rooms. His stories would have to be true because her faith was running out, along with her patience. She got married so she would not have to sleep alone at night. Not to mention, she wanted the feeling of making love to the love of her life night-after-night. Now all she got were the orgasms she gave herself from the countless toys she had purchased.

She picked up her phone and there were no missed calls and no texts. When they first got married, he would call if he thought he would be five minutes late. If it was snowing, raining, or a meeting ran over he would call. He never wanted her to worry or doubt that he was doing anything he wasn't supposed to. It seemed that all changed when he hired Cheyenne to be his executive assistant. She was pretty, young, and seductive. At twenty-five years old, the girl was the epitome of walking sex. Miranda would always see how the men would fall all over themselves at the office. Outside of work, there had been plenty of conversations between her and Israel about her attire and appearance at the office. Miranda understood she was young, however she didn't feel that was an excuse for her to dress like that at the office. Not to mention, she didn't want a half-naked woman flaunting her ass in front of her husband all day long. At the time, she was convinced their marriage was strong and she had no reason to worry about him. However, temptation could only be avoided for so long.

After five years and six months into their marriage, Israel dove head first into infidelity. It started out as late night texts and secret emails on a different phone he had purchased without her knowing. Then it gravitated into him coming home late, to not coming home at all. Initially, he would say he had some big projects to work on at the office. Since he had been on track to become partner at the law firm he worked for, Miranda had no reason to doubt him.

When she found the extra phone, he simply stated, "It was for work."

After three months of his inconsistent behavior, Miranda started to get suspicious. Without him knowing, she sat outside of his job and watched him leave one evening. Convinced she was being paranoid, she followed him to the *Four Seasons Hotel*. She waited for him to check in and then she followed behind him. The entire time she was watching him as she was calling him on the phone. Each time, he would send her to voicemail and then a text would follow stating he was still at work. Miranda's heart sank further into her chest when she spotted the woman at the bar he had walked up to and kissed. At first, she couldn't make out who the woman was and then as they made their way to the elevator, she could see it was Cheyenne. After all the ranting he did with her, telling her he would never consider being unprofessional, here he was being as unprofessional as a motherfucker could be.

Before she moved any further, Miranda had called her sister to tell her what was going on and what she was about to do. In the event, she needed bail money she wanted her sister to be on notice. Standing in that lobby, she could feel herself having an out of body experience and only God himself could intervene on the homicide that was about to occur. Miranda remembered walking up to the front desk and asking the lady for a key. Since his dumbass had checked in under his own name, it was nothing to show she was his wife. The lady happily gave her the room number and key. Prior to going up to the room, Miranda went to get a drink at the bar. She wanted to give them just enough time to get comfortable and let their guards down. She had an ass whooping cooking, and she wasn't leaving there until she served it.

After about thirty minutes and two drinks, she was ready to go upstairs. She told the bartender to put the drinks on the room and made her way to the elevator. Miranda could still remember that ride up to the fourteenth floor and sadly it wouldn't be her last. Each floor the elevator passed, the knots in her stomach grew tighter. Then finally it stopped at the fourteenth floor and she walked off. She and Israel had come here many times and never did the hallway seem so long. It was all or nothing at that point. She could either fight to save her marriage or turn a blind eye and act as if she never saw what she saw.

Miranda looked down at the room key and made her way down the hall. She stopped in front of the door and stared at the numbers in front of her. Room 1414 would always be the room that took her marriage's virginity. She waved the key over the sensor and busted the door down. She flicked on the light and dove head first into the bed, punching anyone she could get her hands on. First, she wrapped her hands around Cheyenne's throat and choked her until Israel pulled her off. As Cheyenne rolled to the floor, gasping for air, Miranda threw everything she could get her hands on at Israel. Every ounce of her body was in pain and all she wanted to do was inflict it all on them. After she finished destroying the entire room, she threw her ring at him and told him to never come home again. Eight months had passed before she let him come back home. Ironically, that had been ten years and two love affairs ago. She wasn't sure if it was his ego or if he just couldn't keep it in his pants. Whichever it was, time was not on his side.

Miranda went to pick up her phone to call and see if Israel was ok and if he needed a change of clothes. Knowing him, he already had a change of clothes there since he never came home in what he left in the night before. Miranda grabbed her phone and dialed his number. The phone rang once and then went straight to voicemail.

"Israel, this is your wife. Please call me back and let me know you are ok," Miranda said calmly.

She was far from calm, but she knew the only way to get him to come home was to remain that way. If he thought for one second she was pissed, he would stay away longer. She would play the concerned wife for now, but she was anything but calm or concerned. The minute he walked through that door all hell was going to break loose. He would either start to fulfill his husband duties by respecting her or pack up his shit and stay wherever he was.

Israel sat in front of the house as he gathered himself. He had spent another amazing night with Nova, and it was one for the books. Out of all the women he had cheated with, she was by far the best one. Everything she did with her hands, her mouth, and her body always made him want more. Nova was a sex goddess, and he was her slave. Once he fixed his tie he looked to see if Miranda was standing at the window waiting for him. He remembered how she would spend countless nights waiting up for him, while he was out with one of his many women. Now most of the time, she acted as if she didn't care anymore. He loved her and even though he cheated on her, it had nothing to do with his feelings for her.

He had tried countless times to stop, but every time he tried he found himself underneath or on top of a beautiful woman. He remembered when his cherry first got popped. It was with Cheyenne Evans. She was young, ambitious, and made him feel like a real man. To be honest, she stroked his ego and then as time passed his dick too. Before he knew it, he was lying to Miranda and spending nights in hotel rooms and her house. Everything was going good until Miranda caught them and all hell broke loose. He was homeless for eight months before Miranda finally let him come home. Sleeping in hotel rooms was no longer once they had become his home. After that incident, he had been on his best behavior for about a year and a half before slipping back into temptation. Now he was more careful about his indiscretions and the places he had them in. Israel opened the car door to get out. There wasn't a million voicemails or texts from Miranda which meant only one thing, she was waiting for him to get home before she chewed his ass out. Israel walked up to the door, opened it, and walked in. The smell of coffee greeted him as he made his way towards the kitchen. Miranda wasn't sitting at the door, which meant he may have dodged a bullet.

He walked around the corner and Miranda was sitting at the island reading her tablet and drinking her coffee. She looked up long enough to give him a sinister smile. He walked over to the coffee pot to make a cup of coffee. He wanted to enjoy the silence just a little longer. He could feel her staring a hole in the back of his neck as he sipped. Miranda had looked him up and down to see that he had on a completely different outfit. He didn't even have the decency to come home in the same shit. He was just plain arrogant about his affairs and what he presumed was her acceptance of it.

"Good morning, Miranda," Israel said.

Miranda sipped more of her coffee. She was in no mood for small talk. Maybe her disposition confused him, so therefore, she needed to make it clear for him.

"Actually, Israel, it's not a good morning. Once again, I wake up to an empty bed and find my husband was not home. So, how do you figure it's a good morning?"

"Miranda, you know I am working on a big case. If I win this case it will guarantee I will make partner. I need your support right now," he said.

"Israel, respect me enough not to lie to my fucking face. I'm pretty sure no one else at that firm isn't going home. Who is it this time? Is it another one of your assistants, co-workers or have you ventured outside of those walls again? I'm getting real tired of your bullshit, Israel!" Miranda yelled.

Israel refrained from commenting on the co-worker and assistant comment. He knew speaking on it would only drudge up old memories and problems, so it was best he moved passed it. No need in fanning a slow burning flame this early in the morning.

"Baby, I promise you I'm not lying. I was at work all night preparing for this big case. My client is up for double murder and it's important that I have everything under control."

"I don't see how not coming home is you having everything under control. Are you seriously willing to let your home life go up in flames so you can make partner? I don't put my career before you. My clients know that I have a family and after a certain time, I'm off the clock. So, help me understand why you can't make the decision to do so as well."

"Miranda, you own your own business, therefore, you can set your own hours. I don't have that luxury because I work at a firm. You know that so why are we even having this discussion?"

"Fine, so, you mean to tell me that your office is full of people at three o'clock in the goddamn morning? Somehow, I do not believe that one bit."

"Miranda, once I make partner then I will have more flexibility. All I need is for you to support me just a little while longer."

She could smell the exotic blend of what seemed like orchids and mandarin from across the room. He thought he was outsmarting her by coming home in some different clothes. Wherever he was the scent was obviously sprayed everywhere because she could smell it from where she sat. Now all she had to do was bade her time, seeing as though he always got sloppy when he thought he was getting away with some shit.

"Honestly, Israel, I don't know how much longer I can hold on. I'm tired of having the same arguments. I'm tired of waking up every morning feeling disrespected and unappreciated. You do whatever the fuck you want and want me to be okay with it. Hear me and hear me good, your time is wearing thin so I suggest you get your shit together," Miranda warned.

Israel reached into his pocket and pulled out the box he managed to smuggle pass her. He realized he had been distant lately and wanted Miranda to know he still loved her. He knew he was fucking up and if he did not do something drastic he would be getting a glimpse at the woman she was a few years ago. He was sure that she wouldn't go to that extreme again, but that didn't mean she wouldn't act a fool if need be. He sat the box on the island and stepped back to lean against the counter. Miranda looked at him and then at the box. She knew it was another please forgive me gift because he's fucking up and wants her to turn a blind eye.

"What's in the box, Israel?"

"Open it and see. I worked hard to make sure it was perfect like you."

Miranda hesitated before she picked up the box. She popped the top open and saw a beautifully set diamond ring. The emerald cut reminded her of the very first friendship ring he'd given her six months into their relationship. She looked up at him and then back at the stone. It was gestures like this that made her love and hate him at the same time. He moved closer to her and held her hand. He took the ring out of the box and placed it on her finger. Israel raised her hand to his mouth and placed a kiss on it.

"Thank you, Israel. I appreciate the gift, but I would prefer my husband come home at night. To me that would be a much better gift," Miranda said.

"I understand, baby, and I will do a better job of making it home at a respectable time," Israel said, placing a kiss on her lips.

No matter how many women he slept with, his heart belonged to Miranda.

Israel grabbed his coffee and headed upstairs to take a shower. He had hoped Miranda didn't smell Nova on him. He didn't mean to sleep passed the time he should've gotten home. He had no time to freshen up or take a shower. He was already late and needed to get home before he reached the point of no return. He was glad he had picked up the jewelry last night before heading to Nova's house. He pulled the receipt from his pocket and smiled. One pair of two-carat princess cut earrings for his mistress and a four-point-five carat emerald cut ring for his wife. He had both of his women at bay and was close to becoming partner. For Israel Cantrell, life was good and getting better.

Chapter 3
Nova Pussy Trapping

"I'll take yo' man, yo' fiancé, ya' husband—"

The music of Mia X blared loudly from the speakers of Nova's brand new Mercedes-Benz CLK. A gift courtesy of an ex-man she had indeed taken from some desperate housewife. Women who had no idea on how to seduce a man so Nova was more than happy to do so. She had a natural gift for making even a regular Joe Blow feel like he was the mutha'fucking man. It was because of that they gave her nothing but the best. Every possession that she owned came from the bank account of some unhappily, attached man.

The twenty-six-year-old, Nigerian born sex kitten fancied the way that Mia X boldly told the main chick to bow down because despite popular belief, the side chick was a factor. Long before the world knew of Olivia Pope and the bizarre side chick super power she possessed, Nova held that title. She had been at the beck and call of her king even before dealing with the average men she was forced to deal with now.

She played upon the hearts of men to ensure that she would always look good while living the fabulous life. Some people were born to be the help and although that was most of Nova's family, she vowed to never have that slave mentality. She didn't give a damn what she had to do or who she had to fuck over, she would always get hers. Sure, she had plenty of enemies because of it but none of them dared to ever approach her. As beautiful and alluring as she was, Nova was also wickedly evil. Her seductive nature could turn into the python's venom in a matter of seconds, but that was only when provoked.

Nova knew that she was far too pretty to still crave the need to get down and dirty. She looked up into her rearview mirror and winked her eye at her own reflection, pleased with what she saw. As a woman who used her looks and unadulterated sex appeal to get whatever she wanted, she kept her shit tight. Women across the world helplessly paid to look like what came natural to her.

A pair of overpriced sunglasses hung low on her milk chocolate, high cheekbones. Nothing but the finest high end designer clothes adorned her toned frame. The sun illuminated her never out of place, short crimson tresses. Her skin glowed from that natural, I'm the shit vibe she felt in her soul. From her full, Ruby Woo painted lips to every perfectly sculptured curve on her body, Nova was the type of woman you never wanted around your man. They knew it, she knew it, and she got a huge rush whenever she thought about it.

Her phone rung, temporarily stopping her flow. She looked down at the screen on her dashboard and immediately laughed at seeing Jamal's number pop up yet again. He was always clingy and never able to grasp ahold of the fact that she only fucked with him when she needed something. That was only when she was in between cash cows and whenever she found a new one, she would forget about him as if he never existed. As soon as she felt like she needed him, he came running back, licking his own balls, and looking even more pathetic than when she dismissed him.

As far as she was concerned, she was over his ass and was sure he knew it but just didn't give a damn. He was hooked, and addicted to Nova's potion of uninhibited lust and wanted more. She could ask him to cut out his wife's heart and he would run and retrieve it like a huntsman.

Men always found themselves perplexed on how they had been left strung out, though Nova already knew what she could and would do without giving two shits about it. Once she got in, got what she wanted, and then fucked up their lives, she was out. Toying with men and their hearts was child's play for her. She hunted them down, studied their asses intently, and before they could see it coming, she'd kill the happiness from their souls. Case in point, her new lil boo, Israel.

His time with her had been slow and tedious on Nova's part. This was a special case for her. One that she wouldn't fail no matter what. She had planned to take her time with this one and that's exactly what she'd done for the past ten months.

She stalked and obsessed with every detail about him before making a move to make him the next man she brought to his knees. Surprisingly, he had some bomb ass sex that left Nova satisfied, but always wanting more. She had to catch herself a few times from craving a sex session with him. He was the first to ever give it to her how she needed. Even still, she was going to juice him for all she could get because men were weak for pussy, especially good pussy.

Thoughts of Israel surprising her with a pair of diamond earrings the night before made her pussy wet. She picked up her cellphone and called him for what she considered, daily ego fucking. Men loved to have their egos stroked and what better way than to make them feel wanted, damn near needed sexually.

The phone only rang once before he answered excitedly.

"Hey, baby!" he all but screamed.

Nova rolled her eyes but managed to still make her voice drip sweet honey.

"Hey, daddy. What you doing?"

"I was just thinking of how good that pussy is. You were amazing last night."

Israel instantly kicked his feet up on his desk. He wanted to call Nova all morning but he knew one of her rules was to never wake her early in the morning. Not to mention, Miranda was on his ass and he didn't need to rock the boat at home at this point. Last thing he needed was her ass pressing him about who and what he'd been doing.

"Ooh, baby. We have one hell of a connection because I was just thinking about how bad I want to feel you inside of me at this moment. I wish I could ride your ass to sleep right now."

"Let me come see you. We can make it happen right now."

"Only if you stay all night. I hate that getting up at three in the morning, creeping out shit."

"Nova, we've had this conversation before. She's still my wife. I cannot do her like that," Israel tried to reason.

He knew Nova wanted to feel like they were more than just sex, but Miranda would burn this city down if he ever pulled some shit like that again. Lately, he could tell by the look in her eyes that her once idol threats now held some validity.

"Oh, I see. I forgot, I'm just the lil' piece of ass, the cum receptacle that he plays with when he's bored with his prudish ass wife," Nova sniffed as if she was crying.

She was proud of herself for putting on such a great performance. She almost believed she gave a fuck about Israel or his ill built ass wife, she was so good. When the truth was, she just wanted the money.

"Damn, baby, I'm so sorry. I didn't mean to make you cry. You know daddy hates when you do that. I promise I'll stay tonight. I want you to be happy. I'll do whatever you want."

Nova stopped her fake tears and smiled at herself in the mirror before opening her mouth to talk some hip stuff.

"You mean it, you'll do whatever for me?"

"Absolutely."

"Anything? What if I wanted to fuck you in your bedroom at home?" Nova tested the waters just to see how far gone Israel was.

"Umm. Why would, umm why would you want me to do that?" Israel asked uncomfortably.

He was crazy enough to cheat, but fucking another woman in the bed that his wife slept in was just insane.

"You said you don't love her so what's the difference. I just think it's exciting and you know how nasty I get when I'm excited."

"Yeah. Believe me, I know how nasty you can get. Shit, I uh guess I'll have to send her out the house tonight for a few hours."

"That's ok. I don't want her calling, waking me up all night. You just give me two hours in your bed and I got the rest."

"Ok, two hours' tops. I know how yo' ass can go all night Nova."

Israel was still reluctant but an image of Nova spread eagle across his bed was pushing away the clouds of doubt and regret. He now found himself excited for the night to come.

"Thank you, daddy. I just need you to love me as much as I love you, Israel. I'll handle the rest of the plans because I'm going to fuck you so good you won't ever touch your wife again."

Nova had her lines rehearsed. She always knew what game to spit at a man. To her, Israel was the type who wanted to dominate everything and the fact that he couldn't tame Nova was a maddening chase. So, she made it her business to take charge as much as possible with him.

"Is that right? You want me pounding inside that tight, wet pussy in our bed?" Israel whispered as he walked to his office door and shut it.

He didn't need anyone in the office suspecting anything was out of place. Everyone respected Miranda there, so he needed to keep his affair quiet.

Israel could tell from the heavy breathing in Nova's voice that his dick would remain rock hard until he stroked himself off. He eased down in his chair and began applying light pressure to his throbbing manhood.

"I do," Nova purred.

"I know your lil' hot ass is wearing either a skirt or dress today. Open them legs wide and tell me what you want me to do to that pussy."

"I want you to lie back and let me feed it to you real nice, slow, and *nasty*."

"Nova, damn girl. I can taste you right now. You taste like magical shit is created between your thighs. I want to suck you dry."

Nova had to stifle her laughter. Israel was always saying shit that he thought was poetic. He assumed that Nova was into this phone sex session just like he was, but little did he know she was absently scratching off a lottery ticket she found in her sun visor.

"Yes, daddy, suck it all up and then flip me over and pipe me down," Nova pushed out amidst fake moans.

"You know this pussy is so damn good, and so damn tight."

"You like that? What you wanna do to it?"

"I'm gonna pound this shit out. I want you on your hands and knees, ass tooted up, and open it up for me. I need to just slide in."

"You got it, baby. Whatever you want. Just cum in me, daddy. Give me all that dick and you betta not fucking stop. Cum in me."

"Say it again, baby. Where you want me to cum?" Israel's voice had become deeper and his breathing labored.

Nova knew that this moment was the perfect time to make her move. Her mother taught her the best time to force a man's hands was when he had his dick in it. It rendered him powerless every time.

"Damn! Shit, baby I gotta go. I forgot to do something so important," Nova feigned panic, changing the mood in one hundred and eighty degrees.

"What? I'm about to cum, baby. Please. Tell me where you want me to cum," Israel pleaded.

He needed to get this nut off. There was no way he would make it the whole day of he didn't.

"No, I have to call Neiman Marcus immediately. They're holding a new Birkin bag for me and if I don't claim it in the next few minutes, they're going to sell it. I've been on the waiting list a long time," Nova whined.

"Damn it, Nova. I'll order the fucking bag soon as we hang up if you'll let me bust my shit before my balls go blue. Where can I come, bitch?"

Nova paused to keep herself from screaming in delight that he would buy the bag. She didn't care about him calling her a bitch because she encouraged him to call her whatever he felt like when they were sexual. Small things like that was something his wife would never agree to, which is why Israel found himself deeply infatuated with Nova. Now that he agreed to what she wanted, she would give him what he needed.

"In my mouth, daddy. Shoot that shit right down my throat."

Nova heard the loud grunt followed by a string of explicit words that she knew would come. Israel's body trembled as he strained to catch his breath. Israel was now soft and mushy as were his pockets. Nova turned her seduction back on and made sure Israel did not forget his promise.

"So, baby when you order that bag, make sure you get me a bonus gift as well."

Chapter 4
Heart Strings

    Five o'clock couldn't get there fast enough for Israel. From the moment, he'd gotten off the phone with Nova he couldn't think of anything but fucking her. He spent most of the day trying to figure out how he was going to get Miranda out of the house for a few hours. God must have heard his prayers because as soon as he went to lunch he heard a commercial on the radio for a concert at a downtown venue. He wondered why his wife hadn't said anything, seeing as though she loved the artists that were coming. Either way it didn't matter to him, he happily bought two tickets to the Mind, Body, & Soul concert with Jill Scott, Erykah Badu, and Anthony Hamilton. He would surprise his wife with the tickets so she and her sister can enjoy a night out on the town. Normally, he would be working until around seven, however, since he had to swing by *Neiman's* he left a little earlier. His assistant had picked up the tickets for him earlier, so he didn't have to worry about doing that. Traffic was backed up and as he inched down the highway he was reminded why he didn't leave work during rush hour. The concert started at 8 p.m. so he would have enough time to drop the tickets off if traffic hurried along. Just as he thought to pick up his phone and call home, it rang.
    "Hello," Israel answered.
    "Hey, baby, I saw you called earlier. Is everything okay?" Miranda asked.
    "Yes, I was calling to tell you to find something sexy to wear tonight. I have a surprise for you."

"Israel, you don't need to buy me anything else," Miranda expressed.

"I know, but I wanted to do this for you. Can you call your sister and tell her to get ready as well?"

"What kind of surprise do you have for me that includes my sister, Israel Cantrell," she teased.

"You'll see so just tell her to be ready. I'll be home in about an hour if this traffic clears up."

"Okay, baby, I love you and I'll see you soon," Miranda said.

"I love you too. See you soon," Israel said, hitting the button on his steering wheel to hang up.

He hated lying to his wife, but the kind of sex game Nova had him wrapped up in caused him to do all kinds of stupid shit. Hopefully, Nova would be satisfied with the effort he was putting in tonight for her. He fully intended on granting whatever wishes she wanted as long as she continued to fuck him like she did.

Israel remembered a time when Miranda was a wildcat between the sheets. There was a point in their marriage they would destroy rooms with all their wild fucking. Miranda had a sex drive that was out of this world, but then out of nowhere it came to a halt. He knew he was mostly to blame with his affairs. The finding out of each one chipped away at her confidence and trust to the point it seemed she wasn't sexually turned on as much as she used to be. Israel wanted to stop and for a while he had, then he met Nova. The milk chocolate sex goddess with crimson hair and an untamable personality to match. Nova had a way of making him feel youthful and to a forty-two-year-old man, that meant a lot. Every time he leaves Nova, he's exhausted and fulfilled all at the same time. The girl had a gift and he was glad she decided to share it with him.

Traffic had finally moved along and he was about ten minutes from his first destination. Luckily for him, he had called ahead to have the purses put to the side. Thanks to his personal shopper, Kyle, he didn't need to order online or wrestle with common shoppers when he wanted anything. When he'd called earlier, Kyle assured him he would put the bag to the side and pull something for Miranda. Israel knew there was no way he could buy something for Nova and not for Miranda. He was fucking up, but he wasn't that damn crazy. Israel pulled into the parking garage so he could get in and out. He wanted to grab the gifts and head home so he could give Miranda the tickets. He was sure she would want to drive his car so he wanted to make sure her night was perfect.

Ever since he bought his Audi R8 Sypder, Miranda jumped behind the wheel every chance she got. Never mind the truck she drove that wasn't even two years old. For months, she begged him for a Porsche Cayenne. Initially, he hesitated to buy it, but when he missed what she felt were *curfews* he purchased it without a second thought. If he did not learn anything from the cheating men in his family, he knew peace at home was a necessity.

His watch read, *6:15 p.m.* He walked into Neiman's and immediately spotted Kyle. Kyle acknowledged he saw him and headed for the back to grab the merchandise. Israel roamed over to the women's shoe section to see if there were any new shoes Miranda may not have at home. His wife had a thing for shoes and he was partially responsible for the addiction. Hell, between birthdays, anniversaries, special occasions, and his *I fucked up/I'm sorry* gifts, she had just about everything a woman could want. Kyle walked out with what looked like two Hermes bags. Israel shook his head, placing the shoe he had in his hand down and walked over to him.

"Mr. Cantrell, here are the purses you requested," Kyle said, handing him the purses.

Israel held up both purses and gave them a once over that any man buying purses would give. He never understood the fascination with purses or why women needed so many. Not to mention, he could not understand why something they threw, dropped, or stuffed into places cost so damn much. Both bags Kyle handed him were bright in color. Still, he could look at the bags and could immediately tell which one Nova wanted. Even though she had a grown as way of fucking, she was still young in some of her ways. By the look on Kyle's face, Israel could tell he was trying to figure out who the purses were for.

"Thank you, Kyle. How much is this going to cost me?"

"Well, the Soie Cool bag is fifteen hundred dollars and the Garden Party bag is four thousand one hundred and twenty-five dollars. With taxes your total is five thousand six hundred forty-seven dollars and fifty cents."

Israel pulled out his wallet and handed him his American Express card. Kyle took the card and purses to the counter to ring out the items. He handed Israel his receipt as he bagged the purses. Israel thought about all the ways he was going to make Nova pay for this bag he just purchased. Seeing as though he just gifted her some diamond earrings, she had plenty to work off. Miranda's bag would simply be a distraction in hopes that she and her sister stayed out as late as possible. He had a long night of sex ahead of him and he wanted to enjoy it without any interruptions. He made sure he checked in with Dillon earlier to see if the property was clear. He and Dillon owned rental properties throughout the city and would occasionally use them for their side action if needed. Since Miranda was an interior designer, she decorated all the homes. Each home was fully furnished for staging purposes. This made it easier if they rented to someone who wanted to buy the home. For Israel, it would serve as the perfect stage for what needs to look like his home.

He knew Nova wanted to come to his house, still no matter how good her pussy was, and it was good, he couldn't risk her being at his house. He did a lot of stupid shit, though bringing his mistresses to his house was never one of them. Miranda loved their home, however she would pour kerosene all over it and light it with a match if she found out another woman had been there. He learned that much from his father. His dad would always say, *Son, don't shit where you lay your head. Whatever you do in the streets, keep it away from home.*

Like most men, he was a good husband and father who had his vices. Some men give into alcohol, gambling, and others to drugs. For most of the Cantrell men, women and power seemed to be their downfall. His father had numerous affairs on his mother and per his aunt, his grandfather was the same. It wasn't until he was in high school that he realized he had another brother across town. The moment he found out about Dillon, they were inseparable. Although Dillon was single, he had his fair share of drama with women too. It seemed the men in their family was cursed when it came to women. Hopefully, Dillon wouldn't make the mistake he made and settle down before he fucks it out of his system. Israel pushed open the garage and pulled in. Tonight, he would let his wife floss in his ride.

Since he would be knee deep in Nova tonight, he had no real need for it. Israel shot Nova a text before getting out of the car. He wanted her to know he had something special for her and wanted her to be primed and ready. He checked his other phone to see the address Dillon said was open for use and then sent it to Nova. Israel grabbed the bags. He turned the phone off, slid it in his briefcase, and headed into the house.

As soon as he walked in, he made his way to his office. He needed to hide Nova's purse until it was safe for him to put it in Miranda's truck. Once he had it tucked away, he headed upstairs to the bedroom to give her the surprise he mentioned earlier. Israel turned the corner of their bedroom to head to the closet. Upon walking into the room, he could smell the fragrances of her body wash and perfumes. There was something about a woman smelling good that turned him on. It was like an aphrodisiac or something. To him, a woman could have on the simplest outfit, but if she smelled good everything else was a go. Israel walked into their closet to see Miranda in a black sheer and lace undergarment set.

Damn, he thought to himself.

Sometimes, he forgot just how beautiful she was. Over the years, her shape had gone from petite and curvy, to full figured and curvy. To put it lightly, she had a grown ass woman's body. Even though he stepped out with other women, he loved every dimple and curve in her body. Whenever she did give it to him, she made the wait worthwhile. Israel had every intention of getting his shit together, he just needed to get Nova out of his system first. Miranda had his heart and soul, but for now, Nova had his dick and that was a power like no other.

"Hey, baby," she said, interrupting his thoughts.

"Hey, Miranda," he said, walking over to kiss her.

He'd thought about getting a quickie in, but he needed his energy for tonight. He would take a stab at his wife tomorrow.

"So, tell me what's my surprise?" she asked, excitedly.

Israel had two surprises for her. He reached into his suit jacket to pull out the first one. He handed her the tickets and her eyes almost popped out her head.

"Oh. my God, baby! I wanted to go to this concert, but since you've been so busy lately I didn't want to bother asking if you wanted to go."

"Damn, Miranda, I'm sorry. I know I've been busy lately and I actually have to go back to the office, but I wanted to come home and give you these first."

Israel could see the excitement in her eyes, but there was a pinch of sadness. Whenever a concert would come to town they would be there. He knew his selfishness was getting in the way, but he couldn't kick the Nova habit just yet. In the meantime, he would just shower Miranda with gifts until he got his shit together. He watched as she pulled the gray tube dress over her curves. He wasn't entirely sure he wanted her going out without him in a dress like that. It showed way too much of her curves and would welcome some unneeded attention. Israel tilted his head back to look at her round booty. Age had done her ass very well. Miranda had been petite up until she hit her late thirties. It was then all her thickness began to appear and land in some favorable spots. Israel stood there as she grabbed some multi-colored sandals to put on her feet. It was then he realized he had another surprise for her. He'd forgotten all about the purse from looking at her get dressed. If today had been tomorrow, she would not be going to a concert and the only Anthony Hamilton they'd been hearing is from a stereo as they made love.

Israel shook the images out of his head so he could give her his next surprise. He pulled the bag from behind the door where he'd hidden it and gave it to her. She looked at him with a confused look before taking it.

"What's this, Israel?"

"Well, it seems I made a good choice considering the shoes you're wearing."

Miranda opened the bag and pulled the suede duffle bag out. She looked at the print on the outer bag and saw it was Hermes. She wondered what he had done to be giving her a bag she knew costed somewhere around three thousand dollars. Miranda pulled the purse out and a smile formed across her face. The purse was perfect and it was a beautiful Kelly green. He was right, it went perfect with her shoes. She looked at him and blew him a kiss. Israel winked at her and handed her his kiss.

Israel smiled and then headed downstairs. He needed a drink and wanted to sit down before he met up with Nova. It was now 7:30 p.m. and Miranda would be leaving shortly. The concert started at 8:30 p.m., and he wasn't sure if she still needed to pick up her sister. For his sake, he hoped she did. This would buy him more time to be with Nova. Israel made himself a drink and sat down on the sofa for a second. He told Nova he would meet her at 9:00 p.m., that way it was dark and she wouldn't be able to tell if it was his house or not.

Another ten minutes passed before Miranda finally came downstairs. She looked sexy as hell and even though it did not seem like it, he was proud to be her husband. She was smart, independent, and loyal as hell. She looked at their marriage as an investment. Something she had committed to and given her all to be in. Israel knew he didn't deserve her, but he would die before he gave her up.

"Okay, Israel, I'm heading out."

"The keys to my car are on the key holder if you want to take my car," he said.

"Well, Mr. Cantrell, you are really going all out tonight, huh?"

"You deserve all of it, Mrs. Cantrell," he said, winking and puckering his lips for a kiss. "Be gentle with her tonight. Bring her back in one piece."

"Are you referring to me or the car," Miranda asked, jokingly.

Israel laughed before responding, "Both of you, please."

"Okay, baby, I promise I'll bring your precious cargo back unharmed."

Miranda walked over, placed a kiss on his lips, and waved goodbye. Israel swallowed the rest of his drink and headed upstairs for the shower. Tonight, was going to be a long night and he was ready to get it started.

⚜

After twenty minutes in the shower, Israel hopped out and dried off. He sprayed on some of his Gucci cologne and lotion himself. He was glad he had stayed in shape over the years. For some men in his age group, they had let their bodies go. Since he was still a part-time ladies man, Israel stayed in the gym. Most of the young guys in the gym still could not believe he had fifteen to twenty years on them. Israel brushed his mustache and his beard. He gave himself a once over before heading to his closet. He grabbed a polo shirt and some jeans to throw on. He needed his outfit to be believable when he came back home in the morning. Since he told Miranda he was going back to work, he would simply explain his outfit change as something he threw on after working out and wanted to be more comfortable in. It wasn't uncommon for him to work in casual clothes. It was just rare.

Israel finished buttoning the last button before turning the lights off in the closet. He made his way downstairs to grab the bag with Nova's purse in it and headed out the door. He pushed the garage open and grab the key to Miranda's car. He hopped in the car and as soon as he started it up his phone rang.

'What's up, man?" he asked when he answered.

"Nothing much, bro. Just calling to see what kind of trouble you're getting into tonight since you needed the property to be empty," Dillon asked.

He knew Dillon liked Miranda, but out of loyalty to him he minded his business and only offered his advice when solicited. He remembered the first time he had got caught with Cheyenne. He was in a bad place and Dillon had been there for him. He had his moments of judgment and sibling reprimands, but he was there. It was that incident that prompted them to start investing in rental properties. After the hefty bill, he paid from living in a hotel room, he decided if he continued down this path, he needed somewhere to lay his head in case he was put out.

"Man, the trouble's name is Nova and I'm fighting to let her go."

"So, you fucking a chick named Nova? How old is this one? You know you good for meeting them young chicks and setting them up," Dillon said, slyly.

"Who cares how old she is. Man, she so damn sexy. She has this chocolate skin that makes me want to lick her from head to toe. Then she has this red hair that drives me nuts feels so good in my fingers when I'm hitting from the back. Bro, she be doing so much."

"Aww yeah, what exactly does this one be doing?"

Israel normally had a rule about talking about the women he'd slept with. He knew his boys and his brothers were always on the hunt. Therefore, he never wanted to give them any reason to go hunting for his selected bunch. Nova was one of his prized possessions, but he knew his brother knew better.

"Hell, what don't she do? I mean, her lips have literally been touched by gods and don't get me started on that voice. Man, when she be riding me, she starts speaking in her native tongue and I lose it. I know I need to let her go, but damn that mouth is God-sent. It's like she has some kind of voodoo over me. Every time I get close to cutting her loose, she does something to suck me back in."

"So, how you meet her?"

"I met her one night when I was out with Ian. I think you were out of town that weekend, so me and Ian went out with the fellas. I bumped into her at the club and before the night was over, I was deep inside her."

"Damn bro, that's ironic."

"What do you mean?"

"Nothing. Well, I hope you keep your shit together because I'd hate to see what Miranda would do if she found out about another one. You know you barely survived Bria, so be careful," Dillon mocked.

"You and me both," Israel laughed, though somewhat bothered by his brother's comment.

He wasn't sure what the sarcasm was about, especially since he had quite the track record with women.

Israel didn't have far to travel to the rental property. This property was within his community which is why he chose it. He had no intention of spending the night with Nova, but he knew it would be a late night so he needed to be close to get home quick. He was surprised this property was open, seeing as though Wildwood was a nice neighborhood. He and Dillon owned properties in about ten different neighborhoods throughout St. Louis.

"Alright, well man, make sure you beat it down and get your ass back home. I don't need Miranda calling me about where you were at."

"Well, in the event I get too deep in it and fall asleep, I worked late, we grabbed some drinks, and I crashed at your house."

"I got you, bro. Holla at you later," Dillon said, hanging up.

Israel hung up and turned into the sunken driveway leading to the back of the house. Nova hadn't showed up yet and he was glad he'd beaten her there. He needed to make sure it looked like he lived there and had been home waiting for her. He got out with the bag in his hand. He opened the door and walked in. The house smelled spectacular. Miranda must have stopped by at some point and swapped out the oil scents. Israel put the bag down and reached to pull out his other phone when he realized he left it at home.

Shit, he thought. He was so ready to get this night started he walked out and left the damn phone in his briefcase. He was glad he'd turned it off, so the chances of it going off were low. On the flip side, he had no way of contacting Nova. He had never called from his main phone and wasn't going to start today. That was the first mistake he made with Cheyenne and was the ammunition Miranda murdered him with. Well, aside from catching him butt ass naked in a hotel room with her. For his sake, he hoped Nova was good at following directions. Otherwise, this night would be a wash.

An hour had gone by and Israel had fallen asleep on the couch. He hadn't even realized he had fell asleep until he was startled by the doorbell. Israel hopped up to open the door. Nova was standing there in a black mini dress with stockings being held up by what he knew was a garter belt. He could only imagine what was underneath it. He stepped out of the way so she could come in.

"Damn, Nova, you look sexy as hell."

Nova formed a devilish smile on her face. She knew Israel was addicted to sex. He loved women, their bodies, and the way each of their shapes curved. She looked at him as he stood there, sexy as ever as well. He had a caramel tone that blended well with his dark brown eyes and coal black facial hair. He knew he was God's gift to women and that's why they were in this predicament. He needed to be taught a lesson. He needed to learn women were not toys to be played with at his disposal. He needed to be broken and she was just the woman to do it.

Nova winked at him, and said, "I know."

Israel loved her confidence. She didn't need him to tell her she was sexy. She already knew it and wore it like the skin she was covered in. Her body was perfection. It was as if God himself carved it out and the devil stood by to watch. Nova looked around before, finding herself at the stairwell.

"Nice house. Where's your wife?" she asked, sarcastically.

"She went to a concert with her sister and won't be back until after work tomorrow. They're having a girl's night so she's going to crash there tonight."

Nova smiled. She knew this wasn't Israel's house, but she would make him pay for that later. Not only was she going to let him believe she thought she was fucking him in the bed he shared with his wife, she was going to make sure he'd spend the night. If he wasn't in trouble at home already, he would be after tonight.

"Shall we go upstairs?" she asked.

Israel held out his hand to her, leading her to the bedroom. He was ready to get this night started. He knew Nova would make this lie worthwhile. The exotic scent she always wore was as alluring as the first day he met her. He wasn't completely sure what it was, but he knew he'd never smelled it before. They walked into the bedroom and he gave her a slight shove onto the bed. He started removing his shirt. She leaned back on her elbows and watched him. She crossed her legs giving him a peek of the thigh that was begging to be freed. She could see his dick imprint rising against his jeans. He was ready for her, but she was going to make this night last. He took his shirt off and revealed his well-chiseled chest and abdomen. She sat up and pulled him close to her. She blew on his stomach and twisted her tongue in circular motion in and around his belly button. She slowly unbuckled his belt and pulled it through the loops. He rubbed his hands through her hair.

Israel had never been a fan of eccentric hair colors, but the way Nova wore it drove him mad. It highlighted her creamy, milk chocolate skin perfectly. Her eyes contained so much depth he often got lost him them. Her high cheekbones formed the smile that hardened and weaken him at the same time. She unbuttoned and unzipped his pants. She removed them, grabbing his briefs in the process. Slowly taunting him, she freed his rock-hard dick that stared back at her. It was a beautiful work of art. A gift and curse to them both. Israel stepped out of his pants and Nova stood up. She moved around him, dragging her hand in slow motion from front to back of his body. She shoved him onto the bed and watched him roll over. Nova had planned to give him the drug he craved, but not before she got her gift. She would tease him and right when she had him where she wanted him, she would ask for a proof of purchase.

"Sing to me Nova. Let me hear that beautiful song you always sing in my ear before you cum."

As she started to serenade him, Nova placed her leg on the foot of the bed. She ran her fingers from her calf to her thigh. Drawing a map for him to place his kisses as she puckered her full lips. Pausing from her song, she played a slight game of tug of war with her lips and she nibbled on them seductively. She moved her leg onto the floor and she slid the straps of her dress playfully over her shoulders. Making sure he could see the danger he was walking into, she turned around as she teasingly slid it over her taut ass. She bent over, exposing the garter belt. Israel eyes almost popped out of his head when he realized she had no panties on. She wore a bra, garter belt, and stockings that were begging to be removed.

"Aww shit, baby, come sit on this dick," Israel said, stroking himself as he became more mesmerized by her body, her scent, and the hypnotic tone of her voice.

He never knew what the song was, but the language in which she sang it in was beautiful.

Nova slid her fingers between her legs. She wanted his attention to be completely focused on her. She was glad she'd gotten that Brazilian wax with her standing appointment. Thanks to one of her old flings, she had a paid spa membership.

"Not yet, baby. I want my gift you promised me," Nova said, pouting.

"Check behind the door," he said.

Nova moved to see there was a bag hanging on the doorknob. She opened it up and saw the bag she had been waiting a year for. She smiled, knowing the bag probably didn't even put a dent in Israel's pocket. She wondered what her bonus gift was.

"What else did you get me, baby?"

Israel smiled.

"A new house," he said, grabbing the set of keys from under the pillow. "Or shall I say our house. Now come over here and jump on this dick," he commanded.

Nova fought to contain her excitement. She told him she wanted a bonus gift, but never did she think he would spring for a house. Israel could see she was trying to act like the house didn't faze her, but he knew better. He had a loft in Lake St. Louis he'd purchased years ago, that neither Miranda nor Dillon knew about. It was paid for and off the books. He only used it as a tax write off or somewhere to duck off to when he didn't want to be bothered. The only person he ever took there was Shelby, his colleague he started sleeping with after Cheyenne. She was the last person he fucked at his job. Women were way too emotional when you didn't want to be bothered with them anymore. Shelby could not understand how her time had expired. Thanks to her, everyone at work knew about their affair and everything else you could think of. He knew he have contributed to her breakdown, but they were both adults, and she knew he was married at the end of the day. Her little public stunt almost costed him his job, but since she resigned instead it blew over. Lucky for him, his boss had been there before and knew affairs never ended well, so he gave him a second chance.

Nova slowly unsnapped each strap holding up her stockings. Israel growing impatient, stood up, pulling her to him as he pushed her towards the bed and bent her over. He ripped the condom packet open, pulling it out. Normally, he liked it raw, but Bria taught him that was a lesson learned the hard way. He rolled the condom on and slid inside her. Israel paused, catching his breath and slowing down his excitement. He began stroking her slowly, creating a rhythm he could control. He had a long night ahead of him and needed to pace himself. Nova responded to his strokes with strokes of her own. She was in no way submissive when it came to sex. She would allow her victims the momentary idea of control only to snatch it away as she rode them to glory, taking pieces of their soul with her. Israel's soul however belonged to someone else. With each stroke, she became more hypnotized by it. Nova wanted him for herself, but as usual the queen bitch had first dibs. Since their time was only temporary, she would enjoy the pleasure as long as she could.

"Ahhhh," Israel moaned loudly.

It seemed like round one was getting close to the end and like him, she knew there would be more to come before the night ended.

Minutes had turned into hours, and hours had become memories he would always have. Moments passed, orgasms were released, and the lust they carried for each other was a beautiful decoration painted on the wall. Israel looked at the clock and saw it was a little past midnight. He wanted more, but he was spent. He figured he would close his eyes for a few seconds to sleep off some of the exhaustion. He would wake Nova up around 2:30 p.m. to tell her Miranda decided to come home instead of staying with her sister. He prayed by morning this night would be worth it and his marriage was still intact.

Chapter 5
Unapologetically Finished

Miranda looked around at the mess she had made. The sun was coming up and she had been up since she'd gotten home. The concert ended around midnight and once she dropped her sister off, she flew home in hopes of having a late-night quickie. She was going to crash at her sister's house, but the drinks she inhaled had her feeling good and she wanted to end her night on top of her husband. Though as usual, he wasn't home. Running the risk of getting a D.W.I., Miranda drove by his office to see if he was there. When she didn't see his car anywhere in the parking lot, she made her way to Dillon's house. She knew if he was up to something that's where he would lie and say he was all night. Miranda sat outside Dillon's house for thirty minutes before she drove off. She fought back the urge to cry in hopes that she missed him in passing and by the time she got home he would be there.

The entire way home Miranda thought about how she had no more energy to endure another affair. As a woman, she had reached her quota. She never believed in divorce, but she didn't believe in being a damn fool either. She had stuck by Israel through three affairs, three counts of betrayal. Cheyenne, Shelby, and Bria were the names etched in the corners of her mind. Their faces haunted her at night and even though she had stayed and forgiven him, they still resided between them. Now she sat in the middle of her room, bottle emptier than she was with a phone that proved her husband was addicted to hurting her. By the time, Miranda had gotten home it was almost 2 a.m., and Israel was nowhere to be found. His phone rang but there was no answer. The idea of what he could be doing or who he was doing it with drove her mad. After leaving Dillon's, Miranda drove back downtown to see if his car was parked anywhere in the Four Season's parking lot.

Miranda realized her search was pointless, so she returned home to start digging. She should have known he was up to something with the sudden gifts he was surprising her with. She was done being the good wife. She had no more masks to wear to hide behind the embarrassment of his infidelities. She would never forget the moment she found out about Shelby.

She was attending a holiday party with Israel and overheard two women who obviously worked there whispering. At first, she couldn't make out what they were saying. Then one of them had the nerve to approach her with a disrespectful comment regarding Israel and Shelby that damn near sent her over the edge. *Was he really having another affair with a woman from his job? Was it possible he had not learned his lesson from when she clowned the first time? Is this what their marriage was going to be like from now on?* For an hour Miranda stood outside in the freezing cold thinking, fuming and on fire from within. To be it honest, if it had not been a work-related function everybody in the party would have been introduced to her Cass and ninety-street background, including the bitch that had the nerve to make the comment. She remembered damn near snatching Israel off the dance floor after calming down long enough to walk back in. The entire way home she slapped him in every way she could, as hard as she could. It was Cheyenne all over again, but this time she was the only one standing on the outside looking in. The whole night all Miranda could think of was how everyone at the party probably knew and here she was, by his side, looking like a fucking clown again. Almost a year had passed before she allowed him back in their house and in their bed that time around.

The tears ran down Miranda's face as her hands grew numb from holding the phone. Everything from naked pictures to oversexed text messages stared back at her. There were phone calls from all kinds of numbers, incoming and outgoing. Picture after picture of women's titties, asses, and even what they possessed between their legs. Miranda could not fucking believe he had the nerve to have pictures of women that were not his wife. One picture really caught her eye since the red headed woman was obviously giving him head. There was another message that particularly stood out since it displayed the address to one of their rental properties. *Was he really fucking other women at the houses they used for income and for how long?*

"God, why? What have I done to deserve this? Why can't my husband be faithful?" she asked as her voice cracked. "I was right by his side and never once did I step out on him. Why can't this man stop hurting me? Lord, I'm so tired."

She placed the phone down to look at the receipt she found his pocket from the other night and a copy of their credit card bill. Israel had spent over fifteen thousand dollars at their personal jeweler. She wouldn't have thought twice about looking for it since the ring that sat on her finger was a pretty nice size rock. What caught her eye was that the receipt said two items, a diamond ring and a pair of earrings had been purchased. Miranda had torn their room apart and there was no trace of any diamond earrings, other than the ones she already owned. Then to add insult to injury, the motherfucker had the nerve to charge two purses to his credit card. It was as if this man thought he was a god of some sort. He walked around like he was untouchable and nothing could destroy him. Miranda smirked at the thought and it seemed she would have to be the hell Israel thought he was above.

Miranda had snatched all his clothes out of the closet and threw them in a pile in their great room. Even the dirty clothes that still carried what she presumed to be his mistress's scent filled the pile. She was done being this perfect wife. If he wanted a crazy, ghetto hood bitch, he was going to get one. Apparently, he couldn't act right unless she pulled a Bernadine from *Waiting to Exhale* on his ass. The empty hangers in his closet reminded her of how she felt. She had held on far too long and enough was enough. Their marriage had run its course. The clock read 7 a.m. and she had already called her sister to tell her to reschedule her clients for the day. They co-owned an interior design company together. Her sister was an architect and she was the interior designer. Together they designed and decorated some of the most beautiful homes around St. Louis. A few of their designs had been featured in

Architectural Digest, *Better Homes*, and a few other magazines. She wasn't an average woman and it was clear Israel had forgotten that very thing. Now it was her turn to show him just how much of a bad bitch she was out here.

"Fuck him!"

She threw the last of his shoes downstairs and then took a shower. She knew he wouldn't see the clothes when he first walked in due to the way their house was set up. She decided to take a shower, get real pretty, throw on some sexy lingerie, and wait for his trifling ass to come home. He would never expect she was angry, sitting there in some sexy undergarments and that's how she wanted it. Little did he know, she was getting ready to destroy his world as he knew it. Her first thought was to leave and go somewhere for a few weeks. They had a vacation home in Miami and some sun would do her good right now, but running wouldn't solve this. It was time to tame this beast right now. This bullshit, his bullshit, was going to stop today.

Miranda stepped over the mess on her floor and headed downstairs. She heard the garage door going up and she wanted to be front and center when he opened the back door. She placed the glass on the counter and hopped onto the kitchen island. Robe open with her titties sitting upright and thighs that welcomed any brave soul who dared to explore her core were exposed. She wasn't as small as she used to be, but she embraced every inch of her body. Miranda thought about all the dick she had turned down because she was a faithful wife. Football players, politicians, and even some doctors had propositioned her for dates. No, she didn't look like any of the young hoes running around St. Louis, but she didn't need to. She was educated, confident, and independent, qualities most of the trash they chased didn't have including her husband's mistresses. All they were looking for was the come up and here she was with her own shit and still couldn't get this bastard to act right.

Israel walked up to the door and prayed to any God who would hear him that Miranda would buy the story he was about to slang her way. He had totally fucked up by falling asleep. He should have set the alarm on his phone, but the one he had was not the one he needed so he couldn't risk Miranda blowing him up and Nova getting mad. When he rolled over it was 5 a.m. and Nova was rocking back and forth on his dick. A normal man who knew he was going to be murdered would have flown home quick hoping to beat his wife waking up. However, Israel was not normal and tested fate every time he could. Nova waking him up on top of him clouded his judgment. Her insides were just as warm as her thighs that pinned him down. The orgasms she pulled out of him caused him to make bad decisions. Israel opened the door and damn near tripped over his own feet. Miranda was on top of the island wearing panties that hardly covered her pussy and a bra that she could have done without since he could see straight through it. He could feel his dick getting hard and he was grateful. After Nova assassinated it earlier, he didn't think it would regain any life until later on today.

With his wife on top of the counter in her *come fuck me* get up, he'd been proven wrong. Israel was relieved to see she wasn't mad. She was obviously still on a concert high and wanted him to lay the *D* down. He threw his wallet and phone down on the counter. He walked over to her and she spun around so he could sit right in the middle of her beautiful place. Israel inhaled her center and she smelled divine. He leaned in to place a kiss on top of her pussy. Miranda pressed his face into her as his soft kisses caused conflicting emotions to stir inside her. Even now, she could smell the orchid and mandarin scent she'd smelled before. Her senses may have betrayed her earlier, but now she was sure of everything she'd known to be true.

"Damn, baby."

Israel sat down on the stool as he moved her panties to the side. He pressed his face into her pussy and kissed her before sticking his tongue inside her. As she bent her head back, tears ran down Miranda's face, causing the moans to crack as they escaped her lips. There was so much pain and pleasure wrapped up in this man. So many good and bad times that disrupted her ability to make sound decisions. She had so much to say, but wanted to live in this pleasurable, chaotic moment just one more time before she said what needed to be said. Just one last time, she wanted to feel her husband touch her soul before she walked away from him for good.

His tongue went deeper inside her as she pushed herself harder against his face. Miranda wanted to him to feel her, feel what he had done to her and was still doing to her. She wanted him to reach deep inside her and taste the remnants of the pain he'd left behind. Miranda freed herself and emptied the love she had saved up for him into his mouth.

"Oh my God, Israel. Ooohh."

Israel continued to lick the walls of his wife's pussy. She tasted like heaven. He wanted to feel the inside of her with his dick. She removed the robe and bra she had on. He stood up, dropped his pants, and pulled his wife off the counter. He slid her panties down so she could step out of them. Pushing her back against the wall, he picked her up and entered her.

"Ahhhhh," Miranda screamed in pleasure.

She wrapped her hands around his neck as he stroked her back and forth. His heavy breathing in her ear was a distraction from the cries she fought to silence. She closed her eyes to stop the tears from falling, but their faces just stared back at her. The women he'd fucked her over for. Opening her eyes, Miranda let the tears flow. She was done fighting them. She was done fighting for this marriage. Wanting to be in control, Miranda pushed him off her. She pulled him down to the floor and straddled him cowgirl style. Although she wanted him to see the pain he'd inflicted on her, she didn't want to look in his eyes. She didn't want him to persuade her to stay in this any longer than she needed to. Israel held onto her hips as she gripped his dick with her pussy walls. He closed his eyes as he fought back his orgasm. He wasn't ready to come. It had been a long time since they had this kind of passionate sex. He wanted this moment to last forever.

Miranda bounced up and down on his dick as hard as she could. When he couldn't take anymore, Israel rolled her over on all fours. The cold tile underneath them provided coolness to their inflamed bodies. Miranda tooted her ass up the way he liked it and he slid in and out of her until he couldn't fight holding on anymore. Miranda didn't want him to come like this. She wanted him to come at the mercy of her lips. The lips that would never touch his dick again after today. The lips that would never whisper I love you into his ears again. She pulled away from him and turned around to finish him off with her mouth. With tongue strokes ranging from fast to slow, Miranda toyed with the mayhem he was fighting inside. When she had him where she wanted him, she released him. Not satisfied about being toyed with, Israel lay her back down and slid in one last time. They would come together like they were supposed to, like husband and wife. Israel leaned down to hold Miranda tight as they gave themselves to one another.

As the last tear fell, Miranda exploded on Israel's dick. Every ounce of her pain, her love, and anger followed. He rolled over onto the kitchen floor to catch his breath and Miranda got up. She grabbed her robe and headed upstairs. In a matter of seconds, she came back downstairs fully dressed with the receipts, the credit card bill, and cell phone. Still lying on the floor, she stood over her husband no longer hiding her tears. Israel looked up completely confused as to why his wife was crying then he looked down and saw her hands. His entire body tensed up because Miranda had totally fucked him and naively he didn't see it coming.

"Miranda, before you say anything let me explain."

"Humph, you actually have an explanation. How is that even possible?"

"Okay honestly—" He started to speak before she interrupted.

"No! You shut the fuck up because it's my turn to talk! I don't want to hear another one of your motherfucking lies. My ears are still bleeding from the last one you told and believe me when I tell you, you don't want to lie to me right now," Miranda screamed.

Israel stood up, trying to get off the floor quickly. He knew he was in trouble and being quiet would help him gage just how bad it was. Miranda walked away from him and headed for their great room. He hesitated in following her because he wasn't sure what kind of trap he was walking into. Feeling as though Miranda would never actually murder him, he followed suit. Once he approached their sunken great room, he could see his entire closet in the middle of it. At a loss for words, he stared into the eyes of the woman he had hurt once again. The tears in her eyes now fell without stopping as the silent tension between them grew. He was still taken back at the fact his wife just fucked the shit out of him and now she was about to rip him a new one. She was definitely a savage and he'd underestimated her skills to move like him.

"Israel, I do not understand. I was good a wife. I gave all of myself to you and instead of appreciating that you took advantage of it. Three women, Israel! Three fucking women I stood by you with as you fucked them and lied to my face! Hotel rooms, busted out windows, false pregnancies, and who knows what else and I was still here. Now we're on woman number four and for what reason I don't understand is that you think I will still be here. How long have you been fucking this bitch?"

Israel looked at his angry wife. Lying was not a good idea right now, but neither was telling the truth. He had been sleeping with Nova for ten months, which in her eyes would be a year.

"It's only been four months, Ran," he lied.

Miranda looked at him and threw the phone at his face. Quickly moving out of the way, the phone missed Israel and shattered the glass vase behind him. Miranda picked up a picture of them on vacation last year and smashed it on the corner of the table.

"You're a fucking liar and incapable of telling the truth! Even when you are caught you still fucking lie!"

"Miranda, you asked me and I told you. Now you want to call me a liar?"

"You've been fucking this bitch for four months and you've spent almost ten thousand dollars on her. Who do you think you're fucking talking too? Have you forgotten I know your black ass? Did you somehow forget who I am? Nigga, I'm not any of those stupid corporate bitches you work with! I was born and raised in the fucking hood and if you think for one motherfucking second I believe you spent ten grand on a bitch you've been fucking for four months you must not know me very well!" she yelled.

Israel could see this argument was only going to get worse before it got better. He knew this version of Miranda and he prayed God hadn't forgotten about him because shit was about to get real. It wasn't often the hood side of her came out, but when it did God help him. Despite where she grew up, Miranda was as classy as they came. However, she could become that girl with her hair braided to the back with Vaseline on her face in a millisecond.

"Baby, I swear I'm telling the truth. I—"

"Oh, so you must be pussy whipped then. My husband is a trick. Not only slanging dick but also our fucking money!" Miranda yelled, cutting him off.

"Please. I don't wanna fight."

"Has that bitch been in my house?"

"No, Miranda, I wouldn't disrespect you like that," he pleaded.

"Fuck you and spare me the respect bullshit. You're fucking another woman and you're married. Nigga, you're already disrespecting me!"

"Miranda, can I say something?"

Miranda shot a look of death his way. There was nothing he could say to her to stop the cracking of her heart once again. She was tired of hurting and pretending she wasn't on account of salvaging their marriage. The days of her putting herself back together for him were over. She deserved a man who loved her. A man who wanted to fuck her and only her. She shook her head and thought about the fifteen years she wasted being faithful to a man who didn't have one faithful bone in his body. She should know since she met his family. His grandfather, father, brothers, and uncles were all whores. This behavior is all he knows and believes to be right. Why she thought he was capable of being a one-woman man was beyond her and she no longer cared.

Miranda took a deep breath before answering, "Get your shit and get the fuck out of my house before I murder you in it."

Chapter 6
Red Moon

"Azora, my sweet. I want to welcome you to my humble abode," King Oyo said, while eyeing her.

Even though he'd studied every spot on her face, he could never get tired of taking in all her rare beauty.

He could tell she'd come from a special tribe that he'd never seen before. The king had been with a lot of women, including the effortlessly beautiful, Nova, but none compared to the dark beauty that was before him. A beauty like hers rivaled Cleopatra's and Nefertiti's. Her face deserved nothing but adoration from the entire world. It was evident to him that she had no clue that she was so magnificent. Life proved her otherwise so it was what she believed.

Azora stood with her head held down and almost in half kneeling position. She was used to being with the queen and knew never to make eye contact or speak even when spoken to. She was not worthy of being a human being because she was a servant. That was what she was taught and she didn't question it. Plus, she was on unfamiliar territory. She wanted to make sure she did nothing that could get her sent back to the queen.

"Look up at me, my kitten."

King Oyo thought she reminded him of a black panther, so he decided she would be his little kitten. He was smitten with her and wanted to explore every crevice of her body and soul. Slowly Azora looked up into the king's eyes and found a look of genuine love not just a lustful stare. At that moment, she knew she would be his forever if he would have her.

"If you are going to be my wife I want to you carry yourself in such a fashion. You will not bow to anyone. This is your home and as your husband I will give you my all. Anything you want is yours."

Azora smiled at her new king. She felt a surge through her body that she had never experienced before.

"Yes, umm, my king," she stated, and then she bowed out of habit.

"What did I tell you about that?"

"I'm sorry, my king. Please forgive me."

Afraid of the lashing she was sure to come for not obeying, Azora dropped down to her knees. She closed her eyes and nervously anticipated the crack of the whip that never came.

"Get up!" the king roared.

He was angry that Azora did not recognize her strength and that she was born to be a queen. He could tell Queen Nzinga had seriously broken her spirits, but he would build her up to be the woman he knew she could be.

In a hurried fashion Azora jumped to her feet but kept her head low. She was confused as her old role embedded in her brain now conflicted with her new role that was awakening a piece of her dead soul.

"I asked you not to bow to me. You are not a slave anymore. You will be my wife, and the wife of King Asya Oyo bows to no man. Not even me. Am I clear?"

He placed his hand under her chin, lifting it so they were looking in each other's eyes. He tried to look past the frightfulness he saw in her eyes in hopes of finding her core.

"Yes, my king."

Azora looked back down to the floor.

He was making her nervous with all his insistence that she should act as if she was some queen. Even with all his reassurance this whole situation was confusing to her, but she didn't want to upset the king any further so she would try her best.

"I will do my best to please you," she muttered.

"Ok," King Oyo replied, and then sighed heavily. "I'll send Nova in to help you get settled in. You two will spend a lot of time together. It would be good to get comfortable with her."

Azora had forgotten all about the Nova girl she encountered earlier. She was so confident that she would be the king's wife. Azora knew from experience a girl like that did not accept rejection well.

Azora looked around her new living arrangements with uncertainty. It was bigger and far more grand than the slave quarters she'd become accustomed to. For some reason the king thought that she deserved all of this. As many times, as she prayed for one of those fairytale things that she heard other slaves talk about, she never thought one would happen to her. She was forever indebted to this man.

Nervously, Azora ran her fingers through the silk curtains that hung loosely around her new bed. She wondered what kind of sexual trysts would be held there. *Would she and her new king consummate their marriage or did he have a more beautiful place in mind when taking her virtue?*

Azora was so lost in her thoughts she hadn't heard anyone come into her room. Startled by the beautiful melody being hummed behind her, she turned around and was face-to-face with Nova. The twinkle she held in her eye an hour earlier was gone. The smile that tugged at the corners of her lips did not match the dull, saddened glare she attempted to hide.

"Your majesty," Nova said tight lipped.

Nova sized up Azora in a different light. Their first encounter she had no clue the shabby, yet beautiful, girl could even be her competition. After the king sent her on her way, she figured it was for preparation of his accustomed daily alleviation of stress from his life between her thighs. *When she first got the news that her spot to be the king's next wife was filled by the peasant she was beyond infuriated but what could she do?* Now with the watchful eye of a jaded, scorn lover Nova could see why he was so smitten with her. Almost instantly, Nova became insecure of her own image. This had never happened to her before. Nova knew she was the most beautiful woman in the kingdom, that was until her eyes landed on Azora.

Nova was only seventeen, but she had already ripped out a few hearts of men with her curvaceous, chocolate kissed body. Her black locks fell perfectly over her high cheekbones that accentuated her full lips. Her eyes were full of wonder that left most men dying to explore them. She could have any man she wanted, still she craved the king. She was willing to do whatever to make sure that she was at least second in line.

Nova glanced at Azora again, this time more openly. She loved the fire red of her hair. Her decision to change hers had been instant. She would become a carbon copy of Azora to get the king to desire her.

"Nova, you don't have to call me your majesty."

"It is the king's wish so I will be your servant, my queen."

Again, Nova bowed in submission. She knew there was no competing with the Amazonian beauty unless she played nice.

"Please don't bow to me, Nova. I am not worthy," Azora said as she put her head down again.

Nova looked up at Azora and rushed to her side. She could tell that transferring the girl from meek idiotic bottom feeder to refined queen was going to be a lot of work. However, she was up for the challenge. Somehow the king had been able to ignore her call to him all day but Nova knew it was only a matter of time before he'd submit.

"Are you crazy? Never let the king see you bow your head to a servant. You are a lucky girl, Azora. You must learn his wants and needs and please him accordingly."

"And how do I learn that?"

"I know him pretty well. No one in this place know as much about him as I do. I was his treasured confidant so—"

Nova made it seem like it was no big deal as she spoon-fed Azora all the right things that only a fool would believe.

"This all so confusing. Will you help me with this?" Azora was almost begging Nova.

"Yes, my queen," Nova replied with a smile.

Though she had been replaced she still held her ranking in the house and she would bide her time until the king grew tired of playing with his new toy or opportunity came knocking.

Azora Oyo stood speechless, staring at all the gifts and love she and her new husband received. She looked over to Nova and noticed her looking at her. She wondered what was she thinking. Azora had a feeling that Nova wished she were dead so she could stand as the queen. Even though Nova was always nice to Azora, she had a feeling that there were ulterior motives for that.

"You look beautiful. Officially my queen," King Oyo said as he took his rightful place next to her.

For certain, he'd never seen a woman more beautiful than Azora. On this day, her beauty shone brighter than the rays illuminating the skies a penetration red. Based on an Oracle, he traveled to see in the land of Greece, the night of the blood moon signified wealth and prosperity, making it the perfect night for their wedding.

"Thank you, my king," she said and smiled at him.

It had taken a few months, but Azora was finally able to look him in his eyes and not cower under the sound of his voice. King Oyo returned her smile. He loved her new found confidence. It turned him on and he couldn't wait to be her first and only lover. Indeed, he had found the one he'd been searching for. The prophecy would finally be fulfilled.

"I hope you are ready for tonight's festivities. Everything will be in your honor. No one deserves this more than you. I hope I am everything and more than you desire me to be," he whispered in her ear.

Azora had more confidence than she had when she first met him but her whole life she'd been nothing but a servant and a slave to Queen Nzinga. Nova had given her a lesson in being a regal woman. Though she had to take Nova's insults and degrading comments, she would do anything to be in good graces with her king. When Nova gave her lessons on giving oral pleasures she thought she would faint for sure. She'd never seen a penis in person let alone had one close to her face. Nova had a great laugh at her expense as she gagged and threw up everywhere when the banana she was practicing on hit the back of her throat. She shook the thoughts of feeling like a dirty peasant again and looked around and smiled in awe at the new life she would be leading.

Now here she was a queen herself. She felt like a small gnat in a world overrun with killer wasps.

"Oh, I know you will by the grace Hecate you were sent to me."

Azora cringed at the mention of the God he prayed to. She always got a bad feeling in the pit of her stomach when he mentioned her. She dared not say anything but now that she was his queen she felt the need to ask.

"My king can you explain to me who Hecate is?"

She faked smiled at him to hide her nervousness.

"All in due time, my kitten."

"But—"

"All that matters now is that I will always love and cherish you in this life and the next. Our souls will find each other no matter what part of the world we end up on for all eternity, my love," he said, interrupting her sentence.

It was obvious that he didn't want to talk about the one he called Hecate.

All Azora could do was smile in return. She was so smitten with his words, she would let it go for now. No one had ever said anything like that to her before. She prayed he meant every word he said.

"Nova!" King Oyo called.

"Yes, my king," she replied as she hurried to Azora's side, knowing she should never be far away from her.

"Prepare my wife for tonight."

"Yes, my king."

An hour later Azora found herself walking through the palace in awe. The red moon shined brightly through the glass ceilings, giving the place an eerie lustful haze. Each room was filled with people in the nude. Wine was poured from fountains as some drank merrily while others drank the flowing juices of the naked women in the center of the room. Moans and grunts of passion filled the atmosphere. The smell was thick and inviting. No matter where Azora laid her eyes, all she saw was sex. The sight of the numerous men that were sweating and growling as they pounded their manhood into the women lying under them, stirred something within her and caused a sudden ache between her legs.

Azora had never seen a man and woman having sex with each other. The queen had shielded her from such acts. Azora was curiously yearning to intake all of this. Slowly, she walked towards a party in the corner. From the count of heads, she could see there were five people. One of the men held a woman by her hips as he thrust himself inside of her while she was on her knees with her face buried between another woman's thighs. Another woman rubbed on his upper torso while she licked and kissed all over his chest area. *The last participant was a man who stood behind the other man, fucking him in what she assumed to be his asshole because what else was back there?* Out of curiosity she stretched her neck so she could see where exactly he was placing his manhood.

"Come on my queen. We can't keep the king waiting," Nova said, looking at Azora awkwardly. "Have you never seen two men fucking before?"

"No I haven't," Azora confessed, lowering her head once more. "I've never seen anyone doing that."

"Oh, so you still fresh? I knew there was a different scent on you. Girlish like, you're not a woman yet."

Nova's sexual confidence scared Azora and made her feel like a fool for being so inexperienced.

"Will you stop it with this bowing to me foolishness. Lift your head. You will not get me beheaded because you cannot accept your new position."

"I'm sorry, Nova."

"What are you sorry for?" King Oyo's voice echoed and ricocheted off the walls of his private room where he and Nova used to spend nights before Azora came about.

"Oh nothing, my love. I got lost and Nova had to show me how to get here for the thousandth time. Neither of us wanted to keep you waiting."

Azora flashed him a confident smile. This time the king recognized the look of lust in her eyes. Being amid the orgy gave her a slight boost of confidence.

"Your smile is captivating and I love when you bless my eyes with the beauty of the twinkle in your eyes. You should do it more often."

King Oyo rose from the bed and stalked towards Azora with an air of confidence that made her feel small again. Nova scurried over to her corner to watch the show that she should have been playing the lead role in.

Azora thought her new husband was handsome beyond measure and she wondered how she ended up with such a man. She had done nothing different than any other slave girl and yet here she stood, delivered to a man who made her feel loved and safe.

King Oyo ran his hands down her arms and she felt goose bumps form all over her body. She'd never felt that before. In the past, she'd only felt disgusted when the queen touched her. Though she knew no other way of life, she knew what the queen was doing to her wasn't right. King Oyo pulled her face to his and kissed her passionately, seeming to have stolen her breath away. She trembled slightly and he sensed her inexperience and decided tonight they would need some help.

"Nova" he called out.

"Yes," Nova replied eagerly.

She knew that Azora wouldn't be able to live up to the sexual appetite that the king had so she prepared her body for this moment earlier in the day. Her skin was smooth and glistened from the tea tree oil she collected.

"It seems my new queen will need some help with getting used to our arrangements. Help her get comfortable."

The king was demanding but gentle in his words as not to embarrass his new queen. He was actually happy her essence hadn't been tainted but a few minutes with Nova and she would be well oiled and ready to ride.

Nova removed her clothes and seductively moved towards Azora. Azora was caught in a trance, watching Nova walk towards her. She heard the king suck in a breath of air and knew that he also was amazed by Nova's body. When she reached Azora she leaned in to suckle at the fullness of her lips but Azora turned away from her.

"Is there a problem, Azora?" King Oyo asked.

"No, I umm, I just thought it would be me and you."

She held her head down.

"Raise your head and I only invited her in with us because I was made aware of your situation with the queen."

Azora felt the blood rush to her face. She was mortified that he knew those things about her. The memories made her cringe and she didn't want King Oyo to think badly of her.

"That was never by choice. I understand and appreciate you wanting me to be comfortable, but couldn't it just be me and you tonight?"

Azora raised her head back up.

If she could help it she would never share her bed with another woman as long she lived. Nova was undeniably sexy, but Azora saw her as a best friend and nothing more.

"Whatever you want, my little kitten. Nova you can retire for the night."

The king dismissed her with a wave of his hand. He didn't even bother to look at or be fazed by the fact that she was naked and dripping wet. Nova fumed on the insides as she retrieved her clothes. She took one last look at the couple and left.

"I know I'm not what you expected in the bedroom. I mean, of course I'm no Nova but I'll try my best," Azora said as she stood timidly in front of her new husband in an emerald green silk gown that flowed down like a waterfall of perfectly woven material yet she felt naked.

"My love, don't worry with frivolous things. I don't want you to be Nova. I want you to be yourself. We will get to where we need to be in due time."

He looked at her lovingly as he began to undo the bun she wore on top of her head. He watched as her crimson red hair fell down around her shoulders. Next, he slid the straps of her dress off her shoulders and watched in anticipation as the fabric slowly slid off her. He stood back and admired her beautiful body. Her skin was the perfect shade of midnight covered in tiny, fine red hairs on her arms and legs. In the middle her woman hood sat covered in what looked like a ball of fire but was her pubic hairs.

King Oyo undid his wrap and let it fall to the floor. Azora eyes widened at what hung between his legs. King Oyo was only at the age of nineteen but his body was that of a man double that age. His confidence had to come from the fact that he would probably win every pissing match. Azora stared in awe. She had never seen a dick in person and wanted to ask if they were all that big.

"Touch it," the king said, startling Azora out of her private thoughts.

Meekly, Azora reached out and held him firmly in her hand. He shivered from her touch and surprisingly, she felt him grow even more. Unable to contain the lust that consumed him, King Oyo grabbed Azora into his arms and walked her across the room. He laid her down on the bed and once again he found himself admiring her beauty. He thanked Hecate one more time for sending her to him before he began to kiss down Azora's body.

Azora wanted to stop him from putting his mouth on her because she'd had enough of that with the queen. It did absolutely nothing for her but make her feel dirty. King Oyo's mouth finally reach her lower region and she felt sparks going off in her body. The queen never made her feel this way. He methodically moved his tongue in and out of her pussy, making it ache and throb. She felt an intense tingle go down her spine so she tried to push the king off. She just knew something was wrong, but he was relentless with his tongue lashing. He wouldn't let up and in turn her body went into involuntary convulsions.

Once the king was sure she was finished he came up face-to-face to see if she was indeed ready for the whole deal. The fire in her eyes let him know she was living up to her words of she would try her best. He could see the fear in her eyes but the way her body heat rose he knew she was ready. He rubbed his hard penis up and down her slit and rested the head at her opening. He lay down on top of her and bit down hard on her neck as a distraction from him inserting himself inside of her.

Azora wasn't sure whether to scream from the bite or him ripping her insides apart. She dug her nails into the soft skin on his back and tried to fight the urge to scream out.

"Let it out, my kitten. Let me hear it purr," the king whispered in her ear as he slowly stroked in and out of her, trying to get her use to the feeling.

He had to bite the inside of his mouth to stop the scream that threatened the back of his throat. He hadn't felt the tightness of a virgin in quite some time, and he relished in the feel of her tight pussy opening and welcoming him.

"Remember, you will be mine forever in this life and the next and the next. No matter what, we will always find each other."

King Oyo knew the moment he saw her she was meant to be his but once he finally pushed all the way inside of her, he felt it. He would do everything in his power to make sure they were never a part.

"Promise me you will find me amid the darkness. Promise me our love will always prevail."

"I am yours forever and I will find you if ever our love is lost," she promised.

"Swear?"

"I swear."

The two of them were lost inside of each other. It was as if no one existed outside of the room but across the palace someone did exist and she could hear their moans of pleasure. Furiously, Nova pleasured herself to the sounds of them. Each flick of her wrist was fueled by Nova's anticipation that soon she would be the one in his bed full-time and it would be her sweet Siren's call that rocks him to sleep each night. The first chance she got the new queen would be history and she would be back in her rightful place.

Chapter 7
Seduction

    Nova was walking on cloud nine. Last night was amazing for her and she wasn't talking about the sex with Israel. Even though that shit was excellent, she was happier about the keys to the new house that she received. True, it wasn't as big as the house that he shared with his poor suffering wife. As a matter fact, it wasn't even as big as the fake house that he took her to last night and tried to pass off as his. She started to bust his ass in a lie but for shits and giggles she went along with it. She would use that for when she needed him to furnish it with every designer piece of furniture she has ever wanted. Besides, she had other plans for him.

    That was the reason she was heading to a place that she hated. She had to tie up her business so that she could move on to other things. This was one debt that she couldn't wait to pay off. She pulled into the driveway off the large mansion and thought about all the times she had come to this place and partaken in the illicit affairs that went on inside of it. The good mood that she was in when she was driving had quickly dispersed as soon as she cut the car off and stepped outside. She could feel the evil wash over her, transporting her back into a time that she escaped from.

    The door opened before she climbed the steps all the way and Tina peeked out her beady eyes at her. Of all the shit that happened in the Smitten Kitten, there was something about Tina that was oddly placed and creeped Nova out. She didn't trust her vibe at all. It wasn't just the fact that Tina was the ugliest woman she'd ever seen, it was the way her eyes studied and envied everyone but

Azora. For Azora her eyes held nothing but lust and longing. Weird shit if you asked Nova.

"Tina," Nova acknowledged the woman as she walked in.

"Ms. Nova, nice to see you again," Tina pushed out while closing the door.

She couldn't stand Nova just as much as Nova couldn't stand her. Both women knew there was no love lost but Tina took her hatred for Nova to another level. At times, it was hard to contain the way she felt, especially whenever Nova would creep over late at night and attend to Azora in a way that she would never let Tina do.

"Where's Azora? She knew I was fucking coming. Why must I wait every single time I get here?"

Tina chose to ignore Nova's bitching. She was used to it by now. It was what she was best at.

"May I offer you a drink?" Tina asked.

"Yeah right. You think I'm crazy enough to drink anything you bitches offer in here? I'll pass. Y'all ain't about to have me tied up fucking some billy goat tonight. Just go tell your boss to move her ass 'cause I have shit to do and better places to be."

"As you wish," Tina muttered with disgust.

Tina rolled her eyes as she climbed the stairs to go fetch Azora. This was not the life intended for her and it burned her soul that she had been trapped with such little purpose. Seeing Nova as much as she did cause her stomach to turn and she hated being fake about it. She wanted Nova dead.

Tina approached Azora's slightly cracked door to her prayer room. Inside Azora stood naked, praying for her ultimate revenge. Tina started to knock, but she was appreciating the sight way too much. Azora's body was amazing. Tina imagined herself running her hands and tongue over every inch of it. She needed to get closer to Azora. She wanted to lay her head between her legs and sniff at the essence of who she was until Azora exploded in her mouth. Tina was lost in her fantasy of having a taste of ecstasy. She didn't even hear Nova approach her.

"My God, lady, you are so fucking desperate. If you want to fuck Azora so bad this is what you need to do," Nova hissed, while pushing pass Tina and walking up to Azora.

Nova grabbed Azora out of her prayers and started kissing her slowly. Shocked, though obviously turned on, Azora responded with a deep moan. Nova turned Azora's back to Tina standing in the door. She glared into her eyes as she grabbed Azora's ass cheeks and spread them apart. Tina could slightly see the wetness that peeked from the chocolate lips of Azora. Tina's mouth flew open as Nova stuffed a few of her fingers inside of Azora. The smell of Azora's scent penetrated Tina's nostrils. She watched intensely as Nova stroked the soft moans out of her. Wanting so badly to join in, she closed her eyes and placed her own fingers inside of herself. She imagined that it was Azora touching and guiding her to the brink of no control. Tina's body shook and she let out a loud yelp. The ringing in her ears plus the swimming of blood in her brain caused her body to rock back and forth. It had been so long since she felt this good. She could have stayed in the moment forever, but the sound of someone clearing their throat shook her back into reality.

"Tina, what the fuck are you doing? Get downstairs and prepare the rooms for tonight. It's obvious you have too much fucking time on your hands," Azora yelled at her.

"Looks like she got more than time on her hands to me. That looks like pussy juice on those fingers," Nova taunted.

Embarrassed, Tina descended the stairs quickly. She could hear the laughter that Nova and Azora shared at her expense. She vowed the day would come when they wouldn't hold so much power over her.

"Girl, I told you that bitch was weird when she first appeared out of no fucking where. You just love a good stray, don't you?" Nova asked her as they sat down on the plush pillows on the floor.

Through each journey of life since meeting, Nova had followed Azora. She was indebted to her and owed her longevity strictly to Azora having connections that she didn't. Nova didn't necessarily control Azora like she did her men, but she used her too in order to remain amongst the living. With her sordid past, she knew her fate was to spend eternity in hell. Doing whatever she needed to, she would prolong the taking of that trip as long as she possibly could.

Nova struck a match to light a joint that she pulled from her purse. She smiled at the memories of home when they would sneak out to the garden for a puff. Happy times, all before that fateful night. Things changed drastically for them both after that night. She looked over at Azora to see if her mind drifted back to the same place, but Azora's face was like stone. She had turned off her emotions a long time ago.

"So, why am I here, Azora?"

"It's time, Nova."

"Time? You said a few more months. Why are you pushing this so fast?"

Azora stood from the pillows and stretched her loins. She looked as if she wanted to be anywhere in the world other than right in this moment.

"Last I checked, I don't answer to anyone, not even you Ms. Nova the seductress. You've been quite busy. So much so, I think you're forgetting what you are here for. Like I said, it's time. I'm just giving you a friendly warning. Consider it a blessing."

Azora didn't bother waiting for a response as she threw her shoulders back, held her head high, and then elegantly sauntered from the room. Nova rolled her eyes as she sat there wondering if it was possible to do the impossible by bringing the mighty queen to her knees.

"Baby, just calm down. I get that you hate your boss but I planned this nice, not to mention, expensive as hell, dinner and you aren't even enjoying the food."

Nova looked over at her new conquest and could tell that he was disappointed. She was mad at herself for even allowing that bitch Azora to get in her head. She was so livid when she walked out of the room all high and mighty that Nova could have killed her if only she wasn't immortal. She really had to work on a way to change that. Azora was feeling a little too high and mighty for Nova's liking.

"I'm sorry, love. You're right. I'm not enjoying this food right now," she said, while putting her utensils on the table.

He raised an eyebrow and looked at her with a mixture of rage and confusion. She could feel that he was seething on the inside. She almost laughed out loud because his anger tickled her soul. These men had no clue of what she was capable of. Nova was about to show them that she was and would always be in charge. She had played the backfield for far too long. It was now time for her to seize, and get back on top.

"Nova, you said you wanted to go home and I can't travel to Nigeria right now so I went through a lot of shit to get you custom food and to have someone make this place look like home for you and you are fucking up my night. Wow!"

Sweat beads tugged around the hairline on his light brown face. His jawline remained tight as he stared her down. Nova smiled sweetly. She didn't need to piss him off. He had been a big help to her, even though he didn't know he was a pawn in her own little chess game. She got up from the chair and walked towards him seductively. He shifted in his chair as if he was suddenly uncomfortable. Nova knew she was wearing the hell out of the short, latex dress. It hugged every single curve on her body and imagination wasn't even needed to know what was going on beneath it. Absolutely nothing because Nova was not the kind of girl who wore underwear.

"When I say that I'm not hungry, I mean for food. However, my mouth is hungry for something else though."

He took in a deep breath as she leaned down and placed several kisses on his lips. He opened his mouth to say something but she silenced him by slipping her tongue in his mouth and hand down his pants. She felt around until she reached the thick rod, freed it, and slightly jerked on it.

"Ooh, baby. You feel so good in my hand. Should I stop and go and eat the rest of my food?"

His breathing was heavy, with lowered eyes he looked at her and responded.

"Don't you dare fucking move. Keep jacking my shit off."

Nova smiled before working him harder. His body shivered from her touch but he remained rock hard. She lowered her head until she was looking directly at the center of him.

"Can you think of anything that I can put in my mouth?" Nova whispered against his tip.

"You are so fucking bad," he managed to say between whimpers.

Nova knew the heat from her mouth mixed with the tiny drops of saliva she put on him was making him sensitive to touch. She pushed her head down further, taking him in wholly. Her tongue tickled the base of his balls. He tried to push her head away but she wouldn't budge. His thighs shook like crazy but never deterred Nova from her goal. Up and down like her neck was made of bungee cords, she gave his ass the business.

"Nova, please, I can't handle-I'm about to cum," his whimpers continued.

Nova heard a loud shrill that sounded like a woman in labor. When she realized that it was him, she almost choked on his nut from laughing. With locked legs and a twisted face, he emptied his entire soul into the back of her throat. Nova welcomed the salty taste in her mouth. She burped loudly as if she just had the best meal of her life.

He stared at her with wide eyes, unable to believe that she could rock his body like that with simply her mouth. He'd heard about her and her mouth. It was what brought him to her. He didn't believe that she was capable of turning a man's entire life upside down but Nova had made a believer out of him. Not only did he feel like he was going crazy with tiny aftershock tremors, he couldn't tell which way was up. He tried to gather himself as best as possible but it was no use.

Nova smiled again and shook her head as she swiped the table clean. She climbed on top of it and spread her legs wide in his face. His eyes were staring directly at her clean-shaven center. It glistened under the light and seemed to have a hypnotizing effect on the man. She stuck three fingers inside of herself and rocked back and forth slightly.

"You like that?" she asked.

He nodded his head, unable to talk.

"You want to taste it?"

There was more nods from him. He was like pure putty in her hands. She would have his ass singing like a canary by the end of the night. Men, were so predictably weak. She grabbed his head and pushed his face onto her. Her hips moved in a circular motio as she used him to get herself off. He did a pretty decent job at working his tongue but the fact remained that he was nothing like his brother. She pushed his head back and placed her hand to cover herself.

"So, Dillion, before I let you finish, I must thank you for giving me that valuable information on Israel. Just like you said, he fell for it and spent the night with me. Thank you, baby. Did you deposit the money into my account?"

"Yes, damn it, just let me finish!" he yelled.

Nova laughed and opened herself back up. She killed two birds with one stone by messing with his ass. She now had ammunition against Israel and more money in the bank thanks to Dillion being a bigger trick than Israel. Yes, this life she was living was a fucking good one.

"Good, boy! You may now eat away."

Chapter 8
Propositions

Azora hated leaving the comforts of her home. This world was so strange to her. She only left the mansion when it was time to lure in her new batch of lambs. This day would be special today. She would finally meet the woman who was living the life she'd longed for half a millennia. A wave of envy washed over her soul as she thought of all the love and affection she was denied because someone was jealous and stole her happiness away. In a matter of minutes her heart had been shattered and she chose never to repair it. For years, she searched for the love of her life King Oyo because he'd told her no matter what their love would prevail and they would find each other. Yet, she sat still broken hearted and searching for the love she'd lost that tragic night. .

She sat in the back of a restaurant, watching a young lady sip her coffee as tears slowly rolled down her face. Azora remembered the last time she cried, the night her beloved King Oyo died in her arms. She still felt a strong love hatred for him because he'd made false promises to her. He was supposed to be her savior. Soon, she would get her revenge even if she had to search to the ends of the earth like she'd promised him all those years before.

The lady was beautiful and tried to keep her make up together as her tears tried their best to rinse away any evidence of there ever being any makeup to begin with. Azora watched the lady's shoulders as they shook from contained pain. Azora could feel her pain from across the room so she didn't need to wonder why the lady was crying. The lady's soul ached from all the pain her husband had been causing her and she was at her ropes end with him. Unbeknownst to her, that is exactly where Azora needed her to be. She needed her over him and want him gone for good. Her chest heaved in and out as if she couldn't find the air that her lungs needed to function. After a few more minutes of crying, the lady stood to leave and wiped away the last of her tears. Azora got up from her table to meet the lady at the trash can before she left out of the coffee shop.

"Excuse me miss. I don't mean to disturb you but I couldn't help but to notice your shoes. They are gorgeous," Azora smiled as the lie rolled off her tongue.

Though the multi-colored Christian Louboutin's were absolutely breathtaking, they were the last thing on Azora's mind. Upon closer inspection Azora could see why any man would choose her as his life's partner. Miranda had a certain innocence to her. Although, Azora knew she was far from it, Miranda's brown doe eyes gave her a youthful look. Her cinnamon-toned skin covered what looked to be two dimples if she smiled hard enough. Azora could tell she had a beautiful smile hidden beneath her pain. She wasn't extremely tall, though her 5'7" frame held her weight and curves perfectly. She looked like a grown woman, graceful and classy. Her bluntly cut bob hung perfectly over her slightly rounded face. On a good day, if everything was going right in her world, Azora knew she could shake the confidence of a few women.

"Thank you," Miranda said with a smile.

She'd finally looked at the woman standing in front of her and immediately her breath got caught in her throat.

The woman standing in front of her was stunning to say the least. Still, not in the mood for small talk, Miranda turned to walk away.

"Can I ask you where you got them from? I know most women don't share their fashion spots."

Azora gave her a look from head to toe again. She had no reason to be envious of the lady physically, but this woman had been living the life she longed for fifteen years.

"Oh, my husband bought them after one his nights out on the town," Miranda said with a roll of her eyes.

"Oh, ok. Well, anyway, they are to die for."

"Humph, right about now, Lord knows I wish he would do just that. Anyway, thanks again," she said, and then again Miranda turned to walk away.

"Excuse me."

"What is it now, lady damn?" Miranda asked with frustration etched across her face.

"I'm sorry. I didn't mean to upset you," Azora smiled, trying to hide her anger from being yelled at.

"Look lady, can you tell me what it is that you want?"

Miranda looked Azora up and down and wondered if this was one Israel's many flings.

"I want to offer you a way out of your current situation."

"And what situation is that?" Miranda asked as she crossed her arms over her chest and she waited for Azora's answer.

"A mister Israel Cantrell and his philandering ways."

"So, you are one of his home wrecking whores?" Miranda scoffed.

"It's funny how women call the side piece the home wrecker. She owes you no loyalty. It was your husband's wandering dick that wrecked your home. What did you do to make him wander? That's neither here nor there, and no I am not one his whores. As I am sure you know your marriage would have been finished if I were in the picture. I am only here to help you."

"Look lady, I don't care to know what you think you know, but stay the fuck out my business. I'll handle my husband, and if you think you are big and bad enough to take what's mine try me."

Miranda stormed out of the coffee shop trying her best not to show her true color in public.

"Miranda Cantrell," Azora called out as she caught up with Miranda.

Not caring about the woman's attitude because she knew that her attitude would never match her wrath, she smiled through her anger.

"How the hell do you know my name?" Miranda asked as she turned on her heels to face Azora.

How did this woman know her and her husband's name? How did she know anything about them? She'd never seen her a day in her life.

"I know a lot of things, Miranda."

"Don't say my name like you know me, lady," Miranda spat.

"Oh, but I do know you. I know that your husband hasn't been able to keep his dirty dick clean for years. I also know you are pissed and want revenge." Azora could feel Miranda' anger rising and it made her pussy wet. "As a matter of fact, I know that I can help you."

"Look, I don't need your damn help," Miranda said as she turned to leave.

"Miranda," Azora sang.

"Yes, what the hell is it now?"

Miranda looked Azora up and down. She really wanted to know the real reason why she following her. She knew for sure she would remember seeing such a work of art. The woman's beauty made her aware of every imperfection she had on her own body. Unconsciously, Miranda pulled at her skirt and fixed the collar of her shirt as watched Azora walk up in what seemed like slow motion. This woman made her feel as if she was inadequate in everything in life.

"No need to be snippy. I'm only here to offer you my services?" Azora smirked.

She liked Miranda's spunky attitude.

"I'm sorry. I don't follow. Do I know you from somewhere?"

Miranda was confused because she couldn't place where she knew Azora from. She seemed to know her whole life's story.

Though she was just as confident as the next woman, she found herself wondering was she really was one of Israel's other women. She said she wasn't, but she knew women liked to play mind games. *Was she here to tell her another secret about her husband? Could she be the mystery woman known as Nova that filled her husband's text messages?* If so she knew her marriage was doomed. She was almost certain there was no coming back after experiencing such a rarity. Miranda could feel the heat coming from Azora's body and she found herself wanting to reach out and touch her. She wondered if the heat was coming from the woman's fire red hair. Azora's presence seemed to drown out everything thing around them.

"No, you do not know me. Let's just say a little birdie told me you could use my help."

Azora's patience was starting to wear thin with Miranda, but she held her temper in place because she needed her. Miranda was a detrimental part in her plan.

"Can you skip with the mind games and tell me what the hell you want lady? I'm not in the mood for any childish games you seem to want to play."

Even though the lady aroused her curiosity she was still getting on her nerves with her roundabout way of getting to the point. With all she had going on, Miranda didn't have a lot of time to waste. She needed to get back to make sure her scumbag ass husband didn't make his way back to their home while she was gone.

"Before we begin let me explain something to you." Azora's smile had faded and turned to slight mask of anger as she appeared in front of Miranda's face only inches away. "Don't ever raise your voice at me."

"Who the fuck—" Miranda started to say.

"Shhhhhh," Azora said as she ran her fingers down the side of Miranda's face, bringing on a sudden calm in her soul.

In a matter of seconds, Miranda wondered why her panties were instantly moist. The ache now pounding in her hot box was almost breathtaking.

"Are you tired of your husband cheating on you yet?" Azora invaded Miranda's personal space as she got close enough to rubbed her lips on Miranda's neck as she talked to her.

Azora breathed in her scent. She could taste the vanilla scent that she'd rubbed on herself from head to toe. Miranda's confusion and curiosity tickled Azora.

"How did you?" Miranda's breathing was labored.

She wanted to pull away from Azora's grasp, though somehow her brain waves weren't hitting her lower extremities. *How had this woman gotten so close to her?* Normally Miranda would never let another woman walk into her personal space without swinging first and asking questions later. However, this woman seemed to take hold of her inner being, rendering Miranda helpless against her advances.

"Shhh, sweetheart," Azora whispered in Miranda's ear, making the hairs on her body stand straight up. "Are you ready for him stop cheating?"

Slowly Azora's hands slid around Miranda's waist as she pulled her into her body. Azora had always been good at seducing anyone in her presence so she knew it wouldn't be hard to get Miranda to do whatever she asked of her.

"Yes."

Miranda had no clue as to how this woman knew her story but if she could help in way she was willing to try. She was too exhausted to even fight the lady standing in front her. Israel had sucked all the life out of her lately. It seemed giving up was the easiest route to take.

"I have a proposition for you. It's your choice and I don't want you to tell me the answer. I'll know what you choose by the end of the night."

"What do you need from me?" Miranda whispered as she prayed the woman took her hands form around her waist.

She was feeling things in her pussy that no one had ever made her feel. The heat from Azora's body was almost suffocating. Still, Miranda wanted to breathe in Azora's every essence and become one with her.

Azora got even closer and whispered in Miranda's ear. As she finished what she was saying, she took her hands from Miranda's body, stepped back, and smiled.

"Oh, in case you were wondering, my name is Azora Monroe."

As Azora walked away, Miranda stood in the middle of the sidewalk wondering what just happened. *Had this woman seduced her in broad daylight and left her yearning for more?*

Chapter 9
Temptations

    Azora hated leaving the comforts of her home. This world was so strange to her. She only left the mansion when it was time to lure in her new batch of lambs. This day would be special today. She would finally meet the woman who was living the life she'd longed for half a millennia. A wave of envy washed over her soul as she thought of all the love and affection she was denied because someone was jealous and stole her happiness away. In a matter of minutes her heart had been shattered and she chose never to repair it. For years, she searched for the love of her life King Oyo because he'd told her no matter what their love would prevail and they would find each other. Yet, she sat still broken hearted and searching for the love she'd lost that tragic night. .

    She sat in the back of a restaurant, watching a young lady sip her coffee as tears slowly rolled down her face. Azora remembered the last time she cried, the night her beloved King Oyo died in her arms. She still felt a strong love hatred for him because he'd made false promises to her. He was supposed to be her savior. Soon, she would get her revenge even if she had to search to the ends of the earth like she'd promised him all those years before.

    The lady was beautiful and tried to keep her make up together as her tears tried their best to rinse away any evidence of there ever being any makeup to begin with. Azora watched the lady's shoulders as they shook from contained pain. Azora could feel her pain from across the room so she didn't need to wonder why the lady was crying. The lady's soul ached from all the pain her husband had been causing her and she was at her ropes end with him. Unbeknownst to her, that is exactly where Azora needed her to be. She needed her over him and want him gone for good. Her chest heaved in and out as if she couldn't find the air that her lungs needed to function. After a few more minutes of crying, the lady stood to leave and wiped away the last of her tears. Azora got up from her table to meet the lady at the trash can before she left out of the coffee shop.

"Excuse me miss. I don't mean to disturb you but I couldn't help but to notice your shoes. They are gorgeous," Azora smiled as the lie rolled off her tongue.

Though the multi-colored Christian Louboutin's were absolutely breathtaking, they were the last thing on Azora's mind. Upon closer inspection Azora could see why any man would choose her as his life's partner. Miranda had a certain innocence to her. Although, Azora knew she was far from it, Miranda's brown doe eyes gave her a youthful look. Her cinnamon-toned skin covered what looked to be two dimples if she smiled hard enough. Azora could tell she had a beautiful smile hidden beneath her pain. She wasn't extremely tall, though her 5'7" frame held her weight and curves perfectly. She looked like a grown woman, graceful and classy. Her bluntly cut bob hung perfectly over her slightly rounded face. On a good day, if everything was going right in her world, Azora knew she could shake the confidence of a few women.

"Thank you," Miranda said with a smile.

She'd finally looked at the woman standing in front of her and immediately her breath got caught in her throat.

The woman standing in front of her was stunning to say the least. Still, not in the mood for small talk, Miranda turned to walk away.

"Can I ask you where you got them from? I know most women don't share their fashion spots."

Azora gave her a look from head to toe again. She had no reason to be envious of the lady physically, but this woman had been living the life she longed for fifteen years.

"Oh, my husband bought them after one his nights out on the town," Miranda said with a roll of her eyes.

"Oh, ok. Well, anyway, they are to die for."

Smitten Kitten

"Humph, right about now, Lord knows I wish he would do just that. Anyway, thanks again," she said, and then again Miranda turned to walk away.

"Excuse me."

"What is it now, lady damn?" Miranda asked with frustration etched across her face.

"I'm sorry. I didn't mean to upset you," Azora smiled, trying to hide her anger from being yelled at.

"Look lady, can you tell me what it is that you want?"

Miranda looked Azora up and down and wondered if this was one Israel's many flings.

"I want to offer you a way out of your current situation."

"And what situation is that?" Miranda asked as she crossed her arms over her chest and she waited for Azora's answer.

"A mister Israel Cantrell and his philandering ways."

"So, you are one of his home wrecking whores?" Miranda scoffed.

"It's funny how women call the side piece the home wrecker. She owes you no loyalty. It was your husband's wandering dick that wrecked your home. What did you do to make him wander? That's neither here nor there, and no I am not one his whores. As I am sure you know your marriage would have been finished if I were in the picture. I am only here to help you."

"Look lady, I don't care to know what you think you know, but stay the fuck out my business. I'll handle my husband, and if you think you are big and bad enough to take what's mine try me."

Miranda stormed out of the coffee shop trying her best not to show her true color in public.

"Miranda Cantrell," Azora called out as she caught up with Miranda.

Not caring about the woman's attitude because she knew that her attitude would never match her wrath, she smiled through her anger.

"How the hell do you know my name?" Miranda asked as she turned on her heels to face Azora.

How did this woman know her and her husband's name? How did she know anything about them? She'd never seen her a day in her life.

83

"I know a lot of things, Miranda."

"Don't say my name like you know me, lady," Miranda spat.

"Oh, but I do know you. I know that your husband hasn't been able to keep his dirty dick clean for years. I also know you are pissed and want revenge." Azora could feel Miranda' anger rising and it made her pussy wet. "As a matter of fact, I know that I can help you."

"Look, I don't need your damn help," Miranda said as she turned to leave.

"Miranda," Azora sang.

"Yes, what the hell is it now?"

Miranda looked Azora up and down. She really wanted to know the real reason why she following her. She knew for sure she would remember seeing such a work of art. The woman's beauty made her aware of every imperfection she had on her own body. Unconsciously, Miranda pulled at her skirt and fixed the collar of her shirt as watched Azora walk up in what seemed like slow motion. This woman made her feel as if she was inadequate in everything in life.

"No need to be snippy. I'm only here to offer you my services?" Azora smirked.

She liked Miranda's spunky attitude.

"I'm sorry. I don't follow. Do I know you from somewhere?"

Miranda was confused because she couldn't place where she knew Azora from. She seemed to know her whole life's story.

Though she was just as confident as the next woman, she found herself wondering was she really was one of Israel's other women. She said she wasn't, but she knew women liked to play mind games. *Was she here to tell her another secret about her husband? Could she be the mystery woman known as Nova that filled her husband's text messages?* If so she knew her marriage was doomed. She was almost certain there was no coming back after experiencing such a rarity. Miranda could feel the heat coming from Azora's body and she found herself wanting to reach out and touch her. She wondered if the heat was coming from the woman's fire red hair. Azora's presence seemed to drown out everything thing around them.

"No, you do not know me. Let's just say a little birdie told me you could use my help."

Azora's patience was starting to wear thin with Miranda, but she held her temper in place because she needed her. Miranda was a detrimental part in her plan.

"Can you skip with the mind games and tell me what the hell you want lady? I'm not in the mood for any childish games you seem to want to play."

Even though the lady aroused her curiosity she was still getting on her nerves with her roundabout way of getting to the point. With all she had going on, Miranda didn't have a lot of time to waste. She needed to get back to make sure her scumbag ass husband didn't make his way back to their home while she was gone.

"Before we begin let me explain something to you." Azora's smile had faded and turned to slight mask of anger as she appeared in front of Miranda's face only inches away. "Don't ever raise your voice at me."

"Who the fuck—" Miranda started to say.

"Shhhhhh," Azora said as she ran her fingers down the side of Miranda's face, bringing on a sudden calm in her soul.

In a matter of seconds, Miranda wondered why her panties were instantly moist. The ache now pounding in her hot box was almost breathtaking.

"Are you tired of your husband cheating on you yet?" Azora invaded Miranda's personal space as she got close enough to rubbed her lips on Miranda's neck as she talked to her.

Azora breathed in her scent. She could taste the vanilla scent that she'd rubbed on herself from head to toe. Miranda's confusion and curiosity tickled Azora.

"How did you?" Miranda's breathing was labored.

She wanted to pull away from Azora's grasp, though somehow her brain waves weren't hitting her lower extremities. *How had this woman gotten so close to her?* Normally Miranda would never let another woman walk into her personal space without swinging first and asking questions later. However, this woman seemed to take hold of her inner being, rendering Miranda helpless against her advances.

"Shhh, sweetheart," Azora whispered in Miranda's ear, making the hairs on her body stand straight up. "Are you ready for him stop cheating?"

Slowly Azora's hands slid around Miranda's waist as she pulled her into her body. Azora had always been good at seducing anyone in her presence so she knew it wouldn't be hard to get Miranda to do whatever she asked of her.

"Yes."

Miranda had no clue as to how this woman knew her story but if she could help in way she was willing to try. She was too exhausted to even fight the lady standing in front her. Israel had sucked all the life out of her lately. It seemed giving up was the easiest route to take.

"I have a proposition for you. It's your choice and I don't want you to tell me the answer. I'll know what you choose by the end of the night."

"What do you need from me?" Miranda whispered as she prayed the woman took her hands form around her waist.

She was feeling things in her pussy that no one had ever made her feel. The heat from Azora's body was almost suffocating. Still, Miranda wanted to breathe in Azora's every essence and become one with her.

Azora got even closer and whispered in Miranda's ear. As she finished what she was saying, she took her hands from Miranda's body, stepped back, and smiled.

"Oh, in case you were wondering, my name is Azora Monroe."

As Azora walked away, Miranda stood in the middle of the sidewalk wondering what just happened. *Had this woman seduced her in broad daylight and left her yearning for more?*

Chapter 10
Ultimatums

    Israel placed the phone down from speaking to his travel agent. He looked around the empty house he was now living in. Life for him had changed drastically over the last couple of days. He had never intended for Miranda to find out about Nova. His plan was to enjoy the easygoing affair and like the ones before her once he was tired of her, he would call it quits. All that went to shits when he made the mistake and got too comfortable. He'd hate to admit it, but that was the affect Nova had on him. He would be out of his mind when he was around her. She had this spell over him and everything that should matter didn't mean a thing, including Miranda. He wasn't lying to her when he said he never intended to leave her for Nova, though Nova was definitely pulling him in that direction. Everything she did drove him mad and he felt like a wild animal when he was with her.

    Interrupting his thoughts, his phone rang and he saw it was Dillon.

"What's up bro."

"Nothing much. I'm calling because I wanted to see what was up with you," Dillon responded.

"What do you mean?"

"I mean, have you figured out how to fix what you messed up so you can go back home?"

"What if I don't want to go home? Maybe I'll just end it all and be with Nova. We seem to click. Maybe it's fate."

Israel heard him chuckle as if to say that wasn't going to ever happen.

"Why you asking me what I'm going to do anyway? You act like you're invested in Miranda or something."

"I'm not invested in Miranda at all. I guess I'm curious as to why this woman of all the women you fucked with is worth leaving your wife for. I know damn well you ain't pussy whipped at forty-two years old."

"It ain't just her pussy, dog. Dillon, I'm telling you me and this girl have some kind of connection. It's like I've met her before, though I can't fathom where I would know her from."

"Man, you know her ass from the damn club and it's obvious whatever you were drinking that night messed up your head. She can't be that damn good. I mean, what's your end game with her?"

Israel paused as he listened to the tone of his voice. He couldn't tell if his brother was jealous or if he was really trying to get him to go home.

"You know it don't even matter 'cause whatever she did to me that night, she keeps doing. I'm trying to resist the urge to call her. I know she's missing me."

"I doubt it. If she's that good she has other people she can call," Dillon said, laughing.

"Yeah, whatever. Well, I got work to do so I'll holla at you later," Israel said, hanging up the phone.

Leaning back in his chair, Israel's thoughts drifted to his brother's comments, then to the day he met Nova. He knew his vow to be faithful would be tested once again. He was at a bar with his other brother, Ian when he bumped into her. He was leaving the bathroom and not paying attention. For a few moments, time had stood still. He had never seen a woman as fine as her. He knew there was no way she was from St. Louis. He'd seen most of the fine women that lived here, so she had to be a visitor. She looked at him with the most intoxicating eyes and his knees damn near buckled. On top of that, she had this air about her that was alluring. The scent she wore caused him to crave tasting her. That night they ended up talking for hours before he found his way back to her house. Drunk and out of his mind, he fucked the hell out of her. To be honest, they fucked each other. For two hours, Nova had him wrapped up in her sexual haven. She'd given it to him so good, a one night stand turned into a regular booty call and before he knew it, ten months had passed him by. She had been the perfect side chick. It seemed they were kindred spirits, though he couldn't imagine how they would have been. Nova was a drug he knew would eventually be the destruction of him, yet he couldn't kick the habit. He'd gone back for hit after hit, not realizing the after effects of overdosing. Now he was in this predicament with no clear idea of how he was going to make it right.

Since Miranda had told him to get out all he could think about was being with her. He was still in shock that she put it on him so good and then told him to fuck off. The woman he saw that day was not his wife, or at least not his wife from the past few years. The woman that fucked him so good and then went bat shit crazy on him was indeed the woman he first married. Now, he definitely wanted her back. He wanted the passion and desire they once had for one another. He wanted the wild, hot nights of sex they would have that led to more morning sex. Although, Nova was a fantasy come true, he was in love with Miranda. She was the woman he pledged his life to and though he was fucking up, he still stood by that pledge. For his sake, he prayed to God this wasn't the end and she was in love with him.

He picked up his phone and texted her, *Miranda, please call me. I love you and I want to come home. I know we can work this out. I promise I won't fuck up again. I will end everything with her if you will just take me back.*

After booking them a trip, he clicked on Facebook to see if she had posted anything. Lately, this was the only way he could see what she was doing. For the last few days, she hadn't posted anything. He would go by the house to grab some clothes, hoping she would be there but she wasn't. He figured she was either meeting with a client or avoiding him. Considering everything he'd done to her, it was probably the latter. When he told her he would do anything she wanted to fix their marriage he meant it. Part of him wanted to just pop up and force her to talk to him, though he knew that wouldn't end well. He looked over and saw the clock read 6:30p.m. He was glad the weekend was finally there. For the past few days, he decided to work from home. He was a mess and he couldn't face going into the office. Nova had made up for some of his sadness, but there was still a void. He wanted to call Miranda again, but he feared she wouldn't answer. He'd gotten lucky when she answered the last time and even though she was pissed, he was glad to hear her voice.

He could tell she was still extremely angry and hurt. The things that were in his phone from Nova were beyond explicit. Nova brought out the porn star in any man, especially him. There probably wasn't a position she hadn't tried on him. He could even remember nights he would try and do to Miranda what she did to him. Nova had awakened the sleeping beast and he got greedy. Now, he was a victim of his own sins. All he wanted to do was repent and gravel at his wife's feet. He was ready to truly be the man she wanted him to be. He was ready to be the man he knew he could be. Thoughts of Miranda with other men had gone through his mind when she wasn't answering her phone. He had gone so far as to ride by their house at night to make sure another car wasn't parked there.

One night, her car wasn't parked in the garage and all sorts of thoughts ran through his mind. For the life of him, he couldn't figure out where she could be at on a Wednesday night at 9 p.m. Israel sat outside their house for three hours until he realized it was midnight and she wasn't coming home anytime soon. All night he called her trying to figure out where she was or who she was with. After several calls back-to-back, Miranda eventually turned off her phone off. It was then that Israel went really crazy. The thought of his wife doing what she did to him the other day to someone else tore him up inside. The way her mouth would cover him, bringing him to the edge of madness as she sucked his soul out. Her voluptuous hips engulfed him as she rode him with satisfaction and control. He could see the love in her eyes each time she exploded over his dick. All of these thoughts forced him to sit outside her house every night since then and he would continue doing so until she let him come back home.

Israel clicked off his computer and made his way to the kitchen. At this point, he needed a drink to calm his thoughts and to keep him from calling Miranda again. He wasn't sure what Dillon's problem was, but he had other things he need to worry about. He wanted to tell her about the trip he'd booked them, but he decided to wait and surprise her. She had always wanted to go to Bora Bora and there was no time like the present. He hoped that by then, she would be talking to him and they could renew their vows. He wanted to show her how he intended to take their commitment serious from this day forth. He wanted one more chance to let her know his life was hers and he would give his last breath fighting for what they had. He wanted to feel himself inside of her on the beach as they gave themselves to one another. Israel could feel his manhood rising as he swallowed the scotch. Dillon had done him a solid and brought him the bottle a few days ago, since he figured he would need something to cope with. At the time, his brother had spared him the big brother talk even though he had forewarned him this could happen. He could see he was a wounded dog and there was no need to kick him any further. Now, he didn't know what the issue could be. He was as low as anyone could get. A man with no place to call home.

Israel rubbed his hand over his manhood. He was trying to resist the urge of calling one of his old faithful's. He'd slipped back a couple times with Nova already and up until then she made him feel like a king, but he felt guilty about being there. He wanted to be available whenever Miranda called, but like any man, he had needs. He was a man who loved sex, lots of sex. Before he married her, he had plenty of it whenever it suited him. His sex drive was a gift and a curse. Had Miranda given him sex on a regular, he would have never found his way into the bed of Nova Sirene.

Now he had two women, one he loved and another one he loved to fuck. He wished he could just put both of them in one bed and they have one hell of a night. Nova's ferocious appetite mixed with Miranda's wild, competitive nature would be a glorious experience. Separately, both women were hurricanes, but together they could be the tsunami of sex. Predators at war with only one outcome, fucking until no one had an ounce of energy left to fight. As much as he would love to have them both, he knew Miranda was never having that shit. She was a freak, but even she had boundaries.

He remembered when he first met Miranda. He was out with his boys at a club called *Plush*. It was a new club that had just opened up downtown on Market and 20th Street, and they decided to check it out. That was the day everything changed for him. He could remember it like it was yesterday, seeing this cinnamon toned woman walk into the club. She had a banging body that any man would love to be inside and under. Her eyes had a brightness about them. It was as if she saw the world differently than everyone else. He watched her dance all night with her friends before he worked up the nerve to approach her. Once he did they were inseparable. It took weeks of him calling her before she finally gave him a chance, but she finally did. Within two dates, he knew she would be Mrs. Israel Cantrell. After a year of dating, he finally popped the question. Israel was so in love with Miranda, he had cut every woman he'd known off. He had the perfect woman and he didn't need any distractions. His life was perfect until they hit the five-year mark. Consumed by work and building their careers, they lost focus of what really mattered and that was how Cheyenne crept in. She had been his assistant for years before he'd even given a thought to sleeping with her. Now ten years later, he was still regretting the day he started down this dark path of infidelity.

Israel's thoughts were interrupted when his phone rang. It was Miranda calling him. He wondered if she was ready to talk to him. He'd hoped she was at least open to giving him some so he wouldn't stray again. His heart was breaking, but there was no need to add his dick to the list.

"Hello, Miranda is that you?"

"Who else would it be, Israel? Are you expecting a call from someone else? Nova perhaps?"

"No baby, I'm not. I'm sorry. I'm glad you called. Are you ready to talk?"

"No, not really. I'm ready for a lot of things, but talking about us is definitely not one of them," Miranda said, sarcastically.

Israel paused before he responded. He wasn't sure where the conversation was going, still he didn't want to be the one to derail it. He was at the mercy of Miranda. His life was in her hands so he had to walk carefully and tread lightly.

"Okay baby, it's your show. I'll let you lead. Just tell me what you want me to do."

Smitten Kitten

"Let me ask you something so I can be clear. What was going through your mind when you fucked all of them? Were you ever thinking about how much it would hurt me? Did you ever consider you would get caught? Hell, did you ever even care?" Miranda asked, fighting back the cracking in her voice.

Israel wanted to answer her, but he didn't know how or where to start. He didn't want to have this conversation over the phone. To him, this was a conversation they should have in person. There was no easy way to explain a fuck-up of this magnitude. He wanted her to see the sorrow and repentance in his eyes. He wanted her to see how sorry he truly was so she would take him back.

"Miranda, I know I made mistakes over the years. I know that right now you have no reason to believe I regret each time I fucked up. I've told you several times I wouldn't do it again, and yet soon after I found myself between the legs of another woman. Believe me when I say I will do anything to make you feel safe again. I realize I have a good thing and I took advantage of it. I just want to fix us."

"Fix us, huh? We weren't broken until you broke us. Tell me Israel, what did this one do for you? Did she fuck you better than I did? Did she make you feel like king of the fucking world? I bet she's a fucking toddler, seeing as though you were running up our fucking bills for her ass. Earrings and purses seem like a young bitch's priority. How old she, Israel?"

Israel hesitated. He knew being forthcoming was the only way Miranda would let him back home, but he feared he would be making it worse by telling her everything.

"Miranda there is no woman who fucks me better than you. You are my soulmate and we have a deeper connection. It's beyond physical with us. No woman will ever have that type of access to my heart. No woman other than you."

"You always know the right things to say. The right words, shit even the exact tone to convince me you're seriously sorry. I mean you're an attorney for fucks sake, of course you do!" Miranda snapped back.

"I'm not a lawyer talking you, I'm your husband telling you how I feel. A broken man pleading with you. I meant what I said, Miranda. I love you and I want to make this work."

"No you don't because if you did we wouldn't be having this same discussion for the fourth time. Each time it's the same routine. You fuck up, I catch you, and put you out. Then you beg and plead for me to take you back and after enough time has passed I do. This time I don't have the energy to do any of it."

"Miranda, please don't say you want to leave me, baby," Israel begged.

"Maybe you need to be single. Maybe you feel like you're missing out on something and you need your freedom. I would say you're having a mid-life crisis, but you did this stupid shit when you were young too. As much as I want to believe you want this, I don't anymore."

A long pause settled between them. Israel didn't know what to say to Miranda to make her see she was the woman he wanted. He knew he couldn't buy his way out of this one. No amount of money, jewelry, or cars would pull him out of this tragedy he created for himself. He knew there was something he could do, he just needed her to tell him.

"Miranda, I don't want to be single. When I put that ring on your finger July 19, 2001, I was sure who I wanted to be with. I want to be married to you."

"No, no, you don't. You want multiple women whenever it suits you. Hell, maybe I should try sleeping with some different men. I mean, I have quite a few clients who have been dying to take me out and show me a good time. Some may even want to fuck me, and maybe some new dick is what I need."

Israel took a deep breath. He knew Miranda had a slew of clients who in the past have tried to holler at her. He didn't want to hear this shit. He was already fighting thoughts of her being on dates when she didn't answer her phone or wasn't at home. He wouldn't stand for her fucking another man.

"Miranda, you are still my wife and I would kill a motherfucker if I ever found out you gave up my pussy," Israel screamed.

Miranda belted out a laugh.

"Wow, you really have a lot of nerve. You fuck whomever you want to fuck, but when I say I want to go on a date you flip out. How is that even possible?"

"Miranda, don't get somebody shot."

Miranda laughed again. Somehow she thought he was playing with her, but he wasn't. He was dead serious. As a criminal defense lawyer, he would do it and get off for it. He played about a lot of things, but Miranda sleeping with someone else was not one of them. It didn't matter how many women he fucked, her fucking someone else was not up for discussion.

"Ok, Israel, that's not what I called you for anyway. Did you mean what you said when you said you would do anything to make this work?"

"Yes, Miranda. Just tell me what I need to do and I'll do it."

"Fine. If you really want to make this work, I will text you an address. Be there by 11 p.m."

"Where am I going?"

"This is a no questions asked deal. You're at my mercy remember, so you don't get to ask questions. You either show up or you don't. Whichever you choose will be on you, but if you don't show up you can rest assured we are done."

Israel heard the phone click and realized Miranda had hung up on him. A few moments later an address appeared across his screen. He had no idea where Miranda was luring him to, but if he wanted his marriage to stay intact he would be there by 11 p.m.

Chapter 11
Nova's Betrayal

King Asya Oyo was tired. He was barely able to drag his aching, naked body to his hidden grotto. When he was younger he always hid out in this part of the palace because few people knew how to get there. It was the place he loved to rejuvenate at after war. It was dark and damp and the only sound heard was the water from the waterfall in the center of the room.

King Oyo walked towards the back of the room where the water was so warm that he always had to gather himself a time or two before he could completely submerge in it. He placed his foot in it but quickly pulled it back out because it burned his skin. He thought about how Nova would always laugh as she would ease her chocolate body in the water with no problem. The softness of her hands rubbing on him as she sung one of her favorite songs about finding the love of her life. Her voice was an airy, soprano that would put him in a relaxed state like a lullaby. It wouldn't be long before the singing would stop and her mouth would be placed all over his body, stopping below his waist and her paying it extra attention. The tightness of her throat and her ability to take his hard, fast thrusts with no complaints were remarkable traits to possess. He felt guilty that a tiny part of him longed to have that moment right now.

It wasn't that Azora wasn't pleasing him because she actually did quite well. She just wasn't Nova. A woman like Nova was born to make a man feel good. She could get into a man's heart because of that but she would never be able to be all of his heart like

Azora. Even still, she was simply the best at draining him of everything and filling him with euphoria.

He placed his hand under the water and slowly started to stroke himself. The heat in the room and the vibrations he was causing his own body made him feel woozy. He leaned against the brick wall and closed his eyes as he continued his strokes. The image of Nova popped in his head again, her hands alternating with her mouth, suctioning away on him. He moved his hips in and out in search of the greatest release. Nova's mouth tightened around him even more and he could no longer stop the shaking of his body. It just felt so, and then his eyes flew open.

"Nova, what are you doing?" he asked.

He pushed her away from him and she fell back under the water. He didn't even hear her come in. He was amazed that he wasn't more aware of his surroundings and pissed at her for catching him in a moment of weakness.

"Get up now," he yelled loudly.

Nova was an excellent swimmer, something she said she learned back in her homeland, and able to hold her breath for long periods of time. He saw the bubbles fly over where she was laying low at the bottom and he pulled her to her feet. She was completely naked with a wicked smile on her face. He wanted to slap the smile from her face, but he was never the type of king who was a tyrant.

"How the hell did you know I was in here?"

"My king, now you know me well enough to know that I can sense when you are in need," she sung her words out.

Out of all of the melodies she sung before he had never heard this one. It was intoxicating and seductive, almost as if the words floated around his veins and slowly seeped into his soul. He felt himself harden again. The needing that shook his core left him in a state of confusion. He loved Azora and the thought of her being disappointed fought against his desire for Nova. Azora was fragile and unable to trust that his love for her was enough. He was willing to love her past her insecurities because to him she worth all that and more. Nova was having a hard time understanding that but he was going to make sure she got it this time.

"My needs have nothing to do with you anymore, Nova."

"They could though. Don't you remember? You used to love me. The way you touched me, no one has ever captivated me like that before."

"That was when I was a boy. I am now a man, a married man at that. I could have any woman in this land but I only chose my wife. She is who I desire and you will respect that."

His voice boomed so loud that Nova shrunk under the words and his glare. All she wanted was to show him that with her he could have more than this boring existence he was intertwined in with Azora. Nova had watched him over the past few months and was shocked to see that he had shriveled into half of the boisterous king who once had parties every night with his soldiers and concubines. She just needed to get close enough to make him remember those times when their passion ran wild and their sinful nights of lust were befitting of a powerful king like himself.

"So, all those times when you filled me with all of you, when you pledged your love for me, does that not mean anything, Asya?"

"We were never meant to be, Nova! Why don't you get that? We tried. You didn't fulfill the prophecy. Azora will. I can feel it whenever I am near her."

King Oyo removed himself from the water. He was done with the conversation. He wanted to find Azora and make sure that she would be prepared for the fulfillment tomorrow night. It was his last chance of seeing the red moon. He had no time to worry about Nova and her frivolous crush.

Behind him Nova exited the water and ran to catch up with him. She grabbed his arm and spun him around. They both felt the electric shock of raw passion ignite between them. As much as he talked the words of his love for Azora only, Nova could tell by his actions that his body wanted her. She moved in closer, erasing the air that stood between them. She placed her lips to his chest, over his heart, and planted soft kisses upon it. Her tongue traced figure eights in light flickers. The humming that lightly flowed from her mouth sent waves of pleasure to his nerves. His senses were heightened. He could now smell the passion and pain that flowed through Nova. He was aware that her love for him was genuine, but yet tortured. Her heart was open but there was no energy flowing in her soul. King Oyo felt a pain of guilt because he knew he was the thief who stole her happiness. He softly placed his hands on her head, rubbing them through her hair. He knew the way to heal her was to dominate her body.

"I missed you," she whispered.

No answer came from his mouth but he yanked her hair, causing her head to fall back. He forced his tongue in her mouth, demanding she kiss him with the same intensity. Nova fell into place with no resistance at all. Her body was his as an offering to do whatever he pleased with her. He didn't want to admit it but he was tired of trying to fight it. He needed her one last time to combat the savage beast she released inside of him. She was his addiction and having her was the only way to dissolve his body's ache to ravage her.

"Is this what you want?" he asked, roughly.

"Yes, give it to me."

In a swift motion he picked her up and slammed their bodies into the wall. Nova winced from the impact but there was no way she would stop him. She prayed and yearned for this moment for the past few months. Watching him with another woman and lying at night hearing them make love was enough to drive her insane. She was seconds from going mad and taking drastic measures to fix this situation. When he plowed himself inside of her she thought she would pass out from the burning sensation that ripped through her vagina.

"Open your eyes and look at me!" King Oyo demanded.

Nova's eyes flew open and locked with his. He was searching for the magic of past times. She felt softer in his arms. She felt more filled out in the curves of her body. There was something off. With the thought quickly dismissed, he slammed in and out of her at a steady pace. Nova's soft moans added fuel to his lovemaking, taking it to a mind blowing fuck. Nova bit his lip, drawing blood. She suckled at it until the bottom lip swelled.

The pain caused darkness to cloud his eyes and it turned Nova on. She used to see that look all the time before Azora came along. He was arrogant and demanding, both great traits he used to enforce his position as the greatest. Nova loved it. The old king was back. This was her king. The beast, the man who took her body to heights that superseded the heavens. She clawed at his back as his pumps slowed into a grind.

"Baby, I've missed this so much. Oh, you're so deep," she whispered against his ear.

"Do you love me?" he asked.

"Yes, I love you so much. Leave her, be with me. I am who you desire. I am who you love. Empty yourself inside of me."

The sound of Nova's voice rung in King Oyo's ear, exposing a demonic undertone. It shocked him so hard that it extinguished the fire that brewed in the base of his stomach. His eyes widened as he went limp inside of her. Years ago, King Oyo began praying to Hecate to reveal to him who his true enemies were. Being king allowed people to have more access to him and he hated feeling vulnerable to exposure. Once he was able to tell friend from foe things got easier, but somehow Nova had fooled him. He pulled himself out of her and dropped her to the ground.

"What, what happened, my king?" Nova asked, full of alarm.

She pulled herself up from the ground and stared at him in bewilderment. He paced the floor back and forth. He was fuming mad and for the first time, Nova found herself afraid in his presence.

"You don't love me. I can't believe I didn't see this all along," he mumbled more to himself than Nova.

"I do love you. I'd do anything for you. Why are you saying that?"

"You want me dead. I saw it. I should kill you!"

He struck her face with a blow that shocked even himself but he felt that Nova was lucky that was all he had done, considering he wanted to kill her with his bare hands.

"How could you betray me this way? Who sent you to me? Tell me or death will be upon you!"

"It wasn't supposed to be like this. I didn't know I would love you. I could never do anything to hurt you now. Please forgive me. I'll do anything. Please," she groveled at his feet.

"Who sent you?"

"Your brother. He was banished a long time ago by your parents. You were just a baby. He wanted to reclaim his rightful spot but only if you were dead. I couldn't do it. I'm sorry," Nova cried.

"Get out and never come back! If I ever hear of or see you again, I will kill you."

He shook his foot loose from her hands. King Oyo was already aware of his brother's situation. He also knew of the prophecy and was in pursuit of fulfilling it as well. That truth was revealed to him years prior but what he wasn't shown was Nova's betrayal. That angered him more than anything else. He grabbed Nova in the air and threw her out of the room. The last image he saw of her before he turned his back was her weeping like a mad woman.

Nova ran from the grotto and down the halls of the palace, dripping wet from water and naked. Her wails were excruciating to anyone who had the misfortune of watching her run out the front doors. Nova didn't care anymore. Her heart was broken into a thousand pieces. She was never meant to be in love, but somehow King Oyo made it possible, only to destroy her with it. The faster she ran the more her hurt turned to anger. The blood boiling in her body caused her legs to pump at the speed of an animal. She was on fire as she made her way across town.

Who does he think he is? He will pay for what he did to me. Azora will too, She thought to herself. Revenge crept inside of her brain, tying her thoughts in a noose. *There has to be some type of way to destroy that sickening love that ties Asya and Azora. I can't let them win and I am left with nothing. They have to pay.*

Nova's thoughts had taken over her body as well. She ran for miles with no destination in mind but stopped short when she hit the palace on the other side of town. The place was dark and lifeless, nothing at all like where she had just come from. It fit Nova's soul perfectly. She walked across the gate and drew her hand to knock but the door opened before she could.

"Hello, Nova. I knew this day would come," the woman said as soon as she stepped in the light.

"Queen Nzinga Anna, I need your help in getting Azora out of the palace."

Chapter 12
The Vow

"My love you are looking breathtaking tonight," King Oyo marveled over his beautiful wife.

She stood flawlessly in the middle of their bedroom draped in Benin's finest silk. The red silk gown hung loosely on her body with parts of her flesh playing peek-a-boo with him. Her signature red hair hung down her back in loose curls. The heat in his groin was building but he needed to refrain from making love to her for they had more pressing issues. Indeed, Azora had lived up to her promise to try her best. She'd been the best thing that had ever happened to him, and he couldn't wait to spend all of eternity with her.

"Why thank you, my king," Azora blushed as she walked in closer to King Oyo.

She couldn't resist being close to him. His presence was almost in intoxicating and addictive. He'd completely stolen her heart and her body craved his touch more than it craved water and food.

"You yourself look good enough to nibble on," she giggled.

Indeed, he did look like a work of art. His muscles bulged out his freshly sewn dashiki that was laced in gold. His beauty never ceased to amaze Azora. Every day she thanked the Gods for sending her into his arms.

"Come my love. It is time to fulfill the prophecy," King Oyo said as he held his hand out for Azora grab a hold to.

"What prophecy do you speak of, my king?" Azora asked before she took his hand.

She'd heard him mention it the night he made the deal with the queen for her but she thought he was just talking.

"The prophecy that me and you should be together forever in this lifetime and the next and the next one after that."

He pulled her in close so they were face-to-face. Their lips were almost touching they were so close.

"I told you before my kitten, I would make sure we find each other no matter what end of the earth we end up on our love will always make sure we find each other."

"Yes, my love," is all Azora could say.

She didn't care what he had had planned for her because at that point she would follow him to ends of the earth to be by his side. He indeed was her one true love and she prayed his prophecy was real so that their love would always prevail.

King Oyo led Azora to a room that took her breath away. She had never been to this part of the palace. The room was covered in beautiful silk curtains of all colors. They floated effortlessly as a soft breeze flowed through the open windows. Fresh flowers practically cover the walls and the flickers from the candlelight danced on the wall and intertwined with the colors of the silk curtains.

"Oh, this room is so beautiful. Why have I never seen this room before?" Azora gave him a questioning eye.

"This room was meant for the purpose of tonight's festivities, my kitten. Don't worry from this night forward you will see a life with me you've only dreamed of," he said with a smile.

The smile he gave her would make any woman agree to anything he suggested.

"Oh," Azora replied as she continued to marvel at the decor.

King Oyo watched her as she walked around room. The natural sway of her hips had started to make his manhood stand to attention. His dick didn't seem to care about the plans for the night. It needed a release and it was pointing right at his sexy wife, Azora. She oozed sex from her aura and the sexiest part about it was she didn't even know it.

"Come to me, my love," King Oyo told her.

He held out his hand as he waited for Azora to reach him.

Azora sauntered over to him, putting a little more swing in her hips. She eyed him hungrily, ready for whatever he had planned. The look in her eyes said she wanted to the same thing he wanted.

"Yes, my king."

She stopped right in front of him as he wrapped his arms around her waist. She shuddered under his touch. She still hadn't gotten use to his gentle affection.

King Oyo lowered his face into the nape of her neck and inhaled her scent. Her essence always drove him into a frenzy. He couldn't explain the feelings she pulled out of him but, he knew she was the only woman he wanted to be with for the rest of his life. Nova had betrayed him but he knew he would be able to trust Azora with his life.

Azora giggle from the light air of breath he breathed on her neck. She reached up, grabbed his face, and pulled his lips down to hers. Their lips touched and both felt a magnetic force pull them in closer to each other. King Oyo took his hand and reached under her dress and found the golden pot he searched for. He could feel her juices running down over his fingers. Gently he pulled and tugged on her clit while he sucked on her tongue. The feeling of his hand exploring her womanhood was making her knees weak.

Like a good wife she pried her mouth away from his and dropped down into low squat in front of him. She smiled at the sight of his erect penis pointing right at her. She move his dashiki up above his waist, took a hold of it, and pulled it up over his head. Before it could hit the floor she'd stuffed his phallus deep into her hot mouth. Azora moved her tongue with expertise. Nova had taught her well and now the student could show the teacher a thing or two. Slowly and methodically Azora moved her head back and forth, and with each movement she was able to get more-and-more of him down her throat. She held on to his thighs as she forced him to fuck her mouth. She could feel his muscle twitch with each flick of her tongue. Unable to take it anymore, King Oyo pulled Azora up and walked her over the bed. He could see the fire in her eyes burning bright. He knew that look of lust all too well and he knew that Nova had taught her that look that drove all men crazy. Pushing Nova out of his head he crawled onto the bed and lay on top of her, placing his mouth up against hers again. She could feel him sliding the head of his dick up her slit. She lost her will to breathe once he inserted himself into her. The heat and passion between the two of them could be felt throughout the palace. Moans of ecstasy bounced off the walls as a heated fog clouded the atmosphere. Their bodies intertwined a lustful and passionate tango as they got in each other's essence. King Oyo began to grind his aching pole gently but hard enough for her to feel it deep within her walls. Both sweated and panted as the red moon settled in the sky right over their room. Remembering why they were there, King Oyo quickened his pace so he could bring them both their point of no return. He could feel her walls constricting around him as she neared her orgasm. He felt a tingle shoot down his spine and settle in the pit of his groin. Not able to hold off any longer he released his load into her, making her orgasm that much stronger. Panting, he stood as he tried to catch his breath.

"It is time, my love."

King Oyo picked up his dashiki, looked out the window, and he could see the blood moon shining brightly through the window. He needed to perform the ritual on them both before the moon went away or he would have to wait a half of century before the blood moon returned.

"Stay in bed, my love," King Oyo instructed but it wasn't as if she could have moved even if she wanted to.

Suddenly, a harsh breeze covered the room and everything stood still. Even the curtains no longer had life in them. The candles blew out and everything went dark. King Oyo fell down to his knees and made an ear piercing wailing sound, making Azora jump she tried to get up from the bed but something was holding her down.

"Asya, what is going on?" in a panic she asked but got no answer.

She could hear him softly chanting something over-and-over again, but she couldn't quite make out what he was saying.

"Hecate, take my offering. I offer you my wife's soul, so that we can begin our journey," King Oyo prayed out loud as he rocked back and forth in a trance like state.

"Oh no the hell you don't!" Azora screamed. "Help! Help! Please Asya, don't do this!"

Azora all of sudden felt the pressure of something getting into the bed with her. Slowly, she felt the slimy scales of a snake slithering up her legs. She tried her best to shake the snake off, but it seemed to grip her body tighter the more she struggled.

"Hecate my lord, take my offering," King Oyo repeated again.

"Asya, please, no!" Azora screamed as she felt the large snake constricting the length of his body around her figure.

She could feel the air her lungs leaving. Dots danced in front of her eyes as she began to slowly fade away. The feeling of the snake sliding into her vagina brought her back to reality long enough to feel the snake stab his fangs into the soft meat inside of her womanhood and release its venom. The pain took what breath she had left in her lungs away. The urge to fight and squeeze her vaginal muscles around the snake's head left her body as she felt the venom begin to burn at her insides.

"Asya, please make it stop," she moaned and clenched her eyes shut as the venom began to make her body feel warm all over.

Suddenly, she felt an ache in her pussy. The throbbing in her clit let her know she was about to have an explosive orgasm. She gripped the sheets as explosive sparks went off in her body and King Oyo chanted in the background, giving her a soundtrack to remember forever. The snake began to release her body as it slithered its way out of the bed.

Exhausted and ready to give up on life, she slowly opened her eyes. She tried to adjust her eyes to the darkness. As her blurred vision became clearer she could see shadows of King Oyo rocking back and forth on his knees as he continued to chant.

"Asya," she whispered, but she got no response. "My king why did you do this to me?" Azora cried.

Heartbroken she couldn't believe he'd offered her soul to his God.

"You never loved me. Why would you do this to me?" she whimpered.

"My love, we'll be together for ever now."

Azora hadn't noticed that King Oyo had stopped chanting and was now standing by her side.

Azora looked up into his eyes and could see the sincerity in them. Though she didn't know what he'd just done to her, she

Smitten Kitten

trusted him and wanted to believe whatever he did was to make sure their love would last forever.

"You are mine forever. We will be together in this life and the next. Our souls will forever be as one. Wherever you go my soul will follow."

"Asya—" Azora's sentence was cut short when all of sudden there was light in the room and they were surrounded by a group of soldiers and in the middle of them stood Queen Anna Nzinga.

Each of the guards stood with torches in their hands and weapons pointed at them.

"What is the meaning of this!" King Oyo roared.

His muscles twitched in anger as he watched the queen stand there with a smug look upon her face.

"It seems your reign has come to an end, King Oyo," Queen Nzinga smirked.

He could tell she was really on her high horse at the moment. She had no idea what she had interrupted. If he made it out alive, he would definitely be ending her life for good.

"What do you want, Queen Nzinga? Why are you in my home?" the king looked around, weighing his options.

On one hand he knew he must survive the night so he could finish his ritual, however he also knew he was out numbered. No one was allowed in that part of the palace, not even his guards, so he knew no help would be coming. *The was question was, how did she know where to find him?*

"I come to get what is mine! You took something that was dear to me and I want it back."

The queen cut her eyes over to Azora who still couldn't move because the venom was still doing its magic on her body.

"All of this over someone you called a peasant!" he scoffed.

At the time, he knew she was lying. The queen wasn't aware of it, but her secret wasn't really a secret. Men from all over knew what her true desires were. Never being seen with a man on her arm was a definite sign. She wasn't fooling anyone but herself with the lies she told. Standing there ready to fight him for Azora proved he was right.

"She was mine and now you've tainted her. If I can't have her no one will."

The king looked over and could see Nova peeking her head into the door. He tried to signal her to go get help but she just stood there. Immediately, he could see in her eyes that she aided the queen in this betrayal.

"You will pay for your treachery," King Oyo stated as he looked Nova in the eyes before he gave the queen his full attention again. "So tell me queen, will she return by your side or secretly in your bed? Maybe I should've taken you to bed. Possibly spread you wide and give your backside something it longs for. It seems you obviously haven't had the right man to rid you of your wickedness or bring you real pleasure."

"Seize him!" Queen Nzinga ordered.

Almost immediately, King Oyo was swarmed by the queen's soldiers. They put him down on his knees in front of her.

"When all of this is over with you will just be another woman trying to walk in a man's shoes. You are pitiful and will never be more than a queen that needs a king," he told her as he struggled against their grip but his efforts were in vain.

"You will not take what doesn't belong to you ever again," Queen Nzinga said with conviction as she raised her hand that held her sword.

He looked back at Azora and wanted to cry. He prayed the ritual finished for the both of them. Otherwise, there would be no next lifetime for them.

"No!" Nova and Azora yelled and both women watched in horror as the love of their lives head went flying across the room.

The soldiers dropped his body and marched out. The queen stood looking at Azora, still mesmerized by her beauty. For a moment, she considered having her seized and brought back, but she knew this betrayal would never be forgiven. Azora was a different woman now and she knew her life would be in danger if she brought her back. Satisfied with her revenge, Queen Nzinga gave Azora one last look before walking out.

Unable to move, Azora passed out from the sight of her beloved King Oyo being beheaded in front of her.

Smitten Kitten

"Yes, you may enter."

A knock at Azora's door shook her from her daydream. She hadn't realized she'd gotten so lost in her thoughts. She longed for her husband's touch.

"Yes, my queen," Tina said, entered the room, and stood stunned at the sight of Azora standing in the nude as she rubbed lotion up her legs.

No matter how many times she'd seen Azora naked it never ceased to amaze her. Her dark skin was intoxicating. She stared in awe, unable to pull her eyes away from Azora's beauty.

"Tina, what can I do for you?"

Azora stood up straight and gave Tina a full view of her body. She tilted her head and could tell Tina was tongue tied and couldn't seem to find her words.

"I-Um, well I um—" Tina paused for a second to get her mouth to actually form the words her brain was trying to get her to say.

She totally forgot why she had even entered the room.

"Tina, do you like what you see?" Azora asked as she began to walk over to Tina.

Tina nodded her head in a yes manner. Tina stood frozen stiff. She wanted to faint as she began to feel light headed the closer Azora got to her.

"Yes, my queen."

"Lay down on your back."

Tina just stood there staring. What the queen had just said didn't register in her head.

"Lay down right here," Azora stated as she pointed to the floor in front of her, and then slowly Tina did what was instructed of her. "I see the way you look at me, Tina. Do you want to taste me, Tina?"

Azora could see the look of lust written all over Tina's face, even though she wasn't saying anything.

"Do you want to taste me?" Azora asked again.

"Yes, my queen."

There was a yearning in Tina's eyes that almost made the queen laugh. She had never seen someone so desperate, unless they were begging her for their life. Azora looked down into Tina's eyes as she lowered her pussy down onto her face. Immediately Tina's mouth began to lap at Azora's womanhood. Azora let the feel of Tina's tongue circling around her clit take her mind off of her current situation as she rocked back and forth. Wanting to please her, Tina munched her on her hot box like a starved child. Azora grinded her pussy all over Tina's face. Tina reciprocated by gripping her thighs and making sure not to let a single drip drop of Azora's essence escape her mouth. She didn't want to anger the queen by not serving her well.

Azora reached down and spread her lips open so Tina could get right to the meat of things. Tina switched between sucking, licking, and nibbling on Azora's clit. Azora had to admit that Tina would definitely make her list of top three. Her desire to please her was proven with each stroke she made.

"Yes, make this pussy cum," Azora hissed. "Suck it like you've been wanting to for all these years."

Azora grinded even harder, but Tina never complained nor did she let up. She had waited decades for this moment. Lost in the moment, Tina flipped Azora over on her back to spread her legs as far as they would go and dove face first back into Azora's honey pot. Tina put her tongue into overdrive, determined to take Azora over the point of no return. Azora gripped the back of Tina's head, excited about Tina's aggression, letting her do as she pleased.

"Yeah, suck this pussy and don't you let up. You suck it like your life depends on it."

Azora smashed Tina face deeper into her aching pussy. She felt the orgasms she desperately needed to let go of building and sitting at the edge of her volcano ready to erupt. Tina's response was to do as she was told as she felt Azora's body begin to shake.

"Shiiiiit! Yes Tina, make that pussy cum!" Azora squealed as she felt her body go into light convulsions

As her orgasm subsided she could still feel Tina sucking on her clit. Regaining her composure, she tapped the top of Tina's head trying to signal for her stop. Though, Tina didn't catch the hint.

"Girl, if you don't let my shit go!" Azora yelled as she slapped Tina on the side of her head.

"I'm sorry, my queen."

Tina jumped as she rubbed the side of her head. She got up, embarrassed that she'd gotten carried away. She hoped she didn't make Azora angry that was the last thing she ever wanted to do. She wanted to make sure she was pleased and would be returning for more.

"Go prepare for tonight," Azora ordered as she pulled herself off the floor.

She watched as Tina scurried out her room. She stood in the same spot for a moment, trying to get the feeling back in her legs.

"Damn, that lil' bitch been holding that good head for all these years. I knew I kept her around for a reason."

Azora dabbled in the world of pussy rarely. Nova was the only woman who could have her any way she wanted with no objections. She'd vowed years ago that she wouldn't share her bed with another woman, and technically she hadn't considering they were on the floor. She had to laugh as she busied herself with getting ready for the main event. Tonight would be something special. Tonight she would get her revenge.

Chapter 13
Next Lifetime

Boom!

A loud thunder reverberated throughout the house. Lightning struck the rooftop over-and-over again, letting the world know that the Gods were not happy with what was going on. Hard rain pounded on the windows as heavy winds blew the trees around and about. The light had gone out hours ago but the sleeping beauty still stirred in her sleep. She'd been sleep for what seemed like an eternity but it was time for her to awaken and walk in her new circle of life.

"Hecate take my offering!"

"Oh no the hell you don't! Help! Help! Please Asya, don't do this!"

Azora shook in her sleep as flashes of her life ran rampant through her mind.

"You will pay for your treachery."

"Seize him!"

"No!" Azora screamed as she was jolted out of her turbulent slumber.

Azora sat up and looked around. The room she was in was big and beautiful, but it was very unfamiliar. Confused, she ran her hands over the soft silk covers that she lay under. She looked down at her hands and then looked up into the mirrors that sat on the wall in front of the bed. Something was different. She couldn't put her finger on it but there was a nagging feeling that she couldn't shake. The house had an eery silence that sent chills up her spine.

"Asya!" Azora screamed. "Asya! Nova!" she screamed again. "Where is everyone?" she asked herself. "Asya!"

She ran her finger through her hair. She got up from the bed and walked around and took in the decor of the home. *No doubt she didn't remember anything about the place so how had she gotten there?*

"Azora, my queen, is everything ok?"

Azora looked to the door to see Nova standing there in a panic. Her eyes were all over the place, and she didn't seem to know what to do with her hands that she constantly played with. She looked different. Her clothes, the way she wore her hair, everything was foreign.

"Oh my God!" Azora shrieked. "What is this place, Nova? This isn't my kingdom. Where is Asya?"

"Are you ok, my queen?" Nova asked again as she gave a perplexed look.

"No, I'm not ok. I'm confused. What is going on?" Azora screamed.

"So, you don't remember anything about that night?" Nova asked.

"What night? You are scaring me? Where the hell is Asya? I need to see him immediately. Have the guards look for him in this weird place," she commanded.

"Calm down. I think this is your home and we've just had to change with the times."

Azora now gave Nova the same perplexed look.

"What do you mean?"

"My queen, the night of the blood moon, Asya was trying to turn the both of you immortal so that you could spend eternity together. He had to summon Hecate to do it. He tried with me before but it only made me immortal and not him. That's how he knew I wasn't the one that the prophecy spoke of."

"What is this damn prophecy that I keep hearing people speak of?" Azora butted in out of frustration.

Taken aback by her words, Nova smiled a little. Azora had always been so meek and quiet that Nova had no clue she even knew of the curse words that the hunters used when they were away from women.

"Asya's parents were promised their son would have a great love that would endure even stronger than Cleopatra and Marc Anthony's. When he was of mating age, he sought out special women like me after that. There were three before me, all unsuccessful. We were purposely created in hopes that we would be the one who would fulfill it. None of us knew that the whole time some peasant girl would be the one, but Asya felt it the moment he laid eyes on you."

Azora felt her heart flush at the thought of how much he loved her. He had saved her life. She wanted to hop off the bed and go find him herself but something about the look on Nova's face troubled her.

"What are you not telling me, Nova?"

"Well, that night Queen Nzinga and her men stormed the palace. Death covered every inch of the place that night. I don't know every detail of what happened but she killed Asya, you, and me. When I awakened we were here in this home. I was by your side as usual. I've always been by your side."

Azora could sense something behind Nova's last remark but she just charged it to the nostalgia she was feeling from just waking up. She was confused by everything. The tears that fell down her face only showed a tiny glimmer of the pain she felt.

"So Asya is dead? Oh my God, I can't believe this. Where is Queen Nzinga? We must kill her!"

Nova shrunk a little under Azora's vengeful glare. She didn't want to show it, but she was nervous about what Azora would do to her when she found out what part she played in his death. It was clear to Nova that this was not the same Azora she knew in her past life.

"My queen, I walked past a monthly chart and it is the year twenty-thousand. She is long gone and never coming back."

"Twenty-thousand, what the hell?"

"Yes, we've crossed over into the next lifetime."

"Well, where is my king? He said he would meet me in the next lifetime," Azora stated to herself more so than Nova.

Nova fumed inside that even after all of this Azora's undying love for the man who was really the love of Nova's life was still front and center.

"There is no king. There is just you and me," Nova said through her own tears.

She felt horrible that the king had died in such a heinous way. This was all her fault and if anyone, especially Azora, ever found out her secret she didn't know what she would do. God forbid that King Oyo had crossed over and he was looking to kill her. She would never forget the look in his eyes when he realized that she had really betrayed him.

Nova's cries tugged at Azora for reasons other than mutual heartache. Azora felt something wasn't right, but without knowing what it wa she shook it off because she was just happy to have a familiar face around. She looked down at the floor again, trying to let everything sink in.

"So, there is no Asya but you're here. I am a queen without a king. How is that possible? Do I still have servants? How do I not remember how I got here? What have I been doing all these years? I need answers, Nova."

"My queen, as I said before, I do not know all the details. I've only been here for about a month. You showed up out of nowhere today but you are still Queen of Benin, which the natives here call Nigeria. Yes, this your palace. Yes you still have servants and I am still one of them. Now that I have you back we need to do something different with this place. It's been boring, not like when King Asya ruled," Nova huffed.

"Well first things first, never make mention his name again! He lied to me!"

Azora was hurt and angry that he hadn't kept up his end of the bargain. *Where was he?* She thought over-and-over. He said they would always find each other and that their love would always prevail, but he'd left her alone with nobody to love. Azora thought back to the night King Oyo died and what he'd done to her. He offered her soul to his God, Hecate. She decided to live as he'd lived and praise the God he called Hecate. She would do as he had. Maybe that would help her get back to the love of her life. Maybe Hecate would bring them back together if she prayed hard enough and showed loved with sacrifices like King Oyo had.

"And second, we will study up on Hecate and figure out how to bring souls to her so that we may continue to receive her many blessings."

Nova nodded as Azora continued to give out orders. She might have been afraid back then but King Oyo would be proud of the way she jumped right into ruling today. Her decision to pray to Hecate would be one that he would love. It could also be a decision that would ruin Nova's life. During one of her last moments with the king, Hecate showed him her true intentions. Nova knew that she would not be able to live here in the palace or commune with Azora daily, surely all would be revealed about her.

"Azora, we will also have to change to match the times here so as not to draw suspicions about us."

"You will address me as queen, not by my first name. I will not tolerate such disrespect."

"There are no kings and queens here. This land is very different but it thrives off a sexual spirit that I've never felt before. It is almost as if everyone is oblivious to the lurking dangers that hang over them."

"What do you mean?" Azora asked.

"The men here are different. Their very bold and rude. They approach women for sexual favors as if they're asking for a random dance. The women are all sexual slaves to the men. They offer their bodies for free. There is no gold here, just some thin green paper that they call money. If you have a lot of that, you can rule this place."

Azora looked Nova up and down from head to toe. If men were looking for a sexual slave she could think of no one more perfect than Nova. However, they would not be getting her for free. She would charge them and they would use the money to find King Oyo. She would kill him for lying to her and leaving her and Nova to fend for themselves.

"Nova, you and I will rule this place. I am still the queen and you are still my maidservant. We will be an unstoppable force that they will write and talk about for years to come. Once we find King Oyo and kill him, no one will be able to get in our way."

Nova smiled at Azora's confidence. She found herself turned on in a major way. She walked to the bed and sat down next to Azora.

"First, let me do something that I have been dying to do since I laid eyes on you," she whispered in Azora's ear as she pushed her down on the bed.

Israel glanced at Miranda as they walked through the carnival. It was the Fourth of July and they had ridden every ride and ate every ounce of junk food they could inhale. Today, marked their one-year anniversary and neither of them wanted to spend it doing something fancy. They wanted to spend it laughing and having as much fun as the day would permit. He squeezed her hand tighter as she went on about the design internship she was almost finished with. He loved listening to her talk about her dreams. She was such a dreamer and that fascinated him. She was full of energy and being around her was contagious. He knew after six months of being with her, she would be his wife. He can remember the night he met her and how much fun she and her friends were having just hanging out. They were dancing, laughing, and not paying attention to anyone in the room. Her confidence was sexy as hell and after tonight, they would be embarking on a new path together.

"I love you, Miranda Blackstone," Israel said.

Miranda glanced at him and smiled.

"I love you too, Israel. Are you okay?"

"Yes baby, I'm fine. I just want you to know I am so in love with you."

Miranda stopped in her tracks and turned to him. She could see the sincerity in his eyes and she wanted him to see it in hers as well. She had fallen in love with him months after they met. If she had to guess, she would say it was probably their second date. There was just something about him. He reminded her of her father and she always knew that was the kind of man she wanted to be with. She would have to admit she played coy with him in the beginning, but now as they stand here a year later. She knew it was worth it.

"I am in love you with you too, Israel. I think I fell a long time ago, but I wasn't sure if you had so I kept it secret," she said, laughing.

"Are you happy with me, Miranda? Do I make you happy?"

"Of course you do, baby. Do you think I would spend a year with someone who didn't make me happy? I think we both know I'm not the type of woman who would settle for being treated any old kind of way."

"Good because I want you to promise me something. If there ever comes a time when I hurt you or I'm not making you happy, I want you to tell me. I never want to do anything to hurt you and I never want you to be unhappy."

"Baby, are you sure you're okay?"

"Yes, Miranda, now promise me we will always be honest with each other about our feelings."

"I promise if there is ever a time when you hurt me or I'm not happy, I will tell you. Now can I ask you something?"

"Yes," Israel said, smiling.

He wondered what was dancing around in her thoughts. She was always so curious and intriguing to converse with. Their conversations would begin one way and drift off to something else. He contributed it to her artistic mind. She was fascinated by the damnedest things. Her carefree spirit pulled him in and on his darkest day she was always a light.

"Will you promise me the same thing? I know that I'm extremely quirky compared to the other women you may have dated, but I always want to be the woman you want to come home to."

Israel figured this would be the perfect time to do it, but he wasn't ready yet. The sunset was on the horizon, therefore the fireworks wouldn't be far behind it. He wanted this moment to be perfect. Every moment he had spent thus far with Miranda had been memorable. He needed this one to be as well.

"Miranda, you are more woman than all of the women I ever dated. I can't think of anything I want to do more than come home to you. When I am having a bad day at the firm, I immediately get excited knowing I'll be coming home to you. You are the best part of my day."

Miranda smiled as she reached up to catch the tear that sat at the tip of her eyelid. She loved this man to her core. She would have never imagined that at twenty-five, she would be this deep in love. This man, her man was sexy, caring, and confident. He was working at a law firm and she knew it was only a matter of time before he made partner. She was finishing up her interior design internship and would soon be on her path to working for herself. They were the perfect couple and she couldn't think of anything that could mess this up. Both of their families loved the other one and without actually writing it down, she could already see their future.

"You complete me too, Israel. If I never love anyone ever again, this would be enough for me."

In the middle of the carnival, Israel bent his head down and placed a kiss on her lips. Their tongues wrestled with one another as if they were in a world of their own. He inhaled her scent as he tasted pieces of her. She was a passionate woman and he couldn't wait to spend the rest of his life keeping the passion burning between them. He broke the kiss and pulled her along as they made their way to the last ride before they found a spot to watch the fireworks. They had save this ride for last since the line had been long the entire time they were there.

Israel handed the young man their tickets and they made their way to their seats. They sat down and Israel buckled Miranda in before fastening his own. They smiled at each other and he winked at her.

"I'll always make sure your safety and well-being comes before mine. Know that, Miranda."

"I do," she said, trying to fight back another tear as she leaned over to kiss him.

The ride attendant came around to make sure they were all buckled in and then signaled the operator to start. Without blinking, the ride took off and they were whisked into the air. He could hear Miranda laughing as he fought to keep his eyes closed. He didn't mind rollercoasters, but he never wanted to actually look down as they were moving. He finally managed to release a laugh due to her being so tickled by everything. He knew in that instance no matter what happened between them, they would always preserve this memory and the laughter captured within in it.

After being tossed up, down, and sideways, the ride ended and they made their way off. Israel touched his pocket to make sure it was still there. He intertwined his fingers with her and guided them to the open lawn where they would be able to watch the fireworks. Dillon and her sister had come along as well, but since they didn't want to ride the last ride, they went to find a spot on the lawn. Israel figured his brother was charming his way into her sister's pants, so he didn't want to intrude on his game. He looked at his watch and saw he had few more hours until midnight. He wanted to propose to her before the night was over and before the fireworks started.

"Miranda, let's make a detour real fast. I want to show you something before we catch up to Dillon and your sister."

"Okay, baby, lead the way."

Israel led Miranda to a private spot he peeped out earlier for this exact moment. He didn't want an audience. He wanted this moment to be between him and Miranda. They would share their news with everyone once they had a chance to revel in the excitement. Israel led her to the spot and then stopped in front of her. Miranda could see the field of wildflowers. The array of colors mixed with the floral scent made her smile.

"Israel, this is beautiful."

"It reminded me of you. A wildflower. You have such a sensitive soul, but there is fire buried inside of you. You are fierce and gentle. I could search in every crack, crevice, and corner of this world and I would never find a woman as majestic as you. I would be a fool to let you go another day thinking that forever with me is not the best decision you could make."

Israel bent down on one knee and pulled the velvet bag from his pocket. He opened it and pulled the most beautiful ring Miranda had ever seen out. A tear rolled down her face as a smiled formed across it. There was no one else other than Israel Cantrell she could imagine spending her life with.

"Miranda Desiree Blackstone, would you do me the honor of letting me be responsible for your happiness forever? Will you spend the rest of your life laughing in my ear and being the best part of my day? Miranda, will you be my wife?"

Miranda's eyes filled with tears as her heart thumped loudly against her chest. She wanted to spend the rest of her life with him, but she didn't want to pressure him into anything he wasn't sure about. Marriage was a very serious commitment to her. When they first met Israel was juggling quite a few women, which lead her to move slowly with him. She needed to be sure he was serious about being with her. She was never into games or being some man's good time. She grew up watching her father revere and honor her mother, therefore she expected the same. After weeks of brushing him off, he got more persistent with his chase. When he told her he had cut off every woman for her, she eventually opened her heart to him. The moment she let him in there was no getting him out. She wasn't sure what lied ahead for them, but she knew it was a ride she wasn't passing up. Whatever happened, they were going to be in it together.

"Yes, Israel Cantrell, I will be honored to be your wife."

Chapter 14
Obsession

Tina lay in her bed with thoughts of Azora running rampant through her head. She couldn't believe after all these years of service and lusting after Azora she'd finally let her get a taste. If she thought she was hooked before, now she craved the taste of Azora on her lips like a crackhead needing its next hit of the pipe. Azora had only merely got a glimpse of the things that Tina wanted to do to her. If only she would give Tina a chance, she would worship the ground Azora walked on. Tina frowned because she knew that as long as Azora's lover Nova was around there would be no chance for her. She thought back to the first time she'd encountered Azora.

"Welcome to the Smitten Kitten. I am your host Azora Monroe."

Tina stood stunned at the radiance of Azora standing at the top of the staircase. Never had she seen a beautiful woman. Tina envisioned herself placing kisses all over Azora's exotic skin. She couldn't even call her skin tone chocolate because it was a color that hadn't been defined before at in her opinion.

Tina had been so caught up in her head, imagining what Azora would taste like, she hadn't noticed that Azora had descended the stairs and was now standing in front of her.

"Tina is it?"

Azora looked down at Tina, making her feeling uncomfortable and horny at the same time.

"Yes, that's my name."

Tina looked down at the floor, ashamed of the thoughts she'd been having. She felt like Azora could read her mind. She'd also didn't know how Azora knew her name. She'd only agreed to come because her husband had begged her and told her this would help with their relationship. He was always nagging for some reason or another. It was like he was the woman and she the man. He honestly believed this little one night retreat would help their failed marriage. Though she doubted anything would help his horrible sexual attributes she still agreed. She knew deep down he could never fulfill her sexual desires. That's why she often found herself in the bed of multiple men on a daily basis, and even then she was still left wanting more.

"Oh, don't get bashful now." Azora pulled her head up they were face-to-face. "Looking down at the floor won't hide what your body is saying, my dear Tina."

Azora ran her finger the side of Tina's neck. Tina thought for sure she would faint. She looked at her husband to see if he watching the exchange. Sure enough the scene had his full attention but he didn't seem mad. Tina could see there was a look of lust in his eyes that she hadn't seen before.

"Hank, is it?" Azora addressed Tina's husband.

"Yes, ma'am."

Tina could see the color drain from his face. She knew a woman of Azora's caliber was too much for him to handle.

"Well, aren't you too cute."

Azora smiled at him.

Tina looked back to her husband and wondered what Azora was seeing. She hadn't thought her husband was handsome in long time. To her he was average looking and the mediocre sex only made him look even worse.

"Well, I will let you all mingle for a while and then Miss Nova will come out and lead you to your destination for the night. Now remember only take one the goodies out of the bowl."

Azora turned and ascended the steps, leaving Tina with all kinds of crazy sexual thoughts running through her head.

Tina walked through the house looking through the glass walls. She could see all kinds of sexual acts happening. They way her pussy was jumping she didn't know if it was the effects of the drugs she'd taken or if she was dying to start participating. She wanted to stop at every room and join in but something kept pushing her along.

Tina's body stopped on it's own in front of room that was laced in dark purple silk curtains. She could see someone having sex but they looked far away. She slowly slid the glass door open and entered the room. Sounds of ecstasy filled the air. She could hear loud grunts and moans coming from a man. She thought they sounded familiar but she wasn't sure. She pushed her way through the curtains only to walk into more curtains. She could the moans getting closer to her.

"Oh, Hank," Tina heard a moan.

Hearing her husband's name said with such desire made her put a little pep in her step.

"Hank!" Tina yelled out.

No that couldn't be my husband the lady was moaning for in pure ecstasy.

"Oh, Hank daddy, give me all that dick, baby. Give it to me. Fuck me harder," Tina heard the woman yelling.

Tina continued to push through the curtains, but it seemed like she was getting nowhere fast. Her attempts to find her husband were futile.

"What's the rush, Tina?" Tina heard another familiar voice whisper to her.

She spun around on her heels but was only met with more purple curtains.

"Where are you?" Tina called out.

"When was the last time you called your husband's name that way?" the voice asked.

"Where are you and who are you?" Tina screamed, frustrated at the situation. "Where is my husband?"

"He's fucking. You don't hear him?"

"You're lying!"

Tina felt her heart fall to the bottom of her stomach. No matter what she'd been doing, he wasn't allowed to do the same. Tina tried to run to her husband's voice but she couldn't seem to find him.

"Hank! Hank! Hank, where are you?"

"He's fucking, Tina. Why are you in such a rush to see him?"

Tina jumped as she felt a hand softly run down the length of her back.

"No, he wouldn't do that."

Tina felt the air in her lungs slowly leaving.

"Yes, he is. Won't you let him finish?"

Suddenly the curtains lifted and the scene before Tina almost made her knees buckled. There Hank lay in the bed with not one but two women on top of him. Tina tried to go to her husband but there was a glass wall in front her. She watched as the women's eyes rolled around in their heads as he fucked and sucked the life out of them. One woman grinded her pussy all over his face as the other did the same on his dick. His hands roamed all over their bodies as he couldn't decide on where to plant them.

"Hank!" Tina yelled as she watched the muscles in his stomach tighten every time the girl riding his dick moved.

He gripped her ass cheeks and spread them apart so he could get in deeper.

"This is what happens when you give a good husband up."

"Shut up!" Tina yelled as the tears ran down her face. "Hank!" she yelled, trying to get his attention.

"He can't hear you. He is in bubble of euphoria that you can't even penetrate."

"Please make it stop," Tina cried as she felt a force making her turn to her left.

When she finally turned there stood Azora.

"My dear, Tina. It can't stop yet. You haven't even began to feel the pain the your husband has felt knowing of your infidelities."

"He knew?"

Tina felt her heart break into a million pieces. She never would have suspected that he knew about her wandering eyes and body. She knew she had problems and wanted to get help, but she couldn't fight the addictive the feeling that sex brought to her.

"Of course he knew, sweetheart. How do you think you ended up here?"

Tina felt she was naked in front of Azora and she could see clear through to her soul.

"He was undecided on whether he wanted to make your marriage work or for you to be gone all together."

"What do you mean gone?"

"I mean, he had the option for you and him to make the marriage work or you live the rest of your days in hell."

"What did he choose?" Tina asked, almost inaudible as she turned to look at her husband.

He looked like he was having the time of his life as the two women rode him into a highway to heaven. The thought of her hurting him to point that he wanted her dead didn't sit well in her spirit.

"He chose to make the marriage work. I didn't agree with him, considering all of dicks you've had in your mouth. I wouldn't dare kiss you in the mouth ever again. However, he's completely in love with you, even though you could be the poster child for the whore of Babylon."

"Why would he do that?" Tina asked herself more so than Azora.

She couldn't understand why he would want to make things work between them two. She would have wished a thousand deaths upon him had she found out he'd been doing the things she been participating in.

"The hell if I know. The heart is fickle thing. Personally, I would've have written it down to the last dot on the sentence on how you would have died."

"Can I stay here?" Tina asked.

"No ma'am I don't take in strays."

"Please, I won't be any trouble. I can't go back and face him. Please just let him go on with his life. I honestly don't want to keep hurting him."

"So, you think you can just run away from your problems?"

"No, I just want to let him go. I know I will never be any good for him." Tina shook her head as she lowered it in shame. "Please, I will do whatever it is you ask of me," Tina pleaded, and she could tell Azora was contemplating her offer. "Please don't make me go back there with him. I will do whatever it is you need."

Tina was desperate and couldn't imagine going back to be with Hank after everything that has happened. *How could she look him in the eyes knowing he knew what she did on the side?* She felt like the lowest form of scum and would kill herself if she had to go to be with him.

"Let's finish watching the show," Azora suggested.

"I don't—"

"Shhhh," Azora stopped her sentence as she turned Tina back so that she was facing the glass wall again.

At that moment, Hank had one of the women bent over the edge of the bed with a tight grip on her waist while he pounded out her insides. *The way he gripped the woman's waist made Tina wonder what happened to them? Did she give up on her husband before she gave him a chance?*

"I can't watch anymore."

Tina closed her eyes tightly to try to get the images out of her head.

"You want it to end?" Azora asked.

"Yes," Tina said, hurtfully not willing to endure anymore.

"As you wish."

Tina rolled over, still remembering that day as if it were yesterday. Azora saved her from herself and she would forever be in her debt. Tina rolled back over again as she went to sleep thinking about the little taste that Azora had given her. For her sake, she'd hope they would meet again in her dreams.

Chapter 15
Atonement

    Azora's anxiety was at an all-time high. She'd waited half a millennium to get her revenge on the person who sentenced her to a thousand life times of loneliness. He promised her love through all eternity, but he hadn't kept up his end of the deal. She busied herself with getting all of her special hell-broths together. She had a special one for everyone tonight. Tonight would be the night that Hecate would reveal all to her and she would exact her revenge on everyone who had ever wronged her.

    Hecate had been revealing small tidbits of Azora's life to her over the years, but she'd never been able to put the puzzle pieces together. Although the clues had been very vague, Azora knew deep down there was something she was missing. The only thing she knew for sure is that Nova had always played a major role in her life and she couldn't imagine life without her. Nova had helped her through it all. At one point she thought confusion would be the end of her. Nevertheless, Nova had stepped in and taken her by the hand and helped her like she'd always done.

    "Azora?" Tina whispered as she stuck her head through the door, interrupting Azora thoughts.

    "Yes, Tina." Azora looked back at Tina and was taken aback at how well she cleaned herself up for tonight's events. "Well aren't you all gussied up. What's the special occasion, Tina?"

Surely she doesn't expect to participate tonight, Azora thought herself. Azora never let her participate in the activities of the Smitten Kitten so why would she think things were going to change that day.

"Well-I um-Thought I would be able to help with the big night," Tina stumbled over her words.

"No, that won't be possible, Tina."

"But I thought—"

"You thought what?" Azora raised her voice as she rose up off her knees. She was working in her garden when Tina interrupted her. "That since you finally got a chance to taste me that things were going to change?"

"No ma'am, I just—"

Azora could see the disappointment in Tina's eyes.

"What I need you to do is go get Nova," Azora interrupted and noticed the sour looked that covered Tina's face.

She dared her with her eyes to speak out of turn.

"Yes, ma'am."

Tina turned away defeated, but her night would not be ending at that moment. She had big plans for the night.

Minutes later, Nova walked into the garden looking like something straight out an African fairytale. The black dress she wore stopped at her calves and clung to her body like second layer of skin.

"You summoned for me, my queen?" Nova's voice dripped with sarcasm.

"You know, Nova, you've been by my side since day one. Always there for me even knowing how our situation started. I couldn't imagine my life without you. Have a drink with me, my friend," Azora said as she began to make them a drink without waiting for her answer. "As I was saying, Hecate has been showing me things over the years. You know the little things that I can't remember."

An uncomfortable silence filled the air. Azora could tell the wheels in Nova's head were turning.

"And you are saying all this to say what, Azora?"

"I'm saying that all the pieces in my life seem to include you. Good or bad Nova, you were there."

Azora smiled as she handed Nova her special concoction. Hesitantly, Nova reached for her drink made from unknown origins.

"Again, what are you getting at, Azora?"

Azora could tell she was making Nova uncomfortable but that was the goal.

"All I'm saying is that I appreciate you always being there for me my friend. Bottoms up," Azora said cheerfully as she downed her drink.

Slowly, Nova placed the cup to her lips and inhaled the fruity scent before throwing it to the back of her throat.

"Come pray with me my friend. For tonight is the night that we will get the answers that Hecate has been trying to show us."

"Hecate isn't my God, Azora. I'll see you at the party."

Nova didn't want to be around when Hecate revealed everything that she'd done. She didn't want a deja vu moment of when Hecate had revealed all to King Oyo.

"Who is your God then, Nova? Because I thought whoever I prayed to you did the same. Now what's changed?"

Azora turned to look at Nova and instead of Nova standing there in her place was the same black snake from the night of the blood moon. Azora closed her eyes and opened them and Nova was there again.

"Never mind, you can go Nova. I need to pray in peace," Azora said, dismissing Nova.

Hecate had already shown her what she needed to know. She didn't know all, but she now knew that Nova was a snake and she would soon know why Hecate had shown her that vision.

"Hecate, I pray to you to reveal all to me tonight. I pray vengeance will be mine. Reveal to me who means no good show me the way to walk in your light."

Azora closed her eyes as she felt a presence come over her.

"You will pay for your treachery!"

Azora found herself standing in the scene where her life had changed forever. Azora's eyes followed King Oyo's eyes and they landed on Nova. Instantly her heart sank to the bottom of her stomach. Of all the things that she expected Hecate to reveal to her, Nova's betrayal wasn't one of them.

"So tell me queen, will she return by your side or secretly in your bed?"

Azora watched the scene unfold before her eyes. Everything fast forwarded in front of Azora's eyes. In horror, she relived the moment her beloved King Oyo was ripped from her life.

"You lying conniving whore. You lied!"

Nova rushed into the room in tears.

"Oh, hush peasant. He was never yours in the first place. He only chose one good for nothing whore over the next!" Queen Nzinga spat.

"That was not the deal, Queen Nzinga. I kept up my end and you reneged."

Azora watched as Nova knelt down in front of King Oyo's headless body and cried.

"Take her."

Nova looked up in time to see the queen's guards walking towards Azora. Azora could feel Nova's anger rising as she watched Nova jump to her feet.

"You people think you can continue to do as you please without any repercussions. You think we don't matter and that our love means nothing. I will show you heartbreak, my dear Queen Nzinga."

It all happened so fast that no one even knew what happened until they heard the queen scream.

"Nooooooo!"

Azora watched the queen's heart break as Nova stabbed the sword she'd just killed King Oyo with through her heart.

Azora stood stunned as she looked down on her dead body. A fire burned deep within her soul as the men seized Nova.

"Why would you do that?" Queen Nzinga asked as she didn't hide the hurt in her eyes as her tears fell for her beloved Azora.

"Ha! Now you go meet him and that black cunt in hell now," Nova sneered. "I was tired of being in her shadow. She can rot in hell with him."

"You are pathetic. He chose her over you. He treated you like you never even existed. You were never anything other than someone he used for a good time," the queen chastised.

"And your precious Azora couldn't wait to have him ram his cock in her rotten cunt," Nova snapped back, scorned from Queen Nzinga's remarks.

"Shut up!"

"Don't shoot the messenger, queen. You took my love from me and I took yours. If you are that sad about it use that sword on yourself and go be with them in hell."

"No, you will rot in hell with them."

Once again the queen in one swift motion, swung the sword and Nova's head went flying across the room like King Oyo's had done only a few minutes prior.

"Azora!" Tina yelled for the third time.

Azora had been standing in the middle of her floor staring off into space.

"What is it, Tina?" Azora whispered, sad that she'd been awaken from her dream state.

"Your guests have begun arriving."

"Thank you, Tina."

At that moment Azora didn't know if she was hurt or angry to find out Nova's true vindictive ways. She felt a heat so hot covering her body, that it felt like she was set on fire. Heartbroken, Azora finished preparing the night's events. Little did Nova know, she had something in store for her as well.

Chapter 16
Revelations

Miranda pulled up in front of the address she had been given earlier. The whole ride over she had been listening to Jazmine Sullivan's *In Vain* and she couldn't stop the tears from falling. From beginning to end the song was her life over the past ten years. Over-and-over, she had been hurt and had forgiven the man she stood in front of God and her family and pledged her life to. This time was different because she was tired. At forty, she had no more energy to fight for something only she wanted to be in. She had a decision to make tonight and whatever she decided, she needed to be okay with it. The days of worrying about what Israel wanted were over. Never once did he consider how she would feel if this all blew up in his face.

"Tell me, is she worth my tears and is she worth the years. Why won't you look into my eyes. Don't turn away, sit here and watch me cry," Miranda belted out.

This song resonated all the way to her core and she was done fighting the pain. Tonight was about making Israel see just what he'd given up for another piece of ass. Miranda decided tonight she would put her sexiest dress on and make him grovel at her feet. Her momma always told her men didn't miss what they had at home until somebody else walked through their front door and put their feet up on their couch. Israel had gotten comfortable and clearly he'd forgotten he came home to a total package every night.

Miranda wiped her face and fixed her makeup. Just as she was reaching for her door, her phone rang. Tasha's name came across her dashboard. She knew she was only calling to see if she figured out what the Smitten Kitten was. She hesitated to answer, seeing as though Tasha was extremely nosey and long-winded. For the sake of an argument later, she answered.

"What's up, girl?"

"Damn chick, I thought you were going to call me back when you figured out what the place was," Tasha said, laughing.

"I never told your ass I was calling you back. You told me to bring you along if I found out not call you."

"Same damn difference, Miranda. Matter of fact, where are you?"

Miranda exhaled before answering. She really didn't want her to know where she was or who she was with. In case something went south, she didn't need anyone incriminated.

"Just out and about. I wanted some wine so I ran out to get some," Miranda lied.

"Yeah okay, heffa. I know you somewhere doing some sneaky shit, but I'm not going to hassle you about it. Whatever you got going on I probably don't want to know until after you finish anyway," Tasha teased.

Miranda laughed.

"Yeah, let's just leave it at that. I'll call you tomorrow and we can talk."

"Okay and don't do anything I wouldn't do."

"Tasha, that doesn't cover much seeing as though you don't have a whole lot of things you won't do," Miranda said, laughing hard.

She was glad Tasha called. It took her mind off of her sadness and helped her focus on having fun tonight. She looked around and saw two other cars parked in front of the house. Neither of them were Israel's. She wondered if he would even come tonight. Part of her didn't care, whereas, part of her did.

"Whatever, slut. Let's not forget you are no angel your damn self. You have secrets too, so let's not throw shade missy."

"Don't we all," Miranda said.

She had quite of few secrets and as long as Tasha kept her mouth closed, no one would find out.

"Okay well, I'll call you tomorrow," Miranda said, trying to end the call.

"Bye, chick," Tasha said, hanging up.

Miranda knew if she didn't end the call, she'd be in the car all night. She checked her makeup one more time and saw headlights pulling up behind her. Her breath got caught in her throat when she realized whose car it was.

Oh, that man, Miranda thought to herself. She took a deep breath and then checked her white fitted dress. Once she was sure she had it together, she opened the door to get out. As soon as she slid her left leg out, Israel was there to open the door and help her out. She scooted out and stood up, moving out the way so he could close the door. She could tell he was speechless by the heaviness in his breathing. It was a warm night for June, so she decided to wear a white, spaghetti strapped jersey dress. A simple, yet very effective dress on the right body. Her black lace bra peeked out just enough and her thong sat perfectly between her firm ass cheeks. Her whole intention was to make him see he had fucked up and this would be the last night he would ever taste or smell her sweet nectar again.

"Damn Miranda, you looking so fucking good. Shit, baby," Israel said, biting his bottom lip.

"Thank you, Israel. I didn't think you would even notice me, seeing as though you have Nova to look at now."

Israel frowned. Miranda knew it was a cheap shot, but she didn't care. She didn't want him to think for one second that she was in a forgiving mood. She moved to start walking and he pushed her against the car, forcing his tongue in her mouth. Miranda obliged him and they went toe for toe until she broke the kiss.

"Israel, what are you doing?"

"What do you mean what am I doing? I'm kissing my fine ass wife, that's what I'm doing."

Miranda shook her head. This was the same song and dance they had danced to plenty of times. The same steps, the same moves, nothing about it had changed. Every time he fucked up, he would be overly aggressive and extremely passionate to win her back over. Like many times before, she fell right into motion. She couldn't do it anymore, but walking away from him wouldn't be easy and she knew it.

"Why do you do this?"

"Do what?" Israel responded.

"Fight so hard for us, for this, when you feel like you are about to lose everything?"

"Am about to lose everything? Are you done fighting for us, Miranda?"

"If I'm being honest, yes I am done."

"Then what the fuck am I here for? What did you have me drive out to the middle of fucking nowhere for?" Israel yelled.

It was so typical of him to throw a temper tantrum when he didn't get his way, or hear what he wanted to hear. Miranda could care less at this point. He obviously had options so she didn't understand what this performance was all about.

"Really, Israel? Are you really going to act a damn fool out here? I asked you to come so we could have a little fun, but clearly you have other plans in mind."

"Fun? You told me if I wanted to make this work to be at this address at 11 p.m. Now you're telling me we're here to have fun. I don't want to have any fun unless you're telling me I'm coming back home."

"You are so fucking amazing to me. You cheat on me and you have the audacity to stand out here and throw a fucking fit! You know what, do what you want but I'm going inside."

Miranda pushed pass him and started walking towards the door. Since he wanted to throw a tantrum, she would show him what a tantrum looked like. He wasn't calling the shots tonight. Either he fell in line or he could take his ass home. Whatever he decided she would still be going back to her home alone. By the time she reached the door, he was right behind her. She looked over her shoulder and smirked at him. She knew the way her ass looked in her dress, he wouldn't be on that curve too long. He wanted another dose of what she gave him on their kitchen wall, floor, and counters.

After ringing the door, a woman immediately opened it and stepped aside.

Smitten Kitten

"Good evening, my name is Tina. Welcome," she said, holding her hand out to usher them inside.

"Good evening, my name is Miranda and this is my husband Israel. Is Azora here?"

"She will be down shortly once all of the other guests arrive. If you'd like, you can wait in the parlor room with the guests who are already here," Tina offered.

"Thank you," Miranda said, following Tina into the room they were being directed to.

They weren't in the room a good second before both Miranda and Israel stopped dead in their tracks. Miranda could feel herself breathing, but was convinced her heart had stopped. She immediately turned around and gave Israel a scornful look. She remembered she saw some extra cars outside and now it made sense as to why.

"You invited her here? What the fuck is she doing here, Israel?"

Israel looked at both Cheyenne and Shelby sitting at the bar. He wasn't sure what the hell was going on, but he was confused at why Miranda was yelling at him seeing as though she invited him here. Cheyenne looked at him with a smirk on her face as if she wanted to say something, but Israel signaled to tell her not to. He knew Miranda didn't recognize Shelby since she never actually saw her at the party she dragged him out of, but he knew that relief was short lived.

"Miranda, how could I invite someone to a place you invited me to? This was your idea so why are you yelling at me?"

Miranda turned around and shot Cheyenne an evil look. She hadn't seen her in ten years when she whooped her ass in the hotel room. She looked a little older, but it didn't matter how much time had passed, you never forget the faces of the women who helped ruin your marriage.

"Bitch, what are you doing here? Who invited you?"

Cheyenne looked Miranda up and down and slid a slight smile across her face. She didn't feel she owed Miranda an explanation as to why she was anywhere. What she was curious about was how Israel knew the woman at the bar with her since he kept looking at her.

"I don't owe you an explanation as to why I am anywhere, Miranda. I received an invitation just like you did. If you have questions as to why I'm here, maybe you should ask the person who invited you," Cheyenne snapped.

Miranda snarled at her and then looked at the woman beside her. She didn't recognize her and figured she must have been Cheyenne's friend or another invited guest. The young woman was gorgeous and looked to be a little older than Cheyenne, but not too far off. She was quiet and wasn't saying much of anything which was not the typical behavior of a friend. At least not any of her friends anyway. The moment somebody would have said something to her, Tasha would have been off that stool or vice versa. She was about to ask who she was when Tina reappeared with drinks on a tray.

"Would anyone like a cocktail? It's the house special," she said, working the room.

Miranda took a drink off the tray, while Israel took two. He was nervous and rightfully so. If he thought this night was going to be easy then he had another thing coming. He was already in hot water about a woman and now two other women from his past was here, front and center.

Tina passed the drinks around to everyone, and then made her way out of the room. She knew more revelations were to come, and she didn't want to be anywhere in the vicinity when they surfaced.

Azora sat at her mirror prepping herself for the night. She could hear the anger downstairs and knew there would be more before the night got started. Tonight, everything done in the dark would be pushed into the light. Tonight, everyone's secrets would be put to rest, especially hers. She stood up at the sound of knocking at her door.

"Come in."

Tina pushed the door open.

"Azora, the Cantrell's have arrived."

"Thank you, Tina. I can hear them downstairs. It seems Miranda has only made one discovery. She obviously doesn't know who Shelby is so why don't you go downstairs and give her a nudge as to whom she may be," Azora ordered.

"As you wish, Azora. Did you want me to tell Nova to join the guests?"

"No not quite yet. Ms. Nova is still getting ready and I'm sure she will be making an entrance when she feels things have gotten good and heated downstairs. She has a knack for inserting herself in the middle of chaos, so she'll be fine."

Tina could sense some distaste in Azora's tone and she fought hard to hide her smile. She never cared for Nova and she prayed Azora was finally coming to her side of the fence. Nova was selfish and she didn't care for Azora the way she did. Tina only wished Azora could see how much she loved her. How she could make her so happy if she would just give her a chance. She licked her lips in hopes that a piece of Azora still lingered on top of them. She had been dreaming and waiting for years for the opportunity Azora gave her. If only she would give her another chance, Tina knew she could take her to great heights of pleasure.

"Tina!" Azora yelled.

"Yes, Azora. I'm sorry I didn't hear you."

"I'm getting really tired of your goddamn daydreaming. I don't know what has your attention, but fix it and fix it immediately. If I have to yell to get your attention again you will not like the consequences."

"I'm sorry, Azora. What did you say?"

"I am a queen and I have to repeat myself due to your lack of hearing? Come in here right now and close the door."

Tina slowly stepped inside and closed the door. She wasn't sure what Azora was going to do, but she was beginning to become terrified. Her annoyance towards Nova was apparent and she didn't want to be the recipient of that anger.

"Azora again I'm—"

"Save it. This is the second or third time you have done this and I will not keep dealing with this behavior. Take off your clothes and lay down on the bed. I'm going to show you what I do to keep the attention of people I am talking to. It seems as if I'm not interesting enough for you, so let's change that right now," Azora said, fuming as she snatched a whip off the wall.

Tina obeyed and did what she was commanded to do. She was both afraid and turned on at the same time. She wasn't sure if this would be painful or pleasurable. She'd hope it was a little bit of both. Azora had never asked her to strip before.

"I don't have all day servant," Azora hissed.

Tina unsnapped the shoulder of the material that was holding up her dress. She crawled on the bed faced down. In one swoop, Azora connected the whip to the top of her ass cheek. Tina gasped as the pleasurable aftershocks went through her body. Tonight, she hoped she would be able to enjoy Azora while the guests gave into their desires.

Miranda looked at her watch and wondered when Azora would be coming down. She thought she heard some screams from upstairs, but dismissed them since her drink was slowly taking affects. In the midst of giving Cheyenne some dirty looks, she caught the other woman there trying not to look at Israel. She couldn't tell if they knew each other, though something seemed off. She figured she would just break the ice since the woman had yet to say anything to anyone in the room and she kept looking at her husband thinking no one saw her.

"Excuse me ma'am, do you know my husband? I've seen you look at him a couple of times and unless you are extremely disrespectful, do you know him?"

"Yes, I do know him," the woman replied.

Miranda shot another deadly look at Israel. She couldn't believe the whole time he knew who she was and he acted as if he didn't. She could hear Cheyenne chuckling and her body immediately tensed up. There were no limits to the embarrassment this man would cause her.

"Who is she, Israel?"

"Her name is Shelby," Miranda heard someone say.

She turned around and saw an unfamiliar woman standing next to Tina. The woman was beyond gorgeous and breathtaking. Her hair was fire red and her skin a smooth milk chocolate tone. Her eyes were mysterious and seductive. She had an aura about her that reeked of sex and seduction. Before Miranda could speak the doorbell rang. Tina immediately moved to retrieve whomever was on the other side. She seemed a bit different than before when she first met her. Miranda assumed whatever screaming she heard upstairs, it had something to do with how she was acting now.

Miranda stood to give Israel a good tongue-lashing, but immediately stopped at the sight of Dillon. *What the hell was he doing here,* she thought to herself. *What kind of games are being played here?* It appeared the unfamiliar woman was just as shocked as she was. Miranda was curious as to how this woman knew Dillon. She looked at Israel and the look of shock and death all wrapped up in one was plastered across his face. It was as if he'd seen a ghost.

"Miranda, what the fuck is going on here? What kind of sick game are you playing with me?" Israel yelled.

"Miranda?" the unfamiliar woman said in a sly tone.

Miranda immediately caught on as to how the woman sounded surprised to hear her name. She looked at her and a sick feeling quickly came over her. The red hair, the brown skin, it all made sense. She was Nova. Miranda tried to catch her breath, but she was falling apart inside. *What the hell had she walked into? What kind of sick and twisted game was Azora playing with her?*

"Israel, do you honestly think I would invite your whores somewhere I would be? Are you that fucking retarded?" Miranda screamed back.

As they argued, Bria peeked from around Dillon. She stood watch as the man she had fallen in love with hadn't even noticed she was there. Bria looked at Nova and Tina as they both formed devious smiles across their faces. She wasn't sure what kind of sick game she had been pulled into but she feared she couldn't back out now.

"Dillon, what are you doing here?" Israel asked.

"What am I doing here? What are you doing here? My girl asked me to come tonight?"

"Your girl? Who in this room is your girl?" Israel looked around, trying to figure out which one of the women from his past was now his brother's sloppy seconds.

"Don't look at me," Cheyenne spouted.

"Me either. I don't even know him," Shelby responded, rolling her eyes.

Israel hadn't even noticed Bria standing behind him. His thoughts immediately went to her since she came in at the same time he did.

"So Bria baby, it's you?"

Miranda looked at him and then at the door. She hadn't even noticed that Bria walked in since she was hidden behind Dillon. She had suffered her wrath before when she showed up on her doorstep announcing her fake ass pregnancy. Miranda figured being severely cursed out once was enough.

"Naw man, I don't know who this chick is," Dillon said.

"Then who is your girl because it's no one else in here," Israel said, looking at his brother and trying to figure out who he could be talking about.

"I'm his girl," Nova said.

Miranda looked at the unfamiliar woman from head to toe and then back at her husband. A look came across his face and she couldn't tell if he was surprised or hurt. It seemed he and his brother knew this woman and obviously it was news to him to find out that Dillon knew who she was as well.

"Dillon, what the fuck is going on?" Israel asked, moving towards him.

He didn't make it far before a voice began to speak.

"Welcome to The Smitten Kitten. Thank you all for accepting my invitations. It seems everyone has become acquainted with one another. I hope tonight all of your desires are met," she seductively spoke, while descending the stairs.

Azora took in her guests that had all been invited. In attendance, were all of Israel's mistresses, along with him, Miranda and his brother. Yes, tonight would be perfect. Azora fought hard to conceal the anger and revenge that circulated throughout her body.

"For those of you that haven't had the pleasure of meeting me, I am Azora Monroe, your host for tonight's festivities. Here behind me are my servants Nova and Tina. They will be able to assist you with whatever you need tonight as well."

Everyone's eyes were glued to Azora as she stood, capturing the attention of everyone. Nova and Tina were hidden behind her statuesque frame. Miranda swallowed hard as she searched for air to exhale. Her beauty was undeniably breathtaking and there were no other words to describe her. She looked at Dillon and Israel, who both seemed to be at a loss for words. Both of them were two of a kind. They stood in the same room with women they proclaimed to be their women, drooling over another woman. They were both so utterly disrespectful and it was obvious they were brothers.

"Tonight, pleasure will be placed at your feet. You are free to indulge in whatever your mind, body, and soul leads you to. Your mind's internal compass will lead you to your proper places. This is where we will part ways. However, we will meet again later tonight. Oh, be sure to enjoy the treats from the bowl at the bar. They will help heighten your experience for the night, but please only take one. I want you to enjoy every waking moment you are here. Whatever your deepest desires are will be revealed. I will know if you decide to be naughty and over indulge."

Azora smiled a seductive smile as she looked Israel up and down. She knew he would break every rule she had laid out. Tensions lay idle as the guests all walked through the golden doors into what they assumed could only be described as a sexual paradise. Unbeknownst to most, this would be a night that would forever change their lives.

"Miranda," Azora summoned.

Miranda moved closer to Azora. She could feel all of her sexual energy with each step. She wasn't sure what Azora was doing to her, but her body was responding in a way she was unfamiliar with. She stopped in front of Azora. Azora moved closer to her and leaned into her as she whispered in her ear.

"Have you made your decision?"

Miranda shook her head as Azora placed a kiss on her cheek. She knew what she would need to do to push her in the direction she needed to get what she wanted tonight. Miranda forced a smile as she walked back to partake of the treats at the bar. Her body needed something to numb the pain. The only thing she wanted to feel tonight was pleasure. She was done being a slave to pain.

Azora turned her eyes towards Israel. After looking at him closely, she could see how easy it was for him to be a womanizer. He was very attractive and for a forty something year old man, he had a very nice body. Azora then looked at Dillon and could see Nova's maliciousness all over him. He and Israel favored each other a lot and anyone could see they were related. Azora raised her eyebrow as she glanced at Nova. She was always greedy and enough was never enough for her.

Tonight, Azora would show her how greed and betrayal would be her downfall. From the looks of everyone at the party, there was a lot of hurt feelings and scornful eyes circling the room. Azora's heart went out to Miranda. She could see the love in her eyes and all over her face. She could also see the sadness behind her eyes due to the devastation of being promised everything by a man only for him to lie to her time-and-time again. Each of the women invited has played some kind of role in her heartache. Azora never intended to add to the immense pain she suffered, but she needed her to be disconnected from Israel.

"Nova, join me upstairs for a moment," Azora commanded as she proceeded towards the stairs. "Everyone, please continue to enjoy yourselves and Tina will be back to release you to begin your night."

Azora climbed the stairs and made her way down the hallway. Once she arrived at her door, she could see it was cracked. Before opening it, she could see that Tina had placed her chalice down and licked her lips. A devious smiled formed across her face. She knew Tina couldn't resist not indulging in the house any longer. She could feel the lustful spirit oozing from her entire being. Azora pushed the door opened and startled Tina.

'What the hell are you doing in here?"

"Azora, I was making sure you had everything you needed," Tina lied.

"I'm sure you were. Please head downstairs and make sure the guests are ready to be released into the house."

"As you wish, Azora," Tina said, hoping Azora wouldn't smell the concoction on her breath.

She knew she was forbidden to go back into the rooms after Azora showed her mercy years ago. However, she needed to free some of the lust she had built up inside. She was hoping Azora would allow her another chance to taste her, but since Nova was here she knew that wouldn't be happening.

"Yeah Tina, go fetch *mommy dearest* pets," Nova mocked.

Tina looked up and glared at Nova. Azora smiled, knowing it was only a matter of time before the two of them cut each other's throats. Tina moved pass Nova and headed downstairs to tend to the guests. Nova entered the room and closed the door.

"You summoned," Nova said.

Azora stood up and handed Nova the chalice. Nova looked at her with a suspiciously. Never before had she drank anything to participate in the house festivities. She wasn't sure what was going on, but she knew she wouldn't be able to object to drinking.

"This is new, Azora. What are we doing tonight?"

"Tonight, we are going to explore our deepest desires and secrets along with the guests."

Azora gave Nova a straight look, not wanting to alert her to what she knew. Nova took the chalice and drank the remaining contents. She noticed it wasn't full, so she assumed Azora had drank her portion before she got upstairs. Nova swallowed the contents and handed the chalice back to Azora.

"Nova, you'll be starting in Envy. See you later on tonight."

Azora dismissed her and then took a sip from her special chalice. She could feel the guests had started to roam as sex, pain, and heartbreak smothered the air. She left her room to join the festivities. After tonight, all wrongs would be made right and everything would be as it should be.

Chapter 17
Sloth

Once Tina gave them permission to explore the house, Miranda decided to explore on her own. Tonight was supposed to be about fun and pleasure, but up until this point all she had done was relive everything she was trying to forget. She wasn't sure what kind of game Azora was playing, but she didn't sign up for this shit. Her intentions for coming were to release some suppressed anger and the horniness she had been feeling since Israel had left. Touching herself had gotten boring. She wanted some good dick to make her mind forget everything her heart wouldn't allow her to. Her first instinct was to follow Israel to see where he was going to end up exploring. He initially tried to pull her in his direction, but she snatched her hand from him. She was angry at how he knew Shelby was the other unknown woman and he said nothing. To Miranda, it seemed there was no end to his lying and deceit. She was at her wits end with him. Every time she thought she had an ounce of forgiveness left for him, he would prove her wrong.

"This room is for you," she heard a voice whisper.

Miranda turned around to see if anyone was behind her but saw no one near where she was. She had obviously wandered off from everyone else. There was a familiar feeling beginning to stir inside of her as she stood in front of the room. Miranda took a deep breath and swallowed. She wished she had taken a few more of those treats, but since Azora said don't over indulge she obeyed.

She looked at the glass door that had *SLOTH* engraved above the door frame. *Such an odd name for a room*, she thought. Miranda moved to see what else the house had to offer when she heard it again.

'This room is for you, Miranda. Come inside and see what it has to offer you."

Azora stood behind Miranda like a cloth of death ready to lay hands on her.

"Who's there?"

"Come inside and find out. I promise you won't be sorry," Azora whispered, tickling Miranda's ear and making the hairs on the back of her neck stand up straight.

Azora could feel Miranda's anxiety go up a few notches and a slight tingle shot through her spine.

Miranda peeked inside the room and saw that no one was in there. The drinks and treat she had at the bar were starting to have an effect on her. She was hearing things and there was no one around. Miranda felt a tug and she gave into whatever force was pulling her inside. Immediately entering the room, she could feel cold air suddenly wrap itself around her. She spun around and could see herself lying on her side as Israel tried to finagle her panties off of her ass. She moved her hand to push his hand off of her waist. She was turned off by him and was nowhere near interested in having sex with him. He had moved back in for the second time and she hadn't quite came around to fucking him just yet.

"Miranda, baby, I want you. I want to feel myself inside you again. It's been almost a year," Israel pleaded, hoping she would finally give in.

He had been trying to make love to her since he came home two months ago, but she wasn't having it.

"Move your hand, Israel. I'm tired and I don't feel like it tonight."

Miranda saw the look on Israel's face that she had never seen before. It was almost as if she'd given him permission to do it again. She couldn't deny she was horny, but her heart wasn't completely fooled and for that reason alone she couldn't push herself to turn over.

"What is going on? Who is doing this?" Miranda yelled.

"Hello, Miranda."

"Let me out of here!"

"You see what you did to him? You're the reason why he cheats on you. If you would only give him sex when he wants it, he wouldn't have to get it anywhere else," Azora taunted.

"Who the fuck are you to tell me when to fuck my husband? You don't know half the shit he's done to me. Let me out of here," Miranda screamed, as she banged on the walls.

Frost began to form on the glass walls that surrounded her. Her entire body began to get cold except for the bottom half. She looked down to see blood running down her legs.

"Oh my God."

Her stomach instantly filled with sharp pains, forcing her to bend over and fall to the floor. Miranda rubbed her hands across her legs to wipe the blood off her. It seemed the more she wiped, the faster it poured out from her body. She had this urge to push, although something instinctively told her not to.

"What is going on? What are you doing to me?" she yelled out. "Somebody, anybody, please help me," she pleaded.

Miranda tried to stand and couldn't find the strength. Her legs gave out and another sharp pain shot through her body, causing her to lie on the floor. The warm blood ran from between her legs as the cold floor provided a piece of comfort to her aching body. Her center burned like a fire that couldn't be put out. She wasn't sure what was happening to her, but the room was freezing cold. After a few minutes, she managed to sit up in the pool of blood that surrounded her. She crawled towards the chair as the trail of blood followed her. She needed something to hold onto. Something, anything to make the pain easier to bear. She was fighting a fight and she was quickly losing.

"Israel, help me! Israel, where are you?" Miranda's voice echoed throughout the room as she fell to her knees. "Israel help me!"

She banged on the glass as hard as she could, hoping somebody would hear her screaming.

"Israel, help me! Help our baby!"

"He's never there when you need him, is he Miranda? I guess there's no such thing as forever," Azora taunted as she sat down close enough in front of Miranda to where she could feel the heat from her breath cover her face.

Miranda looked down to see her nightgown drenched in blood. She knew what was happening to her and she needed help. She had waited so long for this to happen and it couldn't end like this. They were finally having a baby. She was finally getting the family she'd always dreamed of having.

"Israel!"

"He's not here remember, Miranda."

Azora's body heat rose as she felt Miranda's pain and anger getting higher and higher. You put him out. He's probably with Cheyenne, or is it Shelby that he's fucking now," Azora taunted some more.

"No, not like this. God not like this, please," she begged, as the tears ran down her face.

Another severe cramp shot through her body and in an instance she knew it was coming to an end.

Miranda crunched over into the fetal position on the floor. She held her stomach as the life she so desperately wanted was slipping between her fingers. She'd only found out she was pregnant two weeks before the Christmas party fiasco. Her intentions were to surprise Israel for Christmas, but Shelby happened. She just needed more time.

"Please baby, hold on for mommy. Hold on for mommy just a little longer."

"It's over, Miranda," Azora sang in a wicked tone.

"No, God, please don't take my baby," Miranda cried out. "God please help me. What is happening to me?"

"There is no God, Miranda. I am the only one who can save you," Azora's voice seemed to get creepier-and-creepier with every word she spoke.

"Who are you? Why are you doing this to me?"

"Your husband did this to you. Do think he ever loved you? I would think that one would be able to keep to his penis in his pants if he truly loved his wife. He's cheated on you over-and-over again.

All of this is his fault. All of your pain. He doesn't want children. He wants an abundance of women."

"Shut up! That's not true! He wants our child and we're going to be happy together. You don't know what you're talking about," she yelled, looking around the room.

Miranda picked up the phone to call Israel. She needed his help. She needed him to come home to save their baby. She was going to tell him when the time was right. She just needed to get passed the pain. All she needed was a little while longer to forgive him for breaking her heart and for violating their vows. The phone rang and she turned her head as she heard the ringing echo throughout the room. Her tears flowed faster than the blood that now stained her legs. The blood that gave life and meaning to the child she once carried. Miranda knew she needed to look down but the heaviness of her heart wouldn't allow her to. She buried her face in her hands and just let the tears flow as they wanted to.

"Mrs. Cantrell, is your husband coming?" the doctor asked with concern.

Miranda looked up at the doctor, trying to fight through the tears. After trying him three times, she hung up. Miranda sent him a text informing him of where she was and placed her phone on the table next to her. She had kicked her husband out and in her time of need he had abandoned her for sure.

"No, he won't be here so you can begin doctor."

"Is there anyone else you can call, family or a friend?"

"No, there's no one else I want to call. Let's just get this over with so I can move on with my life."

"Okay. I have to inform you that once we finish the D&C, I will need to administer some antibiotics as well. Just as a precaution I ran a blood sample to see what may have triggered your miscarriage and I found that you have contracted gonorrhea."

The tears that Miranda was fighting back fell like raindrops down her face. She was in so much pain and extremely embarrassed. Not only was she lying on the table to have what was left of her child removed, but she was carrying a disease her husband had given her from fucking around. She would never forgive him for this. She would never forget this moment in her life.

"Your Mr. Perfect gave you a fucking STD while you were pregnant. Now let's think about this for a minute." After a slight pause Azora started back in on her broken heart. "I'm right Miranda and you know it. You're here in pain on the floor and where is your husband? I know where he is Miranda, do you?"

"Stop it, please stop it."

"I told you he doesn't love you," Azora whispered in her ear. "He never loved you, Miranda. Look what he did to you."

"Please just stop," Miranda cried but her tears only fueled Azora's assault on her broken spirit.

"Not yet, Miranda. Not quite yet."

Azora wasn't completely sure Miranda was where she needed her to be. Therefore, to be completely sure, she continued. She needed Miranda to be filled with so much hatred and rage, she would be done with Israel. Her heart was already fragile. Azora knew a few more nudges and she would fall right over the cliff she was clearly at the edge of.

"Miranda, are you ready?" the doctor asked.

Miranda nodded as the needle was inserted into her back. After a few minutes, she could immediately feel her body begin to go numb. It seemed now her body matched her heart. Once again Israel was not there when she needed him. Once again, he had broken her into pieces and was nowhere to be found when she needed to be put back together again.

"Let him go, Miranda. Let him be the man you know he is. He doesn't love you. Let him go. He killed your baby," Azora whispered.

"Don't say that! He does love me. He did love me once. I can't let him go. I love him so much. I hate that I love him this much. I just want to be free of this pain, free of this love."

The warm tears made Miranda forget she was even in pain. Her heart was as cold as the metal stirrups her feet occupied. The room got louder as the suction noise reverberated against the walls. She closed her eyes and imagined Israel was there holding her hand, while he told her everything would be alright. Miranda covered her ears with her hands. She didn't want to remember this sound. The sound of her baby leaving her body. The sound of what her husband's betrayal caused. The sound that would always remind her of what a broken heart sounded like.

"Enough! Enough! Stop this madness!" Miranda screamed.

'Why, Miranda? You haven't had enough? You still think he loves you?" Azora mocked.

Miranda still hadn't gotten to the point she needed her to be yet. She could still feel the love she had for Israel exuding from her skin. All Azora needed to feel was an ounce of hatred and she would free her. If she couldn't get it here, she would get it somewhere else.

"Azora, please don't do this to me. Please make this stop."

"Why Miranda? You aren't a victim in this love triangle. You have dark secrets too. Does Israel know? Does he know the lust that lies deep down in your heart?"

"I don't have any secrets from, Israel," Miranda snapped.

"Oh, but you do," Azora whispered.

She knew what Miranda really wanted and tonight she wouldn't be the only person who it was revealed to. In due time, everyone's true desires and deepest secrets would be plastered across the walls.

"I can't take this anymore."

Miranda looked around the room and the walls were as clear as when she walked inside. She looked down at her dress and saw that it was clean. She held her stomach and instantly she thought about that dreadful day.

'The night is just beginning, Miranda. Prepare yourself because you have so much more to explore."

Without a moment's hesitation, she left the room to find Israel.

Chapter 18
Envy

Nova slowly walked the halls of the Smitten Kitten with her eyes closed. The shot that she had taken with Azora was mixed with the Xanax, and had her almost floating towards the end of the hall. She'd made this journey so many times that she could find her way in the darkness. The Envy room was always her playground to roam as free as possible. Azora didn't have a clue that Nova picked that room because she had been envious of her from the moment that King Oyo chose her. She loved making the wives lose their minds and hearts inside of the room, just as she felt when she was ordered to remain by Azora's side. A mentally torturous time that she was still unable to shake.

The red lace fabric of her panties clung to her bottom. She felt hot and flushed after leaving Azora's room so she discarded her robe and matching bra. Her skin was on fire and even though she was always in the mood to get things popping sexually, at the moment Nova's sex drive was through the roof. Just as she reached the door to Envy room, she felt a surge shoot through her body that she had never experienced. With her hand in a tight grip on the doorknob, her body convulsed repeatedly. Saliva dripped from the corners of her mouth as several different passionate trysts from her past shifted through her mind in rapid seconds filled glances. The last one ended with the night she snuck in the grotto when King Oyo tossed her like a rag doll. The tremors stopped just as Nova's mind beckoned her to enter the room. She opened her eyes, slowly pushed the door open and then walked in.

"Welcome, Nova," a soft voice whispered.

It sent goosebumps flaring up in a rage all over her body.

Nova looked around in disbelief. Even without seeing her face she knew that the voice belonged to Azora. She didn't know why, but Nova suddenly had the feeling that she too would be in the sexual matrix tonight.

"My queen, I am here to serve you. Why am I feeling this way?" Nova asked.

Azora emerged from the shadows of the walls but remained hidden from Nova's eyesight. She stared at the woman she shared her deepest secrets as well as love with. She thought she knew Nova but now she was aware that she was sadly mistaken. Nova would pay for her betrayal and tonight was the perfect night for it according to Azora. She smiled at Nova and decided to play deeper mind games with her.

"Don't you like the way this heat feels on you, Nova? Burning, running rampant, and covering you in comfort. That's really what you want, Nova. For someone to completely submerge you in nothing but love. You want something strong like what Miranda has with Israel," Azora whispered in Nova's ear as she placed her body close to Nova's.

The familiar scent of Azora's nectar wafted through her senses and rested in the walls of her pussy. No matter the situation Azora always had a way of making her hot box go crazy with anticipation.

Nova could feel Azora's spirit even though she still hadn't presented herself. She found herself turned on by it but going crazy because of the words Azora spoke. The gush of air that swooshed through the room sent a chill down Nova's spine. Nova tried to find something of substance to cover her but it was too late. She was knocked to the ground by the strong gust from the wind. She felt like she was being swept into a tornado that only lasted for no more than two minutes. When the wind stopped, Nova was face-to-face with Israel and Miranda in the bed.

"Isn't this what you want? Look at the way he's holding her. He loves her. He'll never love you like that."

Smitten Kitten

Nova didn't want to stand there and watch the scene before her but she couldn't tear her eyes away from it. Israel was on top of Miranda and the two of them were moving in beautiful, synchronized movements. Their skin seemed to blend into a caramel, chocolate swirl of ecstasy. Miranda moaned loudly as Israel kissed her deeply. Nova did want that. So much so that looking at the two of them was driving her mad. She ran towards the bed, screaming and yelling for mercy.

"How could you do this? You're supposed to love me. I love you! I've always loved you! Why can't you fucking see me?"

Nova threw punches at what she thought was Israel's back but she was really swinging at the air. Nova knew this, as being the one who basically ran this room but being on this end of the games were clouding her better judgement. Azora had to place her hand over her mouth to stop the laughter that threatened to spew from deep within her belly.

"Poor Nova. He can't see you because a man like Israel does not love with his dick. Yes, he'll give it to you but you'll never get the heart. Women like you are always on the losing end. That Miranda, she has what a man needs to get a heart. Israel's heart."

Nova was in a ball at the foot of the bed. Miranda's and Israel's moans were driving her nuts. To see him totally engulfed with his wife was something she never wanted to witness again. In all their trysts he had never made love to Nova as gentle like he did with Miranda. He not only made love to her but he nurtured her spirit with soft, enduring words. Nova couldn't stand it.

"I want out! Let me out!" she screamed.

The louder she got, the louder Israel and Miranda became. She could smell the scent of their multiple climaxes lingering in the air.

"Aaagh, yes. That's my favorite part. The stench of true love in the air. Doesn't it make your mouth water, Nova? I bet if you could drink from their essence to receive that kind of love, you'd steal it all but he still won't love you. You're nothing to him."

Azora's words bounced around on her eardrums. The sadness that filled her rivaled the anger that caused her soul to tremor. She knew she had to beat the illusions, but Azora was far too powerful.

"You bitch, Azora. Get me out of here. I can't take this shit. I'm done," Nova screamed.

This time Azora let out a loud and somewhat evil laugh. The shrilled sound startled Nova.

"Oh Nova, this shit has just begun. Have a seat. You're gonna want to really pay attention to what's about to happen next."

A chair appeared from nowhere and Nova was forced to sit in it with leather restraints holding her ankles and wrists. She tried to close her eyes but a gust of wind forced them open. Nova was hopeless as a fresh batch of tears drenched her face. She was forced to watch and listen to the kind of love she knew she would never have.

"Please, please. I can't take anymore," Nova whimpered.

"Oh, but you will. This one's just for you, my love," Azora said.

The bed that Israel and Miranda were on top of spun around until it was high in the air on a stage. Miranda's screams of desire continued as Israel picked up the pace on his deep strokes.

Tina roamed the halls of the Smitten Kitten in search of Azora. The elixir she'd drunk behind Azora's back was kicking in and she felt like she had the strength of ten men. She would make Azora hers before the night was over by any means necessary. Door after door she looked into and one sexual spectacle after another played before her eyes, but none stood even close to the scene of her pleasuring Azora.

Azora consumed her every thought, day and night she dreamed of ways to please Azora. Tina wanted to become one with Azora. She wanted to drink in her very essence and savor the taste of her forever. If she could bottle up Azora's nectar for herself she would and drink form it every day until her thirst was quenched.

"Tina."

Tina heard her name whispered. She looked around into the dark hall but saw no one there. Goose bumps formed all over her body. The sensuous melody of Azora's voice sang to her heart like a lullaby to a baby. The aroma of Azora wafted into her senses, causing an immediate ache between her legs.

"Azora?" Tina asked with urgency.

She needed to see Azora and prove to her that she could take care of her.

"I see you've been a naughty little girl. You just couldn't sit this night out huh?" Azora planned to make her regret she ever wanted to participate.

"I'm sorry but I needed to see you."

"But you disobeyed me Tina. I told you not to partake in any of the things that goes on in the Smitten Kitten."

"But—" Tina started.

"But nothing! You are to do as I say and you've even taken some of the special drugs that are designed for my guest."

"Please don't be mad at me."

"Oh no, I'm not mad, but there will be a lesson learned tonight, my dear Tina."

"I'm sorry. I just wanted to see you. I want you to see me!" Tina cried as she realized she'd upset Azora.

That was last thing she wanted to do. She just wanted to prove herself in the worst way.

"You want to see me?"

"Yes, Azora"

"Open the door, Tina."

Hesitantly Tina did as she was told. No, she wasn't allowed to participate in the shenanigans of The Smitten Kitten but she knew what went on behind the doors and she prayed she made it out again with her sanity intact. Azora had spared her before but she knew deep down she was in trouble. She entered the room and the sounds of loud moans filled her ear drums like the soundtrack to a nightmare she'd dreamed a million times. A heart gripping chill ran down Tina's spine as the lights in the room came to life and the scene before her almost stopped her heart. No matter how many times she'd snuck in and watched Azora and Nova together she could never get use to watching Azora being pleased by another woman.

The sight of Nova with her face buried between Azora's thighs angered her to a point of no return. She would never understand why Azora couldn't see how much she loved her. Nova ate at Azora's pussy like a starving child in Zimbabwe. Azora stared into Tina's eyes as she grabbed the back of Nova's head and pressed her face deep into her love box. Nova's back was arched high with her head down low and her ass sat high in the air like she was waiting for something to come and take a ride. The thong Nova wore had disappeared into the depths of her ass crack and the only remanence left out were the strings around her waistline.

"Is this what you wanted to see, Tina?" Azora whispered.

Azora's body tingled all over from the pain that Tina was radiating. The turmoil that wreaked havoc on Tina's spirit made Azora smile on in the inside. *It also saddened her because it made her wonder if the love of her life ever loved her the way Tina did*? Did he long for her touch or wish she was in his arms the way Tina longed for her?

"No," Tina said almost inaudible as she closed her eyes to the sight before her.

The sounds of Azora's moans made her want to vomit. The hatred she felt deep down in her soul for Nova ran rapidly through Azora, and she loved the feeling she was getting. Tina by far had the most hate in her soul in the house that night. Until that moment, Azora never knew exactly how much Tina loved her.

"Open your eyes, Tina. You wanted to participate."

Though Azora liked Tina she had to be taught a lesson. She made rules for a reason and Tina would follow them just like everyone else.

"No, I just wanted you!"

"You could never be what Nova is to me, Tina."

"But why what makes her so special?" Tina was almost pleading with Azora.

"Look, and you can see what makes her so special."

"No, I don't want to see that shit!"

"I said open your eyes!" Azora yelled.

Tina's eyes flew open as if they had a life of their own. Nova had pushed Azora's legs apart as they would stretch. Azora rubbed the back of Nova's head as she grinded her pussy in her face.

"You like watching me get my pussy sucked on, Tina?"

"No, Azora. Why are you doing this to me?"

"Because you are hard headed and need to be taught a lesson."

"Please, I'm sorry. I won't disobey you again. Just let me go."

"My dear Tina, your night has only just begun. You better strap up. It's going to be a bumpy ride.

※

Miranda made her way down the hall in hopes she would be able to find Israel. She wasn't sure what was going on, but this was not what she came here for. She thought this experience would be about pleasure, not some sick and twisted taunting Azora seemed to enjoy. Miranda walked for what seemed like forever before realizing she had made a wrong turn. The hall was dark with red lights bouncing off of the walls. She couldn't see too much and her body was beginning to really absorb the drinks and treats she had. She wasn't sure what was in those treats, but her body was having all kinds of reactions to it. Miranda leaned on the wall to catch her balance when she heard noises echoing from down the hall. Her eyesight was a bit blurry, so she blinked a few times to regain focus.

She traced her fingers against the wall as she made her way further down the dimly lit hallway towards the noises. The closer she got she was able to make out what they were. The sultry sounds pulled her harder as she found her way in the doorway of another room. As she moved further into it, the moans became louder and filled with more passion. The room was dark and she couldn't see much of anything until she turned her head and saw her husband standing butt-naked as Nova pulled him back and forth inside her mouth. His head leaned back as his mouth opened, causing his moans to flow like melted honey.

"Oh shit, Nova. Damn girl, you make me feel so good," Israel said, running his fingers through her red hair.

Miranda covered her mouth in shock as she saw the enjoyment all over her husband's face. His face had no trace amounts of regret like he tried to make her believe he was full of. He wasn't reeked with guilt in the least bit. Nova was giving him unmeasurable amounts of pleasure and he loved every minute of it. Israel moved in and out of Nova's mouth as she slurped louder and faster.

"Suck this dick, baby. Make daddy come like you always do."

Miranda could see Nova look up at Israel, and then she quickly removed him from her mouth. She could tell Nova was the person in control in their relationship. Nova stood up and pushed him onto the bed, but not before she looked over her shoulder to wink at Miranda.

"Look at her, Miranda. She's doing everything to your husband that you won't do. Your husband is a womanizer and no matter how many times you take him back, he will always find another pair of legs to climb between," Azora whispered in Miranda's ear making the hairs on her neck stand up once again.

Miranda wanted to say something but couldn't find the words. Her eyes were fixated on the way Nova was now riding her husband. Her back was to him as she gyrated in the perfect cowgirl riding position. Nova looked over at her and offered her a sinister smile. Israel gripped her ass once she started bouncing up and down on his dick.

"Israel, you fucking bastard! How could you do this to me again. I loved you. I thought you loved me!"

"You will never be like the women he cheats with Miranda. They love to please him and give him whatever he demands sexually. You are the prudish wife who's always too tired and too busy to fuck your husband."

Miranda covered her eyes as she tried to tune out what Azora was saying. She didn't want to believe her husband was so bad off he was incapable of being faithful to her. She couldn't give up on her love for him. They were more than sex. They had love.

"Oh, you still love him don't you? You still want to believe that he will be with only you. Miranda, that will never happen," Azora used the most hurtful words to push Miranda over the edge.

"Shut up, bitch! Why don't you show your face and stop with all the fucking mind games!"

Miranda whipped her head left and right looking for even a glimpse of the mysterious voice.

"Are you sure you want to see me, Miranda?"

"Yes, bitch. Come on out here so I can show you what we used to do to girls like you in my old neighborhood," Miranda threatened.

"Your wish is my command, Miranda."

Miranda looked around, waiting for Azora to show her face. When she turned around she saw something she hadn't expected to see. Azora was mounting Israel and he was literally bending to her will. She looked over at Miranda, forcing her to watch every move she made. She looked into Israel's eyes and saw something she didn't see when he was on top of Nova. It was like there was a connection between them that she hadn't noticed before.

"Open your eyes. You don't want to miss this. You see Miranda, he has no limits to the amount of pleasure he will give into."

"You bitch. Let me out of here now. Get off of my goddamn husband."

Miranda felt herself running towards Azora, but it was like her feet wouldn't go any further than where she was at. She moved within just a few inches of them but she couldn't touch them. Nova climbed back into the bed and Miranda watched as she traced the outline of Azora's lips before forcing her tongue into her mouth. Azora continued to sway her hips against Israel's dick as Nova turned to climb onto his mouth.

Azora placed kisses on Nova's back as they moved in a steady, in sync rhythm on top of Israel. Azora filled up with her husband's dick as his tongue sent Nova plundering over the edge. The ecstasy that filled the room was intoxicating and she fought hard to keep from breathing it in. Miranda could feel anger and desire building up and racing throughout her body. She could see the passion in their eyes as they stared at her with vicious intent. She was jealous at the fact they were enjoying her husband and he was enjoying them. Lust was seeping from their pores and Miranda could feel all of their sexual energy.

"I don't want to watch anymore. Let me out. I want to go home right fucking now."

"Oh no, Miranda. You can't go home just yet. Your night of pleasure has yet to begin."

Azora walked around watching all of the scenes of uninhibited lust take place. She could the feel the sinful desires flowing through everyone in the room. The fire burning within her was something she'd never felt before. The pain and envy of everyone in attendance bounced off the walls and reverberated throughout her nerve endings. There was a great deal of pleasure meets pain in the room tonight, but Azora was nowhere near finished with the people who betrayed her the most.

As the moans of ecstasy pulsated throughout the room she sauntered on towards her next destination. She toyed with the idea of grabbing some popcorn because she was certain the room of Lust was going to be nothing short of amazing.

Chapter 19
Lust

Israel roamed the dark hallways unsure of where he was headed. Once Tina told everyone they could go their own way, he quickly tried to run behind Miranda. Unbeknownst to him, she was ready to get as far away from him as possible. He couldn't understand why she was so upset with him seeing as though she invited him there. He had no idea any of his mistresses would be there and he was still trying to understand who invited them. All Israel wanted to do was get as far away from all of them and find his wife. Seeing them all in one room reminded him of his continuous epic fuck-ups. If he could turn back time ten years ago he would. He would erase the first time he ever slid his dick inside Cheyenne. He could see the hurt in Miranda's face and it bothered him that he was the cause of it. All of that changed once Nova entered the room and announced she and Dillon had been involved with each other. He fought to hide the disappointment and anger for Miranda's sake, but from the looks of her face he didn't do a great job. Knowing that she and Dillon had been sleeping together caused some unsettling feelings to stir inside him.

"Miranda! Miranda! Where are you?" Israel shouted.

His drink was kicking in and the sweets he ingested at the bar weren't helping either. He knew he shouldn't have overdone it, but he was trying to figure out any way to ease the tension that was obviously thick in the room. Israel turned the corner and couldn't see much outside of the light shining from a room at the end of the hall. He had been looking for Miranda for an hour. He would call her name but couldn't hear much over the various moans echoing off the walls.

"Miranda! Miranda! Where are you?" Israel shouted again.

"Oh, right here baby. Come right here," Israel heard a voice say.

"I'm on my way, baby."

As Israel made his way down the hall he could hear Miranda's seductive purr. He always loved when she did that while they were making love. Usually, she would let out a few as he was licking and teasing her spot. He walked into the room and couldn't believe his eyes. Miranda was standing against the wall with her shirt ripped open, exposing her lace bra as her skirt was hiked up and her right leg hanging over a man's shoulder. Her eyes rolled back and then closed and her lips parted to release a moan. She was being pleasured in a way that only he had been privy to seeing. Israel rushed further into the room, trying to grab ahold of the man pleasuring his wife. He couldn't make out the back of his head due to whatever Azora had put into the treats.

He was trying to regain his senses, but everything flowing through his system had him discombobulated. Israel watched as the man's head went faster-and-faster. Miranda's legs were fighting to stand up straight but the pleasure she was receiving was causing her knees to buckle. Israel's lips moistened as his tongue swirled across them. The juices that ran down her legs caused his tongue to start salivating. She had an insatiable aura about her that drove him mad.

"Oh shit, Dillion, that feels so fucking good."

Dillion, Israel thought. He immediately rushed to see if the man between his wife's legs was his brother. Miranda opened her eyes and looked at him, smiling a mischievous grin. She licked her lips as she pushed his head further and harder into her pussy. Her head buckled as he pulled her hips up. She threw both of her legs over Dillion's shoulder as she rocked back and forth.

"Lick that pussy, baby. Lick just like that. Ooooh, your brother never did it this good."

Miranda softly bounced on Dillon's shoulder as his hand squeezed her ass cheeks. His muscular frame held up her curvy bottom as she gripped his head. Israel could feel the anger mounting as he balled up his fist. He wanted to kill his brother, and at this point Miranda too. *How could she fuck his brother? Why would she bring him here to see this bullshit? Is this what she thought would fix what was broken between them?*

Azora could feel the anger piercing through him and she reveled in it. His lustful ways had lead him to this point and now he was going to stand here and watch what lust does to people and how it destroys relationships.

"Miranda, what the fuck are you doing? Are you fucking crazy? I will kill both of you motherfuckers!" Israel shouted.

He could feel his body heating up and he knew it was only a matter of time before somebody died. Fucking the various women, he sought pleasure with was one line crossed, but fucking his wife would get you killed.

"Ahhhhh," Miranda belted out.

Dillon licked what was left of her juices, placed her feet on the ground, and turned her around against the wall. Without pause or hesitation, he entered her from behind.

"Ohh shit, baby, you are wet as hell. I can't believe my brother been fucking around on this good pussy," Dillion uttered as he pinned Miranda's arms against the wall.

"Fuck me harder, baby. Make me forget about him," Miranda begged.

She peeked through Dillon's arms as she glared at Israel.

As Dillon pulled her hair, Miranda screamed with each stroked. Israel lunged forward, but couldn't manage to touch him.

"You bitch! Is this how you do me? You go and fuck my brother?"

Israel turned to leave, but realized he couldn't move. He couldn't watch this anymore. If he stood here any longer he would kill them both. He knew his brother had a thing for Miranda, but he never could prove it. For the longest time his brother was salty about her choosing him. Now he sees she didn't chose him after all. He wondered how long this had been going on behind his back.

"Are you angry enough?" Azora asked.

"What the hell is going on? Who is this talking? Let me out now," he yelled.

"Why? You didn't seem to mind your wife being angry because you were out fucking around on her. How does it feel to see she enjoys your brother more than you?" Azora taunted.

"Who the fuck are you and what are you talking about?"

"Oh, Israel, it seems you don't like to see shit reversed, huh? Well, too bad my dear. Now you get to watch your wife enjoy another man's dick while you sit here in complete disarray."

Israel tried to tune out the moaning, but it got louder in his ears as if harmonies of their love making were made just for him to hear. He wanted to close his eyes, but he had no more control over his body. Thoughts of jumping on top his brother and strangling him until there was no life left in his limbs crossed his mind. Dillion knew better, but it seemed he wasn't happy unless he was fucking one of his women. First, Nova and now Miranda, enough is enough as he fought to look away.

"Oh my God, Dillion. Right there," Miranda moaned.

Israel turned around to see his brother kneeled behind his wife who was now on all fours. Her beautiful, brown ass that he loved to squeeze as he fucked her from behind was now being squeezed by his brother. He felt nothing but anger and a nauseous feeling quickly took over him.

"Look at how she moves in sync with him, Israel. Look at how their bodies are perfect for each other. She is enjoying every ounce of his dick. It seems that had you been home fucking her, there would be no need for Dillion to fuck her."

"Stop it! Let me out of here right now you crazy bitch!" Israel yelled.

The fact that he couldn't see who was talking to him was driving him insane.

"Not until she comes. I want you to see the passion light up her eyes as he brings her to the edge of her orgasm and forces her to explode. Oh God, I'm getting horny just thinking about it," Azora continued to teased.

Azora could feel the eminence heat and passion seeping from their pores as well as the anger that spewed from Israel. She was enjoying the scene that played out before her and considered joining, but decided that watching Israel slowly breakdown was much more entertaining.

"Look at how hard she's breathing. He is really fucking her. God, I wish I could feel him inside of me like he's in her right now."

She wanted him to feel the same pain he had inflicted on Miranda for the last ten years. She needed him to see what it felt like to be betrayed by someone that has your heart and recklessly damages it over-and-over again. Azora could see the tears swelling at the bottom of his eyes, but it wasn't enough. He tried to fight it but seeing them together cut deep. He could see the same look of pleasure she would give him in her eyes and he grew jealous and broken by the minute.

"She looks at you that way doesn't she? I guess what you had with her wasn't so special after all. It seems Dillion has a much better effect on her than you, Israel."

Israel fell to his knees as his wife came over and over again before his eyes. Orgasm after orgasm ripped through her body as she cuffed the back of his head between her breasts. Her voluptuous hips gyrated back and forth as his fingers dug into the skin of her back. His mouth covered one of her breasts as he licked her nipples slowly. Miranda's head tilted back as her body forced her to exhale between each violent wave of pleasure.

"Keep coming for me, baby. Wet this dick up," Dillon said, as he gripped her hips.

The tears seemed to fall down harder on Israel's face as Miranda began bouncing up and down on top of him. His mind flashed back to her doing him the same way weeks ago in their kitchen. He knew what she was doing to his brother. He knew how her pussy walls were gripping him as she became wetter. Not to mention, the heat from inside of her drove a man wild. All of what they shared and he couldn't believe she would actually do this to him. She had to know this would be the end of them. He could never forgive her for this. Maybe for something else, but never for Dillon.

"I know what you're thinking Israel and how dare you? You are such a typical man. You have all your whores and your fun while you expect your wife to be at home waiting for you to come and wash another woman's scent off," Azora scolded.

"I don't know what you're talking about. I love Miranda."

"No you don't, but as you see, things have changed. Miranda has finally seen the light and found her something good to sit on top of. Don't worry, I have plenty more in store for you tonight. You just wait and see."

The sound of Azora's devious laugh faded to the background as the screams of orgasms being freed rang loudly in his ears. He was done watching this shit and was ready to go. Somebody was going to die tonight and whether it was Dillon or Miranda made him no difference. Either way, somebody was going to pay for this pain he was feeling.

Chapter 20
Greed

Israel was completely worn out, but still filled with murderous thoughts in his heart. Foolishly he assumed Miranda invited him here because she had forgiven him again. Thinking with his dick, he just knew he was going to have a night of naughty fun, but so far this place had been nothing more than a nightmare. The memories of Dillon and Miranda making love played in his head again. He felt sluggish and sort of out of his norm and he knew that could only mean the drinks they had were laced.

What the fuck is going on, He thought to himself.

The dark hallway gave him little to no comfort. He tried to grab ahold to anything surrounding him but it seemed like he was standing in a bottomless pit of emptiness. Israel was about to panic when he was hit with a strong force of air. The smell that lingered in the aftermath of the wind accompanied what sounded like beating drums in the near distance. He wasn't sure why but the sound had a magnetic pull over his body. His feet moved in sync to the bass and he felt himself nearing the source. A light appeared from under a door.

Against what was his better judgment, which seemed to be suddenly returning, Israel opened the door slowly, unsure of what awaited him. To his surprise it was an oasis of streaming water, and from what he could tell, naked women bathing in African attire. The steam that came from the water almost made it possible for him to see but he knew without a doubt, Miranda and Nova were frolicking amongst the women. Shocked, he rose an eyebrow and shook his head in disbelief. The scene that played before him was of a dream that he had often. He was a king surrounded by beautiful women, wealth, massive army, and an entire land at his disposal. Although Miranda and Nova were never in the dream, he couldn't believe his luck and had no intentions on complaining. After all, his mind was convinced that he was clearly hallucinating. Quickly, he discarded his clothes and walked around to see which of the women he would sample first.

"Shame on it all, Israel. Just a few seconds ago, you were about to lose your shit and now you're ready and willing," Azora said.

She appeared right in front of Israel, out of nowhere he concluded. He couldn't put his finger on it but something was off about her, yet he wanted to place his mouth all over her. The need for Azora to be the first woman that he would devour almost overwhelmed him. He moved closer, making sure to rub his hardened self against her thigh as he circled to her backside. If he didn't know any better, he would have thought he felt a slight shudder move through her body. He placed his nose against Azora's neck and sniffed. It was the scent, the one from the hallway. He knew it was something that had turned his senses a time or two. The way it captivated his nose, he felt as if he had no other option than to forcefully take Azora. Like a lion smelling the scent of a gazelle, Israel made the move to place his lips on her. The heat from her skin danced near his opened mouth and it drove him insane. With an urgency that even startled him, he grabbed Azora around the neck and forced his mouth to suck hers wholly. The slight shake of the room caused Azora to break from his embrace. Before he had time to grab her, a sudden air attacked him again, pulling him into what seemed like some sort of rapture.

The velocity and force of the wind tossed Israel around the room like a ragdoll. The waters sprouted up, raining down like a thunderstorm. Israel eyes were forced open and focused directly on Nova and Miranda. The two of them were in still waters, unaware of the chaotic scene that Israel witnessed. Their skin, wet and oily, blended together made a swirl of caramel on chocolate. Both of them beautiful in their own right, Israel looked at the two of them longingly. Connected by only the skin from the tips of their areolas, they smiled at each other. The sense of calm that radiated from the two tugged at Israel's heart. They needed him. He had been the best of everything to the both of him, he reasoned with himself. He was sick of the whirlwind he was in. He needed that peace for himself. He fought against the wind to find his voice.

"Put me down!" he commanded.

Just like that the wind stopped, the waters receded, and Israel was back on solid ground. He smiled to himself as an overwhelming feeling of power washed over him, but it didn't last long. He was now in a chair, chained to it. This irked him as he attempted to pull at the chains.

"Calm down, love. I have so much more in store for you. You've never been a patient man, Israel. I think that's the problem in your life," Azora purred.

"Please, take these chains off me. These aren't meant for me. Chains equate weakness and I am not a weak man!" he yelled in return.

"Yeah, for pussy you are. Why don't we watch the show? I have a feeling this is going to be a good one. Nova is exceptional at tongue play."

"I refuse to watch it unless I can join them."

Azora slapped the back of Israel's head before holding it in a tight death grip. She walked around slowly until she faced him eye-to-eye. She squeezed his jaws together so that his lips puckered out like a fish.

"Oh, but the fuck you will," Azora said through clenched teeth.

She released him and then swiftly turned around so that her ass sat luscious and fat right in his eye sight. He felt himself starting to harden but her next words diverted his attention.

"Nova! Eat her pussy, and eat that motherfucker real good," Azora yelled across the room.

"Your wish is my command," Nova meekly answered.

Israel noticed that her head was down and she never made eye contact with either Azora nor him. This was not the Nova that he knew. Not the one who drove him fucking crazy with her arrogant brazenness. Whatever the case, Israel didn't have time to ponder over it because he was now watching in amazement as Nova walked up to Miranda and flipped her over like a well done pancake on a griddle. Israel felt a stir in the pit of his stomach. He knew the goodness that Nova was about to taste. To him, no one in the world had essence as light and airy as Miranda. Nova slowly pulled apart Miranda's ass. She placed her face between her cheeks and began to slowly lick her from the back to the front. Miranda's purrs of delight caused Israel to grow a little harder. Those sounds were his favorite melody.

Miranda tugged at her own nipples as if she was trying to milk them. The feeling was taking over her body as she squirmed and attempted to run away from Nova's ravishing. That didn't seem to deter Nova at all as she locked her arms firmly around Miranda's waist, securing her in a position that would force her to lose control. Israel had never seen her body react the way it was doing. The muscles in her thighs stiffened and shook simultaneously. Nova fastened her licks and added a few slurps of the sweet nectar.

"That's right, Nova, baby. Get it all. Lick her pussy until she soaks your face. You can bring it out of her. She needs this. Her body has never experienced something so magnetic," Azora spoke softly into Nova's ear.

It gave Nova the fuel that she needed to punish Miranda orally. Nova believed that Miranda had the life that she was supposed to live, and Miranda was an uptight woman who had no clue on how to please her man, and that was how Nova found her way in his heart. Nova placed her entire mouth over her clitoris and sucked softly but firmly. With her left hand sitting on Miranda's pelvis, she felt the tremor in her body and knew that a might eruption was on the way. She sucked faster.

"Let it go, Miranda. Stop suppressing what you feel. You know this shit feels good. Let it go! You've let Israel trap you into his idea of what you should be. Let that shit go," Azora now cheered Miranda on towards the finish line.

Miranda shut her eyes tightly and clenched her teeth. She let out a small growl as she began to grind back onto Nova's mouth. The tremors were coming closer to each other as they hit back-to-back. She threw her head back and yelled to the top of her lungs.

"Fuuuuuuuuuck!"

It hit her hard and violently. It appeared as if she was in convulsions that were never ending. She emptied all of her heart and soul through her most precious vessel. She cried. Not because she was in pain, but because she had never ever felt anything more beautiful than what was happening to her. She turned her head to the left and her eyes fixated on a shadowy figure watching on the side. It turned her on that she had an audience but she was now empty and had nothing left to give. Her body was relaxed into a state of total peace.

"Wow, look at how she came for Nova. Kind of makes you wish you had a pussy, doesn't it? You haven't even made your own wife cum like that in all the years you've been together," Azora cackled at Israel.

"Shut up. You must cut these bullshit ass games and let me join them. They need me. They both need me."

Although he was standing, he was still unable to move forward. He wanted to hold Miranda. He would never admit it out loud but he was jealous of what he'd just witnessed.

"They don't even know you exist right now. This is what you've always wanted, to have them both. But this is what the reality would be like, those two together and no you, because you're too weak."

Israel's chest flared in rage. He had to fight the urge to stop himself from placing his hands around Azora's throat and choking the life out of her. He went to speak but she cut him off before he could even get his first word out his mouth.

"Chill, baby, the real show is about to happen now. I know you really want to be a part of this but I'm thinking I'm now in the mood to have a little fun for myself."

Azora slowly took her time undressing. As soon as the last clothing item hit the floor, she turned and went through the water and up to the hidden stones where Nova and Miranda had already started round two. This time Miranda was on her back with her right hand playing between her thighs, and the other hand was gripping one side of Nova's ass as she bounced up and down on

Miranda's face. It didn't take long for Nova's body to respond just the way that it needed to. Azora rubbed her hair as Nova rode the wave of ecstasy. No sooner had her body stopped trembling, Azora's rubs turned from soft and gentle strokes to gripping Nova's hair and forcing her face into her center. Miranda sucked at Azora's nipples while playing inside of Nova's wetness.

Israel felt himself about to bust wide open. He couldn't believe that he was witnessing, something so beautiful and fucking sexy as shit and he couldn't partake in it at all. He grabbed his throbbing dick and tried alleviate the flow of his blood to his member. He tried to move forward but was once again blocked by a gust of wind, a soft one though. The moans and cries that called out to him were driving him insane because there was nothing he could do to make the situation better. He pulled at himself vigorously. He wanted to get his off at the same time that she did. He could feel it right at the tip, but no matter how hard he went Israel was unable to find that satisfaction that he needed. He watched in horror as his dick started to swell from the back up.

"What the fuck is going on?"

Israel pulled and tugged at himself, trying to get the erection to ease. The pain in his stomach made him double over it was just that intense. He needed help and he needed it immediately.

"Miranda, please. Nova, I need you," he begged.

Azora locked eyes with a panicked Israel. His pain was what she needed to get her over the edge. She winked her eye at him as she moved Nova to suck on her nipples and gave Miranda the spot of licking her to the point of no return.

"You know they can't hear you, right? This is what happens when you are a greedy asshole. You brought this all upon yourself," Azora yelled through moans.

She noticed that Israel was sweating profusely and his body started to shake. He could no longer talk but let soft whimpers come from his mouth. She was breaking him down. He was almost at the point where he would be most vulnerable. The thought caused Azora to merciless grind her clit against Miranda's tongue until she felt her damn break. Tears fell from her eyes and she braced herself in preparation. It was time to release her pain. Azora threw her head back and cried out a yell that was a few frequencies below a dog's whistle.

Israel threw his hands up to his ears and closed his eyes. He didn't know what the hell was happening and for the first time, he was scared that Miranda had unwillingly brought them to the devil. The wind started up again and blew him around the room. He started to pray and cry out to the Lord for help. As soon as he finished with the word, Amen, he was released. The room now empty and nothing but black surrounded him. His hands went down to his dick and he felt that it was back to its normal size. He hurried across the room, hoping he was going in the right direction. After finally finding the door knob, he took off running down the hall and steps. He was about to get the hell out of the house even if he had to fight his way out to freedom and sanity.

Chapter 21
Pride

Israel finally made it to the front door. He breathed a sigh of relief because he couldn't wait to get out of the house of horrors. He wanted to try and go find Miranda but said fuck it. Since she brought him here, all this mess was her fault. Never one to take responsibility for his part, he put the blame on Miranda. He grabbed a hold of the door knob and felt a heart gripping chill flow through his body. He let go of the door, too afraid of what stood behind. He took a few deep breaths to gather his nerves and then grabbed the knob again. Once again a teeth chattering chill coursed through his body, but he needed to get out the house so pulled the door open and walked through.

"Babe, did you forget to get the bacon?" Israel heard Miranda call out.

He looked around their home and smiled. Finally, something good awaited him on the other side of the door. It seemed so lively and sun shone bright through the window blinds. Miranda stood in the kitchen mixing up some pancake mix. She looked edible in her camisole and black stretch pants. He hadn't seen her look so happy in a long time. He could smell the pancakes as if he was standing in the kitchen with her while she cooked them.

"Doesn't she look happy, Israel?" Azora snuck up behind him.

"Fuck, not you again," he huffed. "Can't you just leave me and my wife alone."

Smitten Kitten

He watched as Miranda busied herself with making sure the pancakes were cooked perfectly.

"Oh my dear Israel your night has only just begun." She ran her finger down the back of his neck. Her cold finger caused an instant spread of goose bumps all over his body. He could feel her breathing on his neck. Her presence made his body betray him because no matter how much he wanted to hate her, his lower region yearned for her touch. He could feel her looming on his body. Azora's scent brought on a sense of familiarity but he knew he'd never been with her before. Still, her nectar called at him making his thirst for her even more dire.

"I don't know what I did to deserve this. Why me?" he pleaded.

He continued watching Miranda in the kitchen and upon further inspection he could see pictures of three little children on the refrigerator.

"What the fuck? Whose kids are those?"

He tried to walk closer.

"Those are Miranda and her husband's kids."

"We don't have any kids! What the fuck is this shit?" he yelled, getting angry all over again.

"Correction my dear, Israel. You don't have any kids," Azora said, and then she let out a maniacal laugh that made him want to vomit.

"Are you telling me that my wife has children by another man?"

"No, I'm telling you Miranda has children by her husband. A man who obviously loves her and only shares his dick with her."

"But-Who-How?" Israel couldn't even form a sentence.

Her words cut through him like a hot butter knife going through butter.

"Just watch the show. You haven't even gotten to the good part," Azora smirked as Israel watched the scene unfold before him.

"Shit, damn babe I am so sorry," Dillion said as he came into the kitchen in nothing but some basketball shorts.

His body still had drops of water on it from the shower he just taken.

"You want me to go get it now?"

He walked behind Miranda, put his arms around her waist, and kissed the back of her neck.

"You motha'fuck-" Israel roared as he tried to get to Dillion.

"Oh, calm down, Israel. A bit dramatic don't you think, geez!" Azora's words dripped with sarcasm. "You're mad now and the show ain't even got good yet."

"You two snake bastards! I knew y'all wasn't shit! You always wanted to be me mutha'fucka!"

"Looks like he is living better than you, but I'm just on the outside looking though," Azora taunted.

"Would you shut the fuck up!" he hated the sound of Azora's voice.

"No, I can't do that, especially not tonight. I have so many lessons to teach tonight.

"And what lesson is this? That you shouldn't trust your wife and your brother together?"

"No, Israel, that one man's trash is another man's treasure."

"I never treated her like trash."

"But you did. You made her feel less than a woman. Made her feel like she could never be enough of a woman for you. You made her doubt her whole existence at one point. Then when you and your dirty dick killed her child, she knew then that she meant absolutely nothing to you. She knew that you would risk her and her child's life over some sour pussy bitch. Tsk tsk tsk, you've never been worth a shit Israel, and your time has come. Now back to the show.

This next part will be to die for!"

"You sure you don't want me to go get the bacon, babe? I'm sorry."

He slowly licked her neck.

"Ok, you're about to get something started that can't be finished, Dillion. Now stop," she said with a laugh as she pretended to resist his advances.

"Why? The kids are knocked out? There could be an earthquake and tsunami happening and they still wouldn't wake up."

He reached around in front of her and slid his hand down the front of her pants.

"Umm," Miranda let a soft moan escape her mouth.

"Please, no Azora. I can't watch this. Please, not again."

Israel felt the air his lungs evaporating with every passing second.

"Haven't you learned that you don't run shit around these parts, sir. Now sit down and enjoy this show."

Suddenly, Israel was hit with thrust into a seat that wasn't there before.

"Babe, I'm cooking," Miranda wined.

"But what I want to eat is already done."

He started slipping her pants down around her hips. Miranda gripped the counter top, lowered her back, and hiked her ass up in the air.

Azora could feel the hate oozing from within Israel. The only time she'd ever felt that much hate was when Tina and Nova were around. Little did Israel know, Azora was far from finished with him.

Israel watched as Dillion spread her ass cheeks and pressed his face into her honey box. He took long licks from her pussy to her ass, stopping momentarily to tease her asshole. He could see the look of pure lust in her eyes as she reached back, grabbed his head, and pressed his face hard into her ass. Her moans were loud it was as if they'd been put on speakers. His chest heaved in and out in desperation, trying to find some air.

"You remember when you use to treat her like this? Whatever happened to the passion you two shared? Oh, I forgot. You thought it was good idea to go share your dick with the world," Azora scoffed.

"I never stopped loving her," Israel sounded defeated and he fought the tears that were trying so desperately to escape the corners of his eyes.

"Apparently that wasn't enough."

"Umm, baby, I'm about to cum," Miranda moaned.

"Give me what I want," Dillion demanded.

"No, I can't. I'm going to wake the kids."

"Give me what I want," Dillion said as he softly bit down on her clit and began sucking it hard.

Miranda scratched at the kitchen counter top as her body stiffened.

Israel knew what was about to happen. He'd made her body do that many times before. She was about to cum all over his mouth, giving away what was his. He was the only person allowed to drink from her fountain.

"Cum on this tongue."

Israel heard Dillion coaching her. He wanted to jump on top of Dillion and beat his head in. He couldn't believe he was losing the people he loved the most in the world. He knew deep down there was no coming back from what he was witnessing. They'd done the ultimate betrayal.

Dillion stood up and held her close as he slid in from the back. They both let out a loud hiss once he reached the bottom. Israel could tell her pussy was feeling good to Dillion by the way his fingers pressed in the soft meaty flesh of her ass cheeks. Dillion bit down on her shoulder to keep from yelling and Miranda placed the dish towel in her mouth to keep her moans in check. Dillion stroked Miranda's honey pot slow but hard as he reached around in front again and started playing with her clit. He pinched her clit hard and her legs started shaking so hard they almost gave out.

"Stop this, stop this, stop this! I can't no more!"

"Oh, it's just getting good. I mean the way he is fucking her who could blame her for choosing him over you. Shit, I want to join them. I mean, your sex game is good but not that good, yowsers!"

"Just let me out of here."

Israel finally let the tears fall as he as watched his younger brother ravish his wife in the kitchen that used to be his.

"You are being such the party pooper, Israel. Don't be that way."

"If I ever get the chance to wrap my hands around your neck, I'm going to strangle you with my hands," Israel threatened.

"Oh really?"

Azora appeared before Israel, scaring the living shit out of him. He almost jumped out of the chair.

"Let me tell you something, Israel. You are still breathing only because of me. I am the only thing standing in front of you and the reaper. I don't take threats kindly. If you ever put your dirty pussy smelling hands on me, trust and believe you won't ever touch another soul."

Their little banter was turning Azora on to a point she almost wanted to slide right onto his dick at that very moment.

Azora slid onto his lap. She felt his body go rigid but within seconds once again his body was betraying him.

"Get off of me, bitch," Israel knew what he was saying, though for some reason he felt a strong yearning for their bodies to touch.

"You don't really want me to get up," Azora whispered in his ear and grinded her hot box all over his crotch area.

The heat from her body was making Israel sweat as he reached out, gripped her ass cheeks, and began to massage them. His touch brought so many memories of her first love to the front of her eyes. Her first love who made love to her like no other, and her first love who left her brokenhearted and alone for what seemed like an eternity.

Israel didn't know what was going on. It was as if his body was moving on its own. There was a real life tug of war going on within his body. On one hand, he wanted to kill Azora for the heartache she'd caused him thus far, but on the other he wanted to lay her down and make love to her.

Yes, her familiar scent was like a pheromone driving him insane.

"You sure?"

She continued grinding on him as she licked the side of his neck.

"Yes, please let us go."

"You still haven't learned yet!" Azora jumped off his lap furious. She was furious at him for still wanting to save Miranda after everything he'd witnessed and at herself for getting caught up in memories of a life that would never be hers. Her chance with her one true love was over because he'd betrayed her like Israel had done to Miranda.

"You will never leave here!"

Instantly everything went black.

Chapter 22
Gluttony

Israel sat in a dark corner trying to regain his self-control. Anger ripped throughout his body and at this point all he wanted to do was kill someone. Watching Miranda be passionately ravished by his brother and enjoying, caused him to hang from the edge of the cliff. He knew that he didn't have a squeaky-clean past, but it was okay for him to do it. His entire life he watched men provide and take care of home, all the while having a few extracurricular activities on the side. He was a man and the rules were different for him. As a woman and his wife, Miranda had no right to fuck other people, especially his brother since she belonged to him. He wiped the tear that tried to escape from his eye. As much as he fucked up, he never imagined how it would feel if he saw Miranda stepping out on him.

The pleasure that dangled off her lips as she moaned with such aggression still rang in his ears. He wanted to forget the look on her face after each orgasms she released, but he couldn't get the images out of his mind. At first, he was turned on by watching her and Nova, then he got jealous. No one had a right to make her feel that way other than him. He needed to get his wife and get the hell out of this house. It was tearing him apart and if he didn't leave now, there would be nothing left of his sanity. Completely lost in thought, Israel felt a hand on his shoulder.

"What the hell," he said, abruptly jumping up.

"Israel, baby, what's wrong?"

Israel looked up to see Cheyenne standing across from him in a white, lace bodysuit. Even after ten years, she still had the body from when they first met. Her smooth, butterscotch skin sat perfectly on top of her curvy body. She was never extremely thick, but she filled out in the areas she needed to. Her long hair fell past her shoulders, which framed her face perfectly. He looked her up and down as her eyes immediately filled with sadness. It was as if the beauty quickly faded from her face. He remembered the look she was now wearing from a while ago. It was the same look she had when he ended their year-long affair. She was heartbroken and for months she wouldn't let him be. She reached out her hand and he felt himself pushed closer.

"Why didn't you pick me, Israel? You promised me you would leave her. You promised me we were going to be together. Why did you lie to me?" she shouted.

Israel stood still, not sure what he should say next. It had been over ten years since he'd seen her, and he wasn't sure what she was capable of at this moment. She was crying and shouting about something that ended years ago. He'd gotten over it, so why she was still holding on to it baffled him.

"Cheyenne, baby, I didn't lie to you."

"Yes, you did. You never loved me like you said you did. You were my first, Israel. The first man who I loved beyond reason. The first man who I actually saw my future with. The only man I've ever given my heart to," she said as tears continued to swell up in her eyes.

He could see she was hiding something behind her back, but wasn't sure what she had in her hands. He couldn't take his eyes off of her breasts that were now exposed. He remembered how he loved to suck on them. He tried to forget how many orgasms he brought her to the edge of from teasing her nipples. Her dark areolas were staring at him and he couldn't stop the bulge from forming in his pants.

"You see what I mean, you don't love me! You just want to fuck me! I let you fuck me any and everywhere, but that wasn't good enough for you. I gave you everything and I wasn't good enough to marry like your precious Miranda!" she screamed.

"Cheyenne, baby, calm down. I did love you. I promise."

She was getting hysterical and he didn't want her to lose control. He could remember how crazy she could be and the drama she put him through when they broke up. He needed to get out this house and he didn't want anyone to do anything that would jeopardize him leaving. All these women he'd been with were on the verge of losing it, and he didn't want to suffer because of it. His emotions were everywhere and he was doing all he could to maintain control. This night was definitely not going as he expected it to go.

"He doesn't love you, Cheyenne. He never did and he never will. Show him what you do to yourself when he lies to you. Let him see what happened when he broke your heart," Azora said.

Israel looked up to see the blood running down her arms. The diagonal slits on her arms dripped blood as she cut more into her skin. Her legs were covered with the dried blood that stained her thighs. He moved closer to her to see his name carved deep into her arm. He realized she had been hiding a razor blade behind her back. He moved to stop her but felt a force constrict him in the strongest manner.

"Watch her, Israel. Watch her destroy herself on the outside since you destroyed her on the inside. Look at how much she loves you as she bleeds out for you," Azora said, taunting him.

"No, don't let her do this. Don't let her hurt herself like this," Israel begged.

"Why? You don't really care about her. You threw her away the first chance you got."

"That's not true. I did care about her. I did have feelings for her."

Israel watched as she moved closer to him so he could see what his pain did to her.

"I gave you my heart, Israel. I was so in love with you and I believed you when you said we were going to be together. Maybe I was just being naïve, but I fucking loved you. Why did you do this to me?"

It was as if the razor blade had its own sound effect. Cut after cut, he could hear Cheyenne slice into her body. The drops of blood echoed against the walls as they seeped from the cuts. Her arms, legs, stomach, and even her face now bore slices that bled out. Her tears mixed with the blood as they hit the floor. Her lips were covered in blood. She was a wreck and she blamed him for it. All of her beauty was now hidden behind slashes and blood.

"Make it stop! Make it stop right fucking now," he screamed, hoping Azora would show some mercy.

"No Israel, this is what your lustful ways do to women. It kills them. It destroys them until they waste away. Their hearts never heal," Azora mocked.

"No, make it stop! Stop her before she kills herself. Do something, you crazy bitch," Israel shouted.

"Why? You've already killed her on the inside. Now you get to watch as she finishes the number you did on her on the outside."

"Cheyenne, baby, please stop. Don't do this to yourself," he pleaded.

Her body was now full of cuts that spelled his name and I love you. Her hands bled uncontrollably from gripping the blade so tightly.

"No Israel, I want you to see how much I loved you. I want you to see how I would do anything for you. I would die for you," Cheyenne said.

Before Israel could stop her she made the final slit and fell to the floor.

"No, Cheyenne!" he belted out, closing his eyes to her laying on the floor.

Israel crouched over screaming as he tried to erase what he'd just seen.

"Look at her, Israel. Look at what she did because she loves you. Why did you do that to her? Why did you break her heart? You were never going to be with her and you knew it."

"Let me out of here. I'm sick of this twisted ass house. I'm sick of your psychotic ass!"

Azora laughed, "Oh, in due time, Israel. You'll get a chance to leave, but for now just enjoy the rest of your secrets unraveling before your eyes."

Israel felt himself turned around as a chair slid behind him. He looked up as he sat on the other end of a long glass table. The glass vases down the middle blocked his view of who was at the other enough, though the jasmine scent gave him an idea of who it could be. He heard the chair scoot back as she climbed on top of the table. Shelby was the epitome' of a sexy red bone woman. Her tall stature was undeniably alluring. At thirty-seven, and standing at 5'11", she looked better than she did the day he walked out of her penthouse. He had been caught and for him that meant he needed to end it or Miranda would leave him for good.

Israel swallowed as she stood naked on top of the glass table. Her hips still made him turn tricks inside. The warmth that lied between them was always the motivation he needed to come to work. After Cheyenne left his firm, Shelby gave him some more great office memories. He looked away from her to see the rope hanging in the middle of the table. He was unclear to what it was being used for. Whether pain or pleasure, though he'd hope it was for pleasure.

"Shelby, what are you doing here?"

"I'm here for you, baby. I came so you could see me this one last time. Don't you want to see me? Didn't you miss me?"

Israel sat in silence, unsure of what to say. He was still trying to move passed her standing in front of him completely naked.

"Didn't you miss me? You're not acting like you miss me, dammit!" Shelby screamed, kicking one of the vases of the table.

"Shelby, chill out, shit. Of course I missed you," he lied.

"No, fuck you! You don't get to boss me around anymore. I don't work for you or maybe I do. I guess I was nothing more than your little office whore anyway. Is that what I was Israel? Was I your office whore? Was I something fun to do at work? Did you tell all your work buddies about me? Did you tell them how I fucked you so good?"

Shelby picked up another vase and threw it at the wall. She kicked over another vase as she walked towards him. The bottom of her feet were bleeding from stepping on all of the broken glass.

"No Shelby, you weren't my office whore. Please, baby, calm down. You know what we had. We had a house and we were working on our future, remember?" Israel asked, trying to calm her down.

"Future, what future? You left me standing in a penthouse crying and pleading for you to come back. I wanted you to come back and you never did," she said, kicking another vase.

The glass table was now full of broken glass and with each step she made a trail of blood followed her. She made her way to the middle of the table as she stood in front of the rope. A tear fell down her face as she let out a sinister laugh.

"Shelby, please believe me when I say I did want you. I wanted us to have children. I wanted us to start our own firm. I know I fucked up, but I wanted us to work. I really did, baby. Please calm down and let's talk. Let's figure this out," Israel said, hoping she would get down.

He wasn't sure why she still insisted on walking on the broken glass, but he couldn't watch any more blood being shed on his behalf.

"You never fucking loved me. You just loved to fuck me, right? I was stupid to believe you wanted to be with me. I should've listened when they warned be about you. As soon as your future was threatened, you made sure mine came to a halt. Well, now you get to see how my future will go and it's all your fault you selfish bastard!"

Another vase crashed against the wall as she stood in plain sight for Israel to see. She picked up the stone on the table. She slipped the rope around her neck as she tightened the noose. The emptiness that filled her eyes was a clear indication she had lost the battle to her broken heart.

"Shelby, he doesn't believe you really love him. Prove to him that you were his ride or die," Azora commanded.

Without blinking, Shelby threw the rock down hard against the table, shattering the glass. Her body gave way to the rope and she hung, fighting to breathe. Israel heard a laughing sound as Shelby struggled to breathe.

"Look at her, Israel. She's fighting for you. You always did like the fight she possessed and now look at what she does with it."

"Get her down. Please get her down! Shelby, baby hold on."

"No, I won't get her down. You need to see the after effects of your bad decisions. You need to see that your lies didn't just destroy one woman, they destroyed four. Watch her fight to breathe like she did the day you left her standing in her penthouse. She begged you to come back and you turned your back on her. Now sit here and watch her fall apart."

Israel covered his face as he tried to fight the image of what was in front of him. Shelby hanging in front of him fighting to breathe was too much to see. He let out a loud, yet painful scream. He couldn't take any more of this. He was going crazy and the longer he stayed in this house, the quicker he would lose his damn mind.

When I get my hands on her I'm going to kill her.

Azora could feel him thinking about her. He was almost where she needed him to be, but not quite yet. She hadn't scratched the surface of making him pay for how he destroyed so many hearts.

"Israel, what's wrong? Is it you that don't like to face your destruction head on? Well, too bad.

 You still don't have enough regret built up for me to release you," Azora said.

Israel felt a cold cuff around his wrist. He tugged at whatever was restricting him, but it didn't give. He glanced down to see his left arm handcuffed to a chair. When he looked back up, Bria was sitting across from him. What sat in front of them was all he needed to know that he was done with this night and this horrific house. A shiny, silver .38 revolver and one bullet was all that separated them. He wasn't sure if the bullet was for him or for her. He'd hoped neither, but this night didn't seem to be going very well. In less than an hour, he watched two women he loved destroy themselves on account of him. Now Bria looked at him with such disappointment, and he was defenseless.

Bria stood up and grabbed the gun. She scraped it across the table as she walked around it slowly. The bullet remained in the middle of the table, and for now Israel was relieved. "You know, the first time I met you, I felt like the wind had been knocked out of me," she said. "At the time, I thought it was crazy that someone could have such an overpowering effect on another person. I was twenty-four, and to me I figured this is what it feels like to meet your soulmate."

Israel was staring straight ahead, but turned to look at her as she stood next to him. He had no words for what she had just said,

Smitten Kitten

so he remained silent. Out of the other women he'd slept with, Bria was different. If he would have left Miranda, it would've been for her, but she was wild and he didn't have the time or energy to tame her.

"Bria, what are you doing with that gun? Listen, baby, we don't have to do this. We can get out of here right now. This house is making everyone crazy."

"No!" she shouted.

Israel immediately realized another woman was falling apart and going crazy in front of him. He was watching his greed and excessiveness crumble in right before his eyes. Bria walked back around to her chair, but not before grabbing the bullet. Israel prayed she stopped before things got dangerous.

"I know what you're thinking Israel and it's too late," Azora said.

"Please, don't let her do this. She has a son. Don't let her do this."

"She has a son? You don't care about her or her son so shut the hell up!" Azora shouted.

'That's not true," Israel said as he bowed his head.

He wasn't sure if he was going to die, but watching her die was not something he cared to see.

"Bria, baby, put the gun down."

He saw her spin the barrel around before slamming it shut. The loud sound bounced off the walls and caused a sharp pain to ring in his ear. The sound of death seemed to be the theme song for the night. Six chambers, one bullet, and two people who were stuck in the middle of what could soon be the end of them both.

"Why did you lie? Why didn't you want our baby? How could you pay the mother of your child to go away?"

Click!

Israel jumped at the first click of the trigger. She had the gun pointed at her head while her eyes filled with tears. Fear paralyzed him and he couldn't move to help her. He knew what he did was wrong, still there was no way he could tell Miranda that Bria was really carrying his child and she'd already lost theirs.

"Bria, I didn't want to do it, but I was scared."

"Liar!"

Click!

"Bria, stop it! Put the fucking gun down now!"

He could see her hands trembling, however, the grip she had on the gun was strong. He stood up to grab her arm, and she jumped back.

"Move again, and she pulls the trigger," Azora said.

"Bria, didn't I take care of you. Haven't I made sure you and Cairo were okay. I never let you want for anything. Can't you see I really loved you?"

"Loved me, loved me? You never loved me. You just wanted to control me. If you loved me you would've told your wife about our son," Bria cried.

"Bri—"

Click!

Three times the trigger had been pulled and Israel knew he was running out of time. He had to tell her something, anything that would force her to put the gun down.

"Your lies won't work anymore, Israel," Azora whispered in his ear.

She walked around and stood behind Bria. Azora could see how fragile she was, and she knew now was the time to really make him suffer.

"Pull the trigger, Bria. Show him what life without you would be like. Show him what life has been like for you since he walked out on you and your son."

Click!

"Israel, I became a mother because of you. We were happy for two years and Cairo is a perfect example of our love. How could you not want me? How could you not want him? Is it because of your precious Miranda?"

"Bria, what we had was real. Baby, don't you know that? I love you. You have my son and nothing can ever break that bond."

Azora could feel his charms working and she knew she had to intervene immediately. Her brokenness was obviously not as strong as the others.

"He abandoned you. He abandoned your son. Now it's time for him to feel a loss. Show him what life is going to be like without you, Bria."

Click!

Israel watched the tears run down her face. He felt his sanity slipping away as these women went mad.

"Bria, stop listening to her. She doesn't know you like I do."

"Oh, but I do. I know she loved you. I know she bore your child, and then you paid her off like some whore to be quiet. You didn't treat her like you loved her because she was a casualty to you. You are a selfish bastard and all you thought about was yourself," Azora said.

"Wow, that is so true," Nova said, walking up to him.

He hadn't even noticed she was in the room from trying to keep Bria under control. She smiled as she sashayed towards him in next to nothing. The garments she had on resembled something worn in the early Egyptian days. She looked like a queen or at least someone who lived in a palace with one.

"Tell her Israel, tell her how I came after her. Tell her how you swore to Miranda none of them meant anything and you would never cheat on her again. Tell her how many times you moaned, *I am your everything*, in my ears. She looks weak and you don't look like a man who likes weak women. Do you?"

Nova was antagonizing the situation and he was trying to talk Bria off the edge. He didn't need her bullshit crazy on top of the other crazy bitch. Bria was vulnerable and he knew one slight shove and she was falling. Nova moved closer to him as she straddled him. Israel breathed her mandarin scent in and fought hard to exhale it before it took over his senses. Nova was a hell raiser and she served the devil. They were a perfect match.

"Israel, do you love her? Is she telling the truth?" Bria uttered.

"No, she could never be you, Bria."

Nova accepted his challenge and decided to help the poor girl finish what she came to do. She moved off of his lap to unzip his pants, slowly removing his engorged member. She shook her head as a smirk formed across her lips. He was hard and she knew that even at the brink of death, he couldn't fight lust. Nova glanced at Bria as she kneeled down to take Israel inside her mouth.

"Watch how he doesn't need you anymore. Pay attention to how I control everything about him," Nova taunted.

She slid Israel inside her mouth and in a slow, torturous manner she went up and down the shaft with her tongue. Israel fought hard to keep his head from leaning back. He had a moan stuck in the back of his throat, but he couldn't let it go. He couldn't let Nova win this round. With each swallow, he felt his throat swell as his breathing increased.

"Look at him, Bria, he's enjoying her. He doesn't miss you because he replaced you. Just put him out of his misery," Azora commanded.

Israel shook his head as if to stop her. He couldn't open his mouth because then the moan he was trying to hold on to would escape. Nova moved her mouth faster up and down, teasing the tip as her saliva dripped down the shaft. He wasn't giving in fast enough and this needed to end now.

"Nova, you know what you have to do," Azora ordered.

Nova stood up and straddled Israel. With no hesitation, he slid between her warm thighs as if he was always meant to be there. Her back was to him as she faced Bria. She needed to see the pleasure his dick brought her. She grinded back and forth as her hips gyrated in a wave-like motion.

Click!

"Bria, no! Nova get the fuck off me! Get off my dick, now!"

"Why, daddy? Don't you like it this way? You always told me you like when I fuck you like this. Is it not good to you anymore?"

Bria's cries got louder as Nova bounced up and down. She leaned her head back and in a matter of moments she screamed out.

Bang!

"Nooooooo!" Israel yelled out.

Azora laughed loudly as Israel screamed Bria's name over-and-over. She knew all he needed was to feel Nova's seductive tongue and the game would end. Nova finished her orgasm before lifting herself off of him. He was almost on the brink of insanity. Israel feared opening his eyes again because he couldn't bear to see Bria's limp body lie on the table. His sobbing fueled Azora and she had never felt more powerful than she did now.

"Open your eyes, Israel."

Israel heard what sounded like Miranda's voice, but he knew it couldn't be. Bria was the last face he'd looked away from before Nova climaxed.

Bang!

The noise startled him and his eyes flew open to see Miranda standing in front of him behind the table Bria had just pulled the trigger at. Scattered paper, pictures, hotel keys, an old pregnancy test, and his secret phone beneath her hand were all over the table. His lies were in front of him as Miranda's sunken face bore the last ten years of his lies, betrayal, and selfishness. She slid down in the chair, but not before she pushed everything on the table in his face. He saw pictures of him and Shelby, the hotel keys to rooms he would secretly meet Cheyenne at, and the pregnancy test that told the truth about his son. The credit card bills were also proof that he had been a player, a pimp, or whatever else you can think of over the years.

Israel looked at Miranda as she stood in front of him stripping. The white dress she wore had fallen to the floor as she removed the black lace bra and panties that hid beneath it. This woman, his woman, stood in front of him completely naked. She wanted him to see her in a way he hadn't in so long. He saw a shadow come behind her and as soon as the light hit her he could see it was Cheyenne. Then seconds later, Shelby appeared, and then Bria. All of them were naked, faces covered with tear tracks. Each of the women he had stolen a piece of were in front of him.

"Look at them," Miranda said, running her hands down over Shelby and Cheyenne's abdomens. "Look at us. All of the woman you love. All of the woman you lied to and broke in some kind of way. What are you going to do now, Israel? Who are you going to die beside now?"

They all moved closer to him. Each of them crying, screaming, and begging him to love them. The voices in his ears caused them to bleed. They stripped him and touched him. He felt the cuts that were all over Cheyenne's body on his arms. The rope that strangled Shelby tightened around his neck, forcing him to breathe harder. The clicking sounds of the gun rang loudly in his ear. Meanwhile, he watched Nova stand over him and laugh as they ripped him apart.

"Tell them you love them, Israel. Tell each of these women you want to spend forever with them. Feed them more lies!" Azora yelled.

"No, let me out of here! I want to get the fuck out of here!" Israel screamed.

The more he moved to break free of them, the more pain he felt. He eventually wrestled his way into the hallway, quickly running away from them all. He was heading to find Azora and end all of this madness. Azora laughed louder-and-louder as she could feel him breaking down. He had started tearing at the seams and now was finally the time for her to rip him completely apart.

Chapter 23
Redemption

Israel had one goal in mind, get out alive. He tore through the mansion like a madman. The faster he ran, the faster he got back to the room he just left. He looked around in confusion. He was going in circles and there was no way for him to stop the pain and agony that tore through his soul. He wanted nothing more than to wrap his hands around Azora's neck and choke the life out of her.

He had done so much over the years, but he was always careful of Miranda's feelings. Sure, he slipped up a few times, but all men did. That's what he always told himself in order to clear his conscious. He never thought he was actually hurting her or any of the other women. To see their hidden desires and none of them included him, it was overwhelming to say the least.

In total defeat, he gave up, slid down the wall, and allowed the tears to assault his face. He hollered and screamed because there was nothing else he could do at this point but surrender. He was in a walking nightmare. The crying that poured from Israel's mouth was enough to make anyone feel bad for him, anyone but Azora. It was evident that she had finally accomplished what she plotted and planned for so long. Demolish the soul that brought so much pain from being careless and reckless.

Azora walked over to him and kicked his leg, but Israel still continued to cry. He couldn't see pass his own hurt to even acknowledge the disrespect in being kicked like a dog. Azora rolled her eyes at the dramatics and extended a napkin to help him wipe his face. Israel didn't even bother to look her way. It was as if he was deep into a mental breakdown. Seeing him in a state of being so weakened and defenseless really irked Azora and she kicked him again.

"Oyo, get your ass up now," she yelled at him.

The seriousness and the tone in her voice caused him to stop crying momentarily. He looked up at her and stared at her as if she was the one who had lost her mind. The nonchalant look in Azora's eyes caused him to cry out again. Snot bubbles and tears mixed together had formed some sort of allegiance on his top lip. Azora felt sickened just looking at the mess. She was about to tell him how he was a total disgrace when he finally managed to speak through sobs.

"You are fucking evil. What do you want from me?"

"Calm down, my sweet, Oyo. I think you've learned your lesson now."

"Why do you keep calling me, Oyo? My name is Israel."

He wiped his face, somewhat relieved to hear her say she was through with him, but he had a funny feeling that there was still more bullshit to come his way. He looked at her again and for the first time that night, he saw more than ass and titties. In fact, she had a glow about her that he hadn't paid attention to before.

Azora slid down the wall so that she was sitting right beside him. She placed her hand on his arm and offered somewhat of a smile.

"Your name is Oyo. You just don't remember."

"I think I would know what my own name is," he replied as if she was nuts.

"I know I haven't given you much reason to trust me tonight, but I'm now asking that you do. I've only done this so I could strip you of the foolishness that this world has bestowed upon you."

"Trust you? There is no way in hell I would do that and I don't know if you been drinking that bullshit you gave us tonight or what. You sound crazy."

Azora tilted her head back and laughed for what seemed like a very long time. She had tears running down her face. She remembered the very long nights of the two of them talking and laughing until the break of dawn. They would then make love and sleep the day away. She smiled briefly before continuing to talk.

"Let me ask you a question. Have you ever had vivid dreams or hallucinations about Africa? Can't you hear the beating of the drums? Smell the sweet air and reminisce of home? Perhaps you were a king in some of these dreams?"

Startled that she knew about that, he looked at her in shock. He had told no one, not even Miranda, about what he thought were mere fantasies.

"How do you know that?"

"Because they aren't dreams. A long time ago, you were a very powerful king. I was your queen and believe it or not, Nova was supposed to be your queen before me. That's why you haven't been able to shake her. It's also why you've felt yourself attracted to me. Your soul tapped into who you used to be, even when your mind didn't"

"Get the fuck out of here. You really want me to believe this?" Israel asked, while laughing.

He couldn't explain his newfound feeling of peace. He felt slightly bipolar that Azora was now bringing comfort to him when he just wanted to kill her and felt like he was losing his mind.

"I'm serious, Oyo. You have to get your mind back. You don't remember because something went wrong that night. Something went horribly wrong."

Azora fought hard to hold her tears at bay. Whenever she thought back on the night she lost everything and her entire life changed, she broke down.

Israel watched her face closely. The sudden look of heartbreak tugged at his heart's string. He reached out to her but she pulled herself back.

"I'm sorry. I just felt an urge to comfort you. Hell, I almost want to protect you from the pain you're feeling, but I'm not Oyo. I am Israel and I am in love with my wife."

Azora sighed heavily. She was trying to be patient because she knew it would take more than words, but she sort of hoped that their love alone would be enough to jog his memory. She pulled a small container from her pocket and handed it to him.

"Here, drink this. You will get all your memories back."

"Are you crazy? Last time you told me to drink something I damn near lost my mind."

To prove that she wasn't giving him anything poisonous, she opened the bottle and took a sip. She swallowed and stared at him.

"See, nothing will happen to you. It will make you remember. Take it. All of the crazy questions about your life that you told no one, they'll all be answered tonight."

Apprehensively, Israel took the bottle and downed the contents. At first he felt nothing but then his temperature rose. His head felt like a million tiny missiles had erupted. The blinding pain caused his eyes to close and he grabbed his head to cease the thumping.

Scene after scene floated through his mind. Africa! His land! His army! His parents! His enemies! And lastly, his love. The beating of his heart accelerated as he watched him and Azora making love. She was his queen, his everything. Night after night, day after day, he remembered everything about who he was. Including that night when he was seized right before he made himself immortal like he'd done Azora.

His body shook and he now saw the night through Azora's eyes. He could feel each draining emotion that she experienced. More than a few tears escaped his eyes as he watched first Nova's betrayal then the devastation Azora went through watching him be killed.

He was overwhelmed and began to shake his head in an attempt to make the pain go away. The scenes stopped playing and he had to force himself to inhale and exhale slowly so he could catch his breath. He turned to Azora and stared at her with wild, passionate eyes. He would definitely get revenge on those who robbed them of their love, but that would have to come second to loving Azora.

"My love! Oh, baby! I am so sorry," he cried as he pulled Azora into his arms.

This time she didn't shy away from his touch. She welcomed him because she'd been missing the feeling of completion. It is what fueled Azora's passion for revenge. The weight of that was starting to wear her down and she was happy to finally be at a place where she could lay the burden down for good.

Their first kiss was soft and somewhat unsure. They both knew they had lost so much and ultimately were two different people. Oyo had turned into a man that Azora found repulsing. The Israel person was one she would never even consider allowing into her personal space. Azora wasn't innocent either. Oyo wondered how his pure angel could turn into such a devious person.

He pulled back from her and stared at her. The intensity in his eyes made her blush. She lowered her eyes from his sight. The gesture made him smile as he remembered how hard it was to break her from that. To him it meant that she was still all his.

"Look at me," he demanded.

She lifted her eyes to his and from that moment, the two of them reconnected their souls. Oyo kissed her again. His lips were on fire and equally matched the flames that came from her mouth. They kissed so intensely that they bounced through a few dimensions but never losing their newfound connection. Once they were back into their palace, Azora pushed Oyo down on their bed. It had been centuries since they connected there but the familiarity flowed as easy and gentle as a lazy lake.

Oyo was used to being the dominant one who controlled every move, but Azora was not having any of that tonight. She undressed him with the speed of a panther, while her touch was soft as her fingers grazed different parts of his skin.

"I've missed you so much. You just have no clue," she whispered, while fully mounting him.

Azora tugged at the belt around her waist, freeing her chocolate breasts as the silk robe she adorned, fell from her shoulders. She took the pins from her hair and shook her fire red locks lose.

Soft kisses from her mouth made a trail from the top of his head, down his torso and just below his waist. Slowly she dragged her tongue across the thickest vein and worked her way up to the tip. She ran her tongue around the rim before she sucked him wholly.

Oyo whimpered despite trying to not sound like a nursing baby, but he had no choice. Azora made love to him with her mouth as if it was her only purpose in life. He grabbed her by the hair and massaged her scalp in sync with her licks and suctions, encouraging the magnificent job she was performing. The tingling in his toes came without warning. One moment he was amongst the stars and the very next, he was speeding back to Earth, unable to prevent the flow. He spilled inside of her mouth and she happily welcomed his appreciation of her work.

Azora licked any of the remains from the sides of her lips before making wet trails back to his face. She looked him in his eyes and hoped that he recognized, she was no longer that shy and timid girl he once knew. He threw her off for a moment when he first received his memory back, but she would never be that naïve, sweet, or innocent ever again.

"You are an incredible woman, Azora. I knew you would be from the moment I laid eyes on you. I'm in awe of you. You are so strong and fierce," Oyo confirmed he just witnessed her metamorphosis.

Azora smiled at him. This was her man. The man who she pledged to love for all eternity. That, this, and any other life.

"I have a little more that I need to show you," she purred.

Azora leaned forward in order to place him at her opening. She teased him by allowing him to rest there as she flexed her muscles. The warmth and wetness assisted with hardening Oyo solid as a rock again. She slid down on him in one swift movement. An electric bolt shot through them simultaneously.

Oyo held tight onto Azora's hips, his nails breaking through her skin. Her blood spilled down his fingers. It's sticky substance clinging to the hairs on his arms. He brought his fingers to his lips and licked them. A cool shiver ran the course through his body and nestled along the walls of Azora's uterus.

The shift in the atmosphere could not be mistaken for anything other than pure love. For a slight second, the Earth shook. The heavens opened their windows and rained down upon them. Azora moved her hips as Oyo brought himself up and inside her with a force that rivaled a steel battering ram. He felt her body tense on top of him. His pounding slowed to a heightened circular grind.

"Give it to me," Oyo commanded.

Azora arched her back, tilted her head back, and screamed loud.

"Ahhhhh!"

She released her potion down his shaft and around his inner thighs. She didn't know where all of the liquid had been stored inside of her but she gave him every single drop for what seemed like several minutes. Tears poured from her eyes like freed slaves, running towards the promise land. Azora tried her hardest to breathe calmly through her tremors but her lungs couldn't process their own function.

Oyo rubbed her body softly as he assisted with soothing her. He knew that the final part of the prophecy had been fulfilled. The swallowing of her blood and it transferring through his system back to hers is what caused the shifting of the Earth on its axis. He rested his hand upon her stomach before placing soft kisses on the home that will be a safe haven for his future king.

Now able to breathe, Azora looked down at Oyo with tears still in her eyes. She felt it too and even though it had only been a few seconds of conception. She loved her child already. She was now complete and also sorry. As much as she wanted to remain in this moment forever, Hecate appeared in the corner. The signal for the final stage had just been given.

Chapter 24
Wrath

Azora kneeled down in her prayer room with tears running freely down her face. At last she had found her true love, and she had to let to him go all over again. There was no turning back now no matter how much she loved Oyo. He'd done so much wrong in the world and it was now his time to pay his debt to Hecate.

"Hecate, everything is ready. I sacrifice my love to you and I hope I've done everything to your approval and in your image."

Azora bowed her head and kissed the jet black prayer carpet that she kneeled on.

The smell of burning lavender scented candles floated around the room, relaxing her once tense muscles. That moment with Oyo shook her to her core. She'd dreamed of that moment for half of a millennia. His touch still drove her hormones into hysteria and his eyes beautiful brown eyes still burrowed deep inside to her soul. She rubbed her stomach as she looked up and stared into the eyes of Hecate. The piercing red eyes looked back at her with pure fury burning in them. Azora knew it was time to finish what she'd been planning for what seemed like a thousand life times.

A rigid shiver shot down her spine as she felt an overwhelming abundance of hate run through her body.

"My dear Nova, happy you could join me tonight."

Azora felt the hate coursing through Nova as she stood behind her. Hecate had finally let her feel what she'd been blind to all those years. Nova never loved her and was never loyal to her. She hated her and wanted her dead and it hurt Azora to her heart.

"Hello, my queen. How is everything tonight? Are things going as planned?"

Azora could sense something was up by the tone in Nova's voice.

"Everything is going great. I finally have Oyo where I want him. He finally remembers everything, even the night he was taken from us."

Azora stood and turned so that she was facing Nova. She needed Nova to see the pain in her that she'd caused her.

"Oh, really? Well, what did he say?"

Nova shifted her gaze, hoping that Azora couldn't see the guilt in her eyes.

"He didn't have to say anything to let me know that you're more venomous than an Egyptian Horned Viper," Azora hissed.

Nova's head snapped up and she was now looking in Azora's eyes and could see the pain and hatred seeping from her eyes. Nova returned the same hate filled look that Azora never noticed before.

"Fuck you, Azora. You stole my life and expected me to just bow down and let you have what was rightfully mine!" Nova yelled.

Now it was her time to let her true feelings out. If Azora wanted to go to war tonight she was prepared.

"You are such a petty and miserable little bitch," Azora scoffed. "Who the fuck holds on to jealousy for half of a millennia. I mean really, over a man that never wanted you."

"He was mine till you came along."

Nova felt a release on her spirit as she let out her true feelings.

"Ha! Bitch I took him without even uttering a word. I wouldn't go around telling folks that story. It's not a good look for you, my dear Nova. The temptress, the Siren of all men. Should I say succubus or whoremonger? I mean, let's call a spade a spade, no need to sugar coat it," Azora taunted her, digging deep into Nova's wounds.

"Doesn't matter now because he will never belong to neither of us. I just saw him racing to find his dear wife. You thought your little moment was going to change things?"

Nova gave her an unbelieving look.

"The funny thing about moments is my little moment always seemed to bring about something good." Azora rubbed her belly and watched a coat of sadness cover Nova's face. "The moment he laid eyes on me he knew I was the one. The moment he laid eyes on me I was named his queen." Azora smiled at her. "The moment he laid eyes on me you ceased to exist in his world. The moment he realized who I was he made sure I was the only woman to bare his child." Azora paused for dramatic affect. "Your little moments are what treachery is made from. From the moment you met him you tried to weasel your way into his heart. The moment you realized that wasn't going to happen, you chose to take him from the world. Just like a bitter, pussy bitch," Azora gritted.

"You pathetic, ungrateful, bitch!" Nova yelled as she revealed the knife she been holding been behind her back.

"And what are you supposed to do with that?"

Azora laughed at Nova's moment of bravery.

"What I've been wanting to do since the moment you walked through the palace doors."

"Again, you with your moments. Bitch, you haven't learned yet that you mean absolutely nothing to the world? You are a mere pion, a bug that I stepped on and got stuck to my favorite pair of shoes that I couldn't throw away." Azora smirked as she saw Tina sneak into the room behind Nova. "I loved you Nova. I would have given you the world, but you must pay for treacherous ways."

Nova froze when she felt Tina wrap her hand around her throat and a knife slice through the soft flesh of her back.

"Bitch, I've been waiting to do that since the first time I laid eyes on you," Tina hissed.

A feeling of triumphant joy surged through her body. Finally, she was rid of Nova. Now there stood no one in her way of love. Azora would be hers.

"You little peasant. You can't kill me!"

Nova turned around and swung the knife she was about to use on Azora and slit Tina's throat in one swift motion. A look of surprise spread across Tina's face as she grabbed for her throat to stop the bleeding. She pleaded for Azora to save her life as she fell to the floor gargling on her blood.

"I told you to- Get-Rid of—" Those were the only words Tina could get out before dying.

"What's going on?" Nova asked as she turned slowly and looked at Azora.

She felt light headed. She coughed up blood and a feeling of dread washed over Nova.

"Death is going on. Hecate is not pleased with you, Nova."

"But I can't die. Don't do this me. Don't do this to us, Azora. We've been through too much together to let it end like this."

Nova let the tears fall from her eyes. She knew one of these days her deception would catch up to her.

"But you can die and you will die, my dear Nova."

Azora walked closer and kneeled down in front of Nova. She looked at her lovingly. Yes, Nova had betrayed her in the worse way but she was right, they'd been through a lot together so seeing her taking her last breaths tugged at her heartstrings. However, it was time for Nova to pay for her deeds.

"Hecate has spoken, my love."

Azora ran her fingers through Nova's short hair for the last time.

"But—"

Azora silenced Nova for good with the last kiss she would ever feel. She placed her lips on top of Nova's and inhaled the last of Nova's soul. The kiss of death is what Nova once called it. Azora stood and loomed over her once lover, best friend, and the other woman who was obsessed with her. When Nova drunk the potion earlier, it stripped her of her immortality. Her cockiness and deceit was her undoing.

Poor Tina didn't deserve the hand she'd been dealt. She only wanted to be loved and to prove her love to Azora. Indeed, life would be different without them around but she would get over it.

"Azora!"

Azora heard her name being yelling by the love of her life.

"On to the next one," Azora said to herself out loud as she went to find Oyo.

She walked slowly through the halls of the Smitten Kitten. She had grown accustomed to her new life but it was to be no more. Yes, after that night she would leave them and never return. She smiled as she rubbed her stomach, thinking about her unborn son. She knew she would have a son. Hecate had already shown her.

"Azora, my love," Oyo called out again.

Azora turned to find him standing behind her. He smiled in her direction and her heart melted.

"Yes, my king. What is it that you need?"

Azora fell right into their old routine as if time hadn't stolen a lifetime from them.

"I've been looking all over you," he confessed.

"Well, you've found me. What can I do for you, Oyo?"

She looked at him lovingly. She could feel the love radiating from him but she could also feel a hatred in the air.

"I wanted to tell you what happened that night was a total mistake. When I made you immortal, my love, I was going to make myself immortal but the queen stopped before I could."

"I know all this now, my love."

"I told you we would find each other no matter what ends of the world we end up on, in this lifetime and next one. My heart still beats for you, my love."

"Your love!" Miranda yelled as she stood there with tears running down her face. "Your love? You love her, Israel?" she questioned in almost an inaudible tone.

"Miranda, let me explain."

"Explain what, Israel? Explain why I was never enough for you? Why you never loved me completely like I loved you. I gave you all of me, while you only gave me parts of you."

"Miranda, baby, wait."

"No, Israel. Your lies mean nothing to me now. I see now you will never change and I will never be enough for you. My heart can't take you anymore." She pulled out the gun she'd been holding and aimed at him. "You are the lowest form of human being that the devil ever created."

"Don't do this, Miranda."

Azora stood off to the side, watching the exchange between the two. No, she wasn't going to intervene. Everything that was happening had been a part of the prophecy. It was out of her hands. She didn't know how things would end but she knew she would have to live with whatever decision Hecate made.

"Don't do what, Israel? Don't unbreak my heart? Don't get you out of my system for once and for all? Don't put me before you? Don't what, Israel?!"

She was crying so hard she could barely see. The gun shook violently in her hand as if she would drop it at any moment.

"Let me explain, Miranda. Please!"

"Explain what? How you thought you were about to run off into the sunset with this bitch! You ain't shit and you ain't never gonna be shit, Israel. You think it's ok to stomp all over a woman's heart and just move on with your life without a care in the world."

"I'm so sorry, baby. I'm so sorry for everything I've ever done to you, but I am not Israel," he pleaded.

"I've heard that before."

"But I've never meant it before," he admitted.

"Fuck you, Israel!" she yelled as she pulled the trigger shooting him in the chest. "How does that feel, Israel?"

Instantly Israel's body crumpled to the floor. Azora felt a horrible pain in her heart watching him dying in front of her all over again. Israel would be taken from her again, only this time she was prepared.

"You've broken my heart for the last time, Israel," Miranda declared as she stood over Israel and shot a bullet in him for every time he'd broken her heart.

Once she emptied her clip, she dropped down to floor next to him and pulled him into her arms. She cried a cry of excruciating pain. She poured out her soul as she rocked back and forth with him in her arms.

Azora watched and wanted to go to her king and hold him one last time but she bowed out gracefully. Hecate had spoken and so she let it be as she turned and walked out of the room. She would let Miranda mourn in peace.

Azora's job was done there. She could now move forward in her life. She thanked Israel one last time for her child and never looked back.

Epilogue
Phoenix Rises | 10 months later

Code pink! Code pink! We have code pink. All personnel please be on high alert. The hospital is now on lockdown," the voice over the loud speaker said.

Azora woke up startled as the flashing lights blinked over her door. Still groggy from giving birth, she could see the hospital staff moving quickly back and forth on the other side of her door. She wasn't quite sure what was going on, but she knew it had to be something of urgency since everyone was running back and forth. In the midst of the chaos running through the hallways more flashing lights caught her eye from outside the window. Immediately, Azora slowly rolled out of bed to see what the ruckus outside was all about. Six police cars were parked in front of the hospital. Panic quickly consumed Azora as she moved towards the hallway to find out what happened. Midway to the door she bent over, cringing in a bit of pain. The aftershocks of childbirth still pained her, though what was going through her mind seemed to hurt a lot more.

She wasn't sure what code pink was, but something about the panic that surrounded her made her feel it was nothing good. Azora finally made it to her door, opening it to see the nurse's faces wreaked with fear. Her body senses were all over the place and she feared the worst. A sick feeling sat at the back of throat, making its way to her stomach. There were several nurses at the nurse's station being questioned by police officers and she saw one of them point in her direction. Azora could feel the tension rising as the nurse was speaking in an alarming tone and seemed very afraid of what may be coming her way. Azora walked closer to the desk so she could hear what was being said.

"Yes officer, I had stepped away to help another patient. At the time, she was sleep in her room and there was no one in there with her," the nurse said.

"Okay, is it possible to get a copy of the visitor's log, please? We need to check all visitors to that room."

"Yes officer, I can get you that, but I assure you she hasn't had one visitor since we admitted her. It's actually quite odd that she hasn't had anyone come by."

"What do you mean odd?" the officer asked.

"Well, usually most women that come in here have a least some friends or family come by. Whether it's from her side of the family or the father's, but she hasn't had anyone from either."

"Would you be able to tell me if anyone visited her child in the nursery?"

"No, we don't allow anyone in the nursery that is not staff other than parents or legal guardians and they are required to wear wrist bands and must be scanned in."

The police officer nodded his head as he continued to write down information regarding whatever seemed to be going on. Azora leaned on the desk for support as she continued to listen. She still couldn't make out what was going on, but it seemed to be extreme since the police were now involved.

"Okay is there anything else you can tell me that you feel may be helpful? Could there have been anyone who may have come in while you were on break or making rounds?"

"No, that's all that I can think of. It's only a couple of us here at the desk and on duty right now. You can probably ask the other nurses, though I doubt they will tell you anything other than what I've already told you."

"Thank you, ma'am. I'll go deliver the news to the mother now. If you think of anything else, please give me a call," the officer said, handing the nurse his card.

Azora watched as the nurse nodded at the police officer. She looked around and saw the other mothers on the floor peeking outside of their rooms. It was clear everyone was startled and trying to understand what was going on. Azora quickly read the terror across most of their faces and instantly caught on to something was wrong with one of the babies. Realizing she wasn't going to get any answers out of anyone, she made her way back to her room. Her body never betrayed her and she started feeling as if she was about to hear something that would shake her to her core. She closed the door and moved towards her bed. She sat down slowly as she scooted further into her bed.

The reflection from the flashing lights bounced off her window, preventing her from falling back to sleep. Not to mention, the mayhem that was going on outside of her room had her thoughts in a frenzy. Quickly needing something to calm her down, she picked up the phone to dial the nursery. She needed to see her beautiful baby girl. The moment she pushed her out everything about her life changed. She thought she was having a son, but obviously, fate had other things in mind. Her daughter was the most beautiful creature she had ever laid eyes on. Her eyes had variations of blue and gray that caught the light as Azora looked into them. They reminded her of something she had seen in the sky before and in that moment she knew her name had to be Aurora. She could see Israel embedded in her features and knew that she would always have a piece of her great love with her.

"Hello, this is Azora Oyo in Room 1540. I was wondering if you could bring my daughter to my room please."

"I'm sorry, Ms. Oyo. We are on lockdown right now so no children can be moved at this time. Once the lockdown is lifted we can move around throughout the hospital," the nurse told her.

For some reason, Azora sensed there was something off about how she was speaking to her, but she couldn't put her finger on what it was.

"Okay, thank you. I'll call back at another time."

Azora hung up the phone as she heard a knock at her door.

Come in," she said.

Her door opened and her doctor along with the police officer who was speaking to the nurse earlier now stood in front of her. She wasn't sure what was going on, but she definitely didn't think she could be of any help.

"Ms. Oyo, can we speak to you for a moment?" her doctor asked.

"Yes," Azora replied, feeling her body negatively responding to their presence.

As she turned towards the door, she noticed a note sitting on her dresser.

"Good evening, Ms. Oyo. My name is Detective Tillman. I'm sorry to disturb you, but we have some unfortunate news and a few questions for you if you are able to answer them."

"Detective, you're scaring me. What's going on?"

"Well, Ms. Oyo, if you haven't already heard the hospital is under a code pink. Do you know what a code pink is?"

"No I don't, but I'm assuming it is something terrible if you're standing in my room. Detective, what's going on? Is everything ok with my daughter? Please tell me what's going on," Azora said, fighting back her panic.

"I'm sorry to have to tell you, Ms. Oyo, but your daughter has been abducted. Do you know of anyone who would want to take your child? A family member? A friend or someone else worse?"

Azora felt numb and could barely process anything the officer was saying to her. Anything he said passed her daughter had been abducted she didn't hear. She couldn't think of anyone who would come steal her child. Israel was dead, Nova was dead, and Tina as well. There was no one left who would have the gall to steal her child or even know where she would be. Azora could feel the anger boiling beneath her skin. Her rage was slowly seeping through the seams and she was doing all she could to remain calm in front of the police.

"What do you mean someone has abducted my child!" she yelled. "How could you incompetent people allow someone to take my child. What kind of fucking people do you have working here?" she shouted at the doctor.

"Ma'am, I need you to keep calm," the officer in the room said.

"Keep calm! Keep calm! Are you fucking kidding me? Do you have any idea what you just told me and you're standing here asking me to keep fucking calm?"

"Ms. Oyo, I understand this is traumatizing news, but we need you to keep calm so we can get all the information we need to find your child. It's the only way we can do our job effectively."

Azora was a mess. She couldn't lose her baby girl before she even got to know her. Aurora was all she had left to remind her of the love she shared with Asya. She knew she needed to keep it together so she could find out what the police knew. Anything that would give her some clues to help locate her child worked in her favor. Azora nodded, letting the officer know she would calm down and cooperate.

"The nurse informed me that you haven't had any visitors since you've been here. Is that true?"

"Yes officer that's true."

"Is there a reason no one has come to visit? Do you have parents, siblings, or friends? It's very uncommon for a new mother not to have a plethora of visitors."

"No, I moved here from a different state; therefore, I don't have any family or friends here," Azora said, glancing at the note again sitting on the nightstand.

She was curious to what it said, but decided she would look once the officers left her room. She didn't know if it was a ransom note or not, but whatever they wanted she would give it to them then make them suffer.

"Ms. Oyo, is the father of your child in the picture?"

"No, he passed months ago, so he couldn't have done this."

Both officers jotted down her responses. Azora wasn't sure if she should ask them questions or if she should just keep quiet and feel them out. Up to this point, they hadn't given her any information that would be helpful to her figuring out who had her daughter.

"Detective, how could this happen? I was told the nursery is watched around the clock so how could anyone walk out with my child?" Azora asked, sobbing.

"We're doing everything we can to find out what happened. As of right now, it appears whoever took your baby was inside the hospital and in uniform so that's how they were able to get passed security and the necessary checks."

Azora looked at him as he told her someone who disguised themselves as hospital staff stole her child, but why her child? There had to be other children in the nursery and not that she wished this on someone else, she needed to know why her daughter was targeted.

"Were there any other children taken?" she asked.

"No ma'am, just your daughter. Did the father of your child have any family that would come and take your child?"

"No officer. No one knew I was pregnant. The last time I saw him before he died we weren't on good terms. Soon after I heard he had been tragically killed, so there was no one for me to tell."

The officers looked at each other and jotted down more information. Azora could feel their curiosity and she knew they would be looking into what she just said. She never listed Israel on any of her admission information so unless they asked, they had nothing to look for.

"Ms. Oyo, that will be all for now and we apologize again for this. We will be doing all that we can to return your daughter to you and to make sure the person who did this is prosecuted to the fullest extent of the law."

Azora fought back a tear as the officer handed her his card. The two men nodded at her and then left the room. Once the door was closed, Azora picked up the folded paper left on her nightstand. She opened the paper to see a phone number listed on it. She picked up her phone and dialed the number. The phone rang three times before someone answered.

"Hello ,Azora," the voice said.

Azora recognized the voice and terror spread rapidly through her body. What she didn't know was how this person got within five feet of her to even leave a note.

"Don't speak, just listen. I'm sure by now the hospital is on high alert and the police have been to your room. I'm also sure you've given them very little information, seeing as though you really didn't have much to give them. I know you're also trying to figure out how I played a part in all of this and it's simple."

"What do you mean it's simple? How is this simple?"

"Easy. You let your guard down. You see you thought I would take what you did to me lightly and I didn't. You played your games which in turn ruined my life, so now I want you to feel the helpless pain I feel every day. I want you to know what it's like to have a piece of your heart ripped from your chest. You sent Nova to us, knowing he would be weak and fall for her. You played with my head and caused me to kill the man I love, so now I'm taking someone you love. Don't bother saying shit to the police, otherwise I'll point them in the direction of your little house of horrors. Goodbye, Azora. I'll be sure to raise my husband's daughter as if she were ours because you will never see her again."

Click!

"Miranda!"

Who Do You Love Now?

SNEAK PEEK

SHADRESS DENISE

I found refuge in their kisses. The hypnotic strokes of their tongues gave me strength. Her tenderness, his love, their sexual energy wrapped itself around me while the pleasure they gave me rejuvenated my soul. Somehow I had gotten lost in it all. Lost in the feeling it gave me. Lost in the coverage their shadows provided. The clouds of smoke I had exhaled hid my fears. The countless orgasms were my shield from a broken heart. I figured the more distance I put between me and love the better off I'd be. They were all masks I hid behind. The betrayal I had turned my back on years ago had finally found me again. Now the glass ceiling had been shattered and my world lay in broken pieces at my feet.

You didn't have to be perfect. You just needed to believe I loved you that way.

Micah's words lingered as regret held me tight. My eyes filled with memories as the past rolled down my cheeks. His words, the anger they were wrapped in pierced me to my core. The previous scars of distrust I caused had healed, but they hadn't disappeared. I wanted to forget any of it had happened; though, somehow the ghosts of my past would not let me be. Trent, Zoe and Cree had all found their way back into my life. I ran away from it all and it ran even faster to catch up. My own demons and issues surrounding love consumed me. I was so afraid of being hurt, I caused even more damage. Love, sex, lust, and betrayal had made up the chapters of my life for the past eight years. I never dealt with what had occurred between me, Trent and Zoe. I never processed the emotions behind walking away from Cree. I just compartmentalize everything, packed my shit and moved away. I figured leaving everything and everyone in L.A. would be the fresh start I needed. I never allowed myself the time I needed to heal. I denied myself the chance to grieve the many losses I suffered, and above all; I never admitted to myself I needed closure.

Now, I was paying for it.

Even sitting here now, I could still hear Micah yelling. The hurt behind his eyes was unwavering as the betrayal falling from his lips left me emotionally traumatized. My body went completely numb as my secrets slipped between my fingers. My heart trembled as his fist went through the wall. The blood ran down his hand and onto the floor as the tears flowed down my face. I covered my face in shame as time seemed to stand still. The words I wanted to say got lost in the deadly silence that settled between us once the yelling stopped. My lips were frozen and I had run out of I'm sorry and pleas of forgiveness. I had no more explanations as to why this reckless behavior kept occurring. The excessive amounts of second chances he was going to give me had run out. He had nothing left to give. I had taken everything from him. I was selfish and there was no other way to explain it. I could offer him a million forms of rationale, but it would only fall on deaf ears. From the beginning, this game was set up for me to win. Not once had I considered losing. I had never anticipated love nestling itself within my core. I loved Micah. I loved Cree. They were both the light I needed to find my way out of the darkness. However, Niko was a completely different story.

He was darkness. I had no real way to describe him other than to say; he was the kind of darkness that consumed you, trapped you, and caused you to lose your mind. Niko was the drug your mother warned you about. Even at the risk of consumption, he was the kind of intoxication that felt good, but ended badly. The first time we found ourselves wrapped up in each other was an honest mistake. I was hurting, high, and to the drunken eye, completely unaware he wasn't Micah. To no avail, that wouldn't be the last time. I knew that night the end was nowhere in sight. He had penetrated the surface and whether I wanted to or not, I couldn't fight the urges. The distance worked in my favor until it didn't anymore. It was as if gravity had it out for me. He was a combination of them all. He possessed the right amount of arrogance, passion and tenacity that drove me mad. The games he played made him a worthy opponent. His beliefs regarding love made him addictive. I knew he would be the death of me. I knew my curiosity would blind me. I should have walked away. I should have listened to Taylor. I let my greed get the best of me. I let lust rule my behavior. I challenged love and my luck ran out. I underestimated time. I believed I was in control of my destiny and fate played its hand. Forever doesn't last too long and now I have to deal with the reality of it all.

No matter how fast I ran, it all caught up with me in the end. I didn't know it yet, but the love I had given up on years ago would somehow be my saving grace.

COMING 2017!!!

The Devil's Pie

SNEAK PEEK

CHRIS RENEE

Kirby

"swim the river, climb the hill.... complacency, you ain't gone get me.... no, no, no.... 'cause I gotta get up...." Jill Scott

The screaming sound of the alarm clock, on the nightstand next to my bed, scared the shit out of me. I literally jumped so hard that I was a tiny inch or so in the air, almost as if I levitated. I angrily smacked the clock with more intensity than I intended, but in my mind, it deserved it for being such an on time nagging heffa. I grabbed my head as an instant headache began to percolate around my brain. Too much tequila and not enough sleep. I massaged my temples to alleviate some of the pain caused by the instant rush of pressure, but that didn't work. Either the walls were spinning or I was, whichever way, it made my stomach churn. I closed my eyes, took a deep breath, and found a happy place for my exhale.

"Today will be a good day. No, today will be a great day," I chanted softly.

With one eye opened, I glanced around at my surroundings, hoping that I willed the universe with my affirmation of greatness. Sadly, the god awful Pepto Bismol pink colored walls still spun just as furious as they had seconds ago. I blew out an air full of frustration, pushed the blonde tipped curls of my hair out of my face, and slowly counted to 10 before pulling myself to the edge of the bed. Just when I thought I could turn this hangover around, the scene from last night sucker punched my optimism like a heavyweight.

It was a complete disaster and not the normal, daily disaster that somehow became a part of my life. I already knew my karma was all fucked up and just waiting to get in my ass. I tried to avoid the inevitable for as long as possible, but she came snatching my pride, edges, and a damn brand new pair of heels I'd just purchased. I didn't know what happened to that whole, repent and forgive, preachers used to whoop and holler about, because even with all the good deeds I'd done in the past few months, I still got what was coming to me.

I shook my head and looked down at my naked body. I knew I must have consumed a serious amount of liquor in order to wake up like that. It creeped me out to sleep exposed on the sheets even if they were mine. I always had a firm belief that anything could crawl inside of you.

"Damn it, Kirby," I scolded myself as I staggered from the bed.

I was determined to get in and out of the shower in a record time because being late to work was never an option. I continued towards the shower but was momentarily sidetracked by the blue, blinking light from my cellphone on the floor. I didn't even bother to pick it up to check the pending notifications. I knew that most, if not all, were more than likely from Michael. The lying, cheating, piece of shit who I assumed would be married to by now, but he turned out to be some other lady's husband.

We had 8 wonderful months of wining and dining, mind blowing sex and mutual likes in just about everything. We were what people considered, the perfect couple in a perfect relationship. All of that was taken away by a knock on the door from a crying woman and some snot nosed kid. It took several minutes of attempting to decipher her hysteria and recognizing Michael's features in the boy before I realized, Michael belonged to them and had made me his side piece of ass. I called it off immediately and refused to answer any of his calls. I returned all of the gifts he sent me and even went so far as to change my phone number. When I was done with someone, I was finished without any dipping back. That was almost a year ago and I'd finally restored my heart from the damage he caused, only to sit across from him and his wife in a restaurant last night.

I was livid as she disgustingly fed him food, forced kisses upon him, and pretended that she wasn't bothered by my presence. Sadly, his clown ass went along with the freak show to appease her, as if he didn't keep his face between my thighs every single day, sometimes twice. I used to have to beg him to stop but how quickly he seemed to forget as he loved all over his boring, president of the Missionary Board looking ass wife. She hated me because she thought I signed up for the bullshit. I hated her, even though she did no wrong, and I still felt she took away my chance of finally being happy. Petty and childish thinking but damn it, I'm not known for being in control of my emotions.

Michael solidified how much I hated men. I was done with them all. Every single man who ever touched my life, from my absent ass sperm donor, to the bellman, who hated to sign for my packages, at my apartment, they all let me down. Well, not my best friend Raheim because he was a horse of another color. However, that damn, Michael, he stomped a mud hole in my heart and walked that bitch dry.

If watching their fake love display wasn't enough, the ever so vindictive karma kicked me in my ass even further. I made the stupid decision to quickly down two glasses of wine before sashaying my plump ass away from the table to show him what he'd been missing. Unfortunately, my heel got caught in the carpet, my ankle twisted and I found myself tumbling towards the ground. I tried to grab the nearest thing to me for security and that was the table cloth which was covered with food. As I sat there with chocolate soufflé covering my hair, I had to hold back tears while the entire restaurant erupted in laughter….

COMING SOON!!!

P.O.V

SNEAK PEEK

JOHNNA B

Chapter 1
Felacio

"So Doc, what do you think is wrong with me? I mean like in real life I love sucking dick. I think I'm addicted to it, I swear!"

Doctor Elaine Harrington sat across from her newest patient. She'd been a sex addict therapist for almost 11 years and the things she heard from her patients still amazed her. She met people from all walks of life and all sexual orientations and needless to say they were the entertainment in her mundane life. The young lady sat poised as if she were sitting upon her throne and not in a therapist room trying to figure out where her obsession with giving oral pleasures had come from. The pin striped suit she wore had a bit of a stretch to it so it clung to her body's curves perfectly. She was a deep shade of bronze with dark brown eyes that looked they would put any man in a trance. Though the woman was pretty Elaine thought she could use a good body scrub to get some of the over used tanning lotion off of her skin.

"I see, so how did you come up with this conclusion?" Elaine fought to stifle a slight chuckle that wanted to escape from between her lips. The young lady looked desperate for answers as she shook her left legs as if she were tweaking to suck a dick at that very moment.

"Listen Doc if you had a dick I'd be sucking it right now. Like this shit is unreal. Have you ever heard of such a thing?" She threw her hands up in exasperation. "Doc I love the way the veins ripple up against my throat. The way my tongue tickles his balls when I go all the way down on it. The feeling of a man grabbing the back of my head, pulling me in so he can go deeper send me into overdrive.

"Well, Melany I've heard of a lot of different things but each case is different. Now can you tell me where this all started from?" Elaine looked at the beautiful young lady with a little envy in her eyes. She wished she had the gall to let go of her sexual inhibitions. Though she was a sexual therapist she knew she was a prude in bed and needed to spice up her life in the worst way. If she didn't find a penis with a pulse soon she knew for sure old Arthritis would be kicking in sooner than later. She'd used her dildo affectionately named Long John so much the vibrations had stopped long ago. She'd fiddled her clit with her thumb so much it often got stuck in the hitch hikers thumb position. She didn't know if another human could ever bring her an orgasm. She had no clue as to when she'd lost herself in her work. But she hoped she hadn't ruined her poor little kitty.

"It started in high school I would just walk up to any boy that I chose for the day and pull him into the stairwell and suck him until I came. Didn't matter if he came or not, as long as I got off. He was only a means to an ends just a fixture in my fantasy." She fidgeted in her chair as she played with imaginary lint on her clothes

"I see, continue." Elaine sat silently doing Kegels in her chair she didn't know why the young lady's story was stirring something deep inside of her love canal. The stories she heard always made her feel some type of way but the thought of sucking a dick at the very moment made her pussy ache. It had been so long since she'd seen a real penis up close and personal she didn't know what she would do if she ever got a hold to one again.

"I mean I wasn't molested, didn't have a tortured childhood. I was a happy little girl that happened to like sucking dicks. Didn't matter the size or even it was circumcised. If it was a dick with a pulse it was for me." Melany's shoulders fell in defeat.

"Ok well I have a different way of doing things as I'm sure you've heard." Elaine gave her a questioning look.

"Yes Doc, that's why I'm here, fix me, I want a damn husband soon. Won't get one sucking off every man I see that walks pass me." The desperation was evident in her tone.

"Ok," Elaine put up one finger signaling her to wait a minute. "Noki can you send in Juno." Elaine asked as she pressed the button on the intercom to get her secretary's attention.

"Yes ma'am." Noki's deep but sultry voice came through the speaker.

A minute later in walked Juno. He stood a solid 6 feet tall and was thick in all the right places. His muscles had muscles there wasn't an imperfection on his body. His jet black hair brought out his high cheekbones and perfectly arched eyebrows. He walked in and stood in front Melany stark naked. Elaine watched as Melany's mouth began to water and drool dripped from her bottom lip.

"What's this about Doc?" Melany tore her eyes away from Juno's dick long enough to give Elaine a confused look. Juno's hard love log in her face was causing all kinds of ruckus in her lower region. Instantly she sized it up and knew exactly how she would attack the masterpiece. The vein going the middle and side taunted her screaming at her to lick it.

"How is his dick in your face making you feel Melany?" Elaine knew it was driving her crazy because the gods had blessed him tremendously and she herself had started to get wet. She had to stay professional so she averted attention back to Melany.

"What do you mean?" Melany's leg started to shake with anticipation.

"I mean what do you want to do at this very moment?"

"I want to suck it so bad. I mean really, really, reeeeaallly bad!" Melany whined. She almost reached out to touch it but she stopped herself.

"I want you to think of something else that makes you happy Melany." Elaine stated calmly.

"Nothing else makes me happier than when I'm sucking dick. Can I just lick it?" She looked over to Elaine with tears in her eyes. She had ache in her stomach that wouldn't let up like a real live crack head going through detox withdrawals.

"No you cannot, I want you to fight it. What else makes you happy?"

"Nothing dammit. Bitch this is bullshit!" Melany yelled in frustration.

"Calm down Melany. Take deep breaths and relax." Elaine tried to bring about a calmness in the room.

"Look doc I don't know what the fuck you think you are going to accomplishing. But this is bullshit and it's only making things worse."

"Touch it."

"What?" Elaine could see the confusion etched across her face.

"Touch it. But don't suck it." Elaine demanding softly.

"No, that's a got damn tease lady!"

Excerpt: P.O.V.

"Touch it but do not suck it." Elaine said as she got up from her seat and sat next Melany.

"You sitting over with them ugly ass glasses on the tip of your nose looking like a damn school teacher and shit. Like you gonna scold me if I even think about touching it. Nope you won't be giving me no damn electric shock therapy. Nah I'm cool on that." Elaine could tell her frustration was turning to anger.

"I don't do electrotherapy here Melany." Elaine had to chuckled a little. "Now do as I asked of you."

Melany stared at Elaine for a few seconds before responding. "Ok." She reached out took a hold of Juno's massive penis. The ache that radiated throughout her pussy was about to send her over the edge. She licked her lips to keep the drool from falling again. Slowly she ran her hand up and down it, testing its weight as she let it sit in the palm of her small hand.

"How does this make you feel?"

"Look doc don't keep asking me that dumb ass shit."

"Lick it."

"See now I know you being funny. What the fuck am I paying you 300 an hour for if you ain't here to help me?"

"Lick his dick Melany." Elaine knew she wouldn't want to do it because she had made her feel like it was something dirty. And now Melany felt uncomfortable. Elaine had gotten use to her clients cursing her out. Their frustrations always came out in her office and she understood they needed someone to take them out on.

"No." Melany shifted in her seat still holding on to Juno's manhood. Her hand wouldn't release it; it was like they had become one.

"I said lick his dick Melany, now."

"I said no dammit. You are crazy. I am done with this shit." Melany stood up, took one last look at Juno's manhood and stormed out of the office.

"You can go now Juno." Without a word he retreated back to his room to wait for another session with Elaine.

She watched his ass cheeks as he walked out her office. She loved the way his all his muscles flexed with each step he took.

Elaine Harrington was the top sex therapist in St. Louis Missouri and she took pride in her work. Yes she was very unconventional but she got results. She had to laugh to herself because she knew Melany would be back and she would most likely report that she hadn't given oral pleasures since their last session. Elaine was very good at what she did but some days she wanted to give it all up to focus on her own wants and needs. The things she heard from her patients made her feel like she hadn't been living at all. Compared to them she would be considered a nun. Her little kitty cat hadn't been penetrated in so long she could be considered a born again virgin. She prayed for some sort of sexual relief......

COMING SOON!!!

Made in the USA
Lexington, KY
08 April 2017